Lost dogs

Lost dogs

a novel by

Lucie Pagé

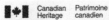 

The publisher gratefully acknowledges the support of the Canada Council
for the Arts and the Ontario Arts Council for its publishing program.
We acknowledge the financial support of the Government of Canada through
the Canada Book Fund (CBF) for our publishing activities, and the
Government of Ontario through Ontario Creates, an agency of the Ontario
Ministry of Culture, and the Ontario Book Publishing Tax Credit Program.

LIBRARY AND ARCHIVES CANADA CATALOGUING IN PUBLICATION

Title: Lost dogs / a novel by Lucie Pagé.
Names: Pagé, Lucie (Lucie A.), author.
Identifiers: Canadiana (print) 2023013078X | Canadiana (ebook) 20230130798 |
ISBN 9781770866690 (SOFTCOVER) | ISBN 9781770866706 (HTML)
Subjects: LCGFT: Novels.
Classification: LCC PS8631.A3353 L67 2023 | DDC C813/.6—dc23

Library of Congress Control Number: 2023932284

Cover image and design: Angel Guerra / Archetype
Interior text design: Tannice Goddard, tannicegdesigns.ca

Manufactured by Houghton Boston in Saskatoon,
Saskatchewan in January, 2023.

Printed using paper from a responsible and sustainable resource,
including a mix of virgin fibres and recycled materials.

Printed and bound in Canada.

CORMORANT BOOKS INC.
260 ISHPADINAA (SPADINA) AVENUE, SUITE 502, TKARONTO (TORONTO), ON M5T 2E4
www.cormorantbooks.com

To family who said I should,
The friends who said I could,
And Bill who kept me going after that.

1
Points of View

THERE WERE PERFECT BLUE skies, but Becca wasn't in the mood for them.

She was walking. Not because she wanted to but because the only things you control when you're fourteen are the music you listen to and how your personalized avatar is put together.

She'd made it to Queen Street faster than she'd imagined, given that she'd been home sneaking gummies, and scrolling through TikToks on her phone just twenty minutes earlier.

Becca hadn't reacted when her mom had read the weather forecast out loud. Sometimes Caroline was weird. But there had been a reason.

"When was the last time you were outside, Becca?" Caroline had asked.

Becca had thought back. "When I took out the garbage?"

"No, I mean out getting fresh air. It's going to get rainy soon. It'll be grey for months, right?" Her mom had gone on, talking up the sky, the trees, the fall colours. She'd even used words like *fresh* and *crisp*.

"Wait," said Becca, clueing in. "Is this you saying you're not giving me a ride?"

Caroline pressed her lips together in a smile, confirming. "I'm going to the garden centre."

"The garden centre," Becca repeated, struggling to believe she'd heard her mom correctly. Caroline was a serial plant killer. "So why can't you give me a ride before you go stalking flowers?"

"You wanted to do your own thing? Do your thing. I'm going to do mine."

"Are you punishing me?"

Caroline stamped out another smile as she shut off her tablet. "Okay, I'm not stopping you from going, Becca. You're free to ignore my advice. But if you want this, you'll get there under your own steam. I'm not getting involved." She rose to her feet and walked toward the kitchen.

"Can I Uber?" Becca called after her.

And because her mom had wasted so much time trying to convince her she had an urge to walk instead of just telling her she was SOL on the ride, Becca had run upstairs, changed out of her car outfit, put on her outside clothes, and wrecked her messy bun in the process.

Instead of discovering colourful fall scenery, there was autumnal carnage all around. The temperature had dropped overnight, and all the foliage on the gnarly little city trees had fallen en masse. There were curled-up yellow leaves all over the place. As she walked, Becca watched them catching the breeze and skimming over the sidewalks like they were crossing the river Styx only to come to rest on the garbage piles that sat near the curb.

It was grim, but it was the way Becca had started to see everything around her. Like, there could be a bunch of flowers in a yard, but she'd zero in on the one whose head had been lopped off. She'd see a puddle, but rarely the sparrows drinking from it. And whenever there were old people around, she couldn't stop thinking about how soon they would die.

Clearly, she needed to talk to someone.

Obviously, it couldn't be her mother.

For one thing, Caroline solved everything with diets. For another, every piece of advice her mother had given her so far had been wrong. Like picking prestige friends. And wearing showy clothes. And how everything would be fine. Everything was not fine. Her life was a disastrophe.

Becca had done a lot of work trying to figure out which therapy clinics were the most discreet. Eventually, she'd found one on Queen Street that felt right. It had a spa-grey website that was super understated. There was barely any writing about sadness anywhere on it. Sadness was implied.

What had impressed her most had been its test for depression. It was totally free. She went through all the questions and got a seven out of ten, which was like a B-minus. Normally, that grade might have upset her, but this wasn't school. This was life, and all she needed was a pass.

The therapists who worked at the clinic had posted pictures of themselves smiling. It was probably how they'd smile at you if you were talking to them IRL. There were blurbs beneath their pictures, but they were all blah-blah-blah brags. All Becca wanted was a doctor who would really listen to her. She'd carefully studied their profiles and eventually settled on this one therapist who had long earlobes. He wasn't smiling as hard as the other doctors were, but something about that was okay.

Her mom had taken one glance at his picture and said, "Keep looking."

It had been offensive on so many levels.

Caroline had been all: "Men with beards look reasonable on the outside, but they're only happy when they dominate."

Which had made Becca roll her eyes because there was no way her mom could actually tell all that from a beard.

Although. It was Caroline's job to know people. Like, really know them. Becca could barely decide what kind of gum she should chew, but Caroline could tell what people wanted even before they knew because she did marketing. She was so into people, sometimes she'd go right up to total strangers like one of those psychics with a message from someone who's passed away and say things like, "Okay, you don't know me, but you one hundred percent need an avocado hugger. It. Will. Change. Your. Life." And people would freak out and be amazed.

And yet, when it came to knowing what Becca wanted or needed, Caroline was usually wrong. No matter how closely Becca followed her mom's advice or recommendations, it always ended up as a huge personal fail. So, in spite of how much her mom had immediately disliked her chosen therapist, Becca had gone ahead and booked an appointment with him.

Naturally, Caroline had insisted on going with her to her first session to check out the doctor and then ended up using most of Becca's session, but Becca could tell Doctor Schofield was okay. She was also pleased his ears looked just like those in his picture.

All the way home, Caroline had kept trying to change Becca's mind about going back to see him. She'd said Becca would get over whatever was bugging her, but Becca had ignored her. Besides, the receptionist had Caroline's credit card number, so it didn't matter what her mother thought anymore.

She was around three blocks away from the clinic when a giant grungy ice cream cone folded open onto the sidewalk, revealing itself as the door of a store. It was sort of mind-blowing, like a secret world being revealed, only instead of a wizard with an owl appearing, it was a guy cracking open a pack of smokes.

Becca had to look inside. She slowly pulled the door open for a sneaky peek, and a way-too-happy recorded greeting blasted, "Hello! Welcome! Come i-in!" She spotted a lucky cat's paw waving hello with great enthusiasm from over the Cheetos. Then the guy at the cash register made eye contact. She was one hundred percent busted. She couldn't *not* go in.

Becca wended her way through the maze of chip racks toward the front counter. Behind the Hickory Sticks, she saw a photocopier.

On the right, just past the Bacon Ringos, were a couple of coolers. She knew she had to get something so she didn't seem like a complete freak, so she headed toward the bottled water.

The walls were covered floor to ceiling in random little bags filled with cell phone cases, safety pins, ant traps, and shower caps. So. Sketch. She wondered what was in the dusty plastic baggies by the ceiling. Maybe antique gummy worms?

Taking a small water bottle from the fridge, she returned to the counter to pay. As she put away her change, she noticed that taped to the back of the lottery monitor was a poster of a lost dog.

Becca immediately recognized the big white pit bull with the stupid grin and the white eyes. She'd seen the dog a bunch of times around High Park. It was legit blind. She'd seen it walking around with some guy, gently bumping into things, although this one time they were out in a field and the dog started leaping straight up. It must have known where it was. Then the guy had said something, and the dog had taken off galloping. Like, with no fear of hitting anything. Just crazy. They must have had a signal, because the dog stopped and came running right back. You could tell it knew it wasn't going to get hurt. Ever.

Suddenly, Becca felt tears in her eyes. She didn't know what was going on, but the counter clerk had started to stare, which could only mean he could see her tears. He'd started to look alarmed, and then his face unexpectedly burst into an awkward smile. "Okay. Thank you," he said, pointing to the door, inviting her to leave. "Thank you."

She nodded because she got that he wanted her to leave, but she was not in control of what was going on with the crying situation. She *def* didn't want to deal with it in front of the entire world. *Almost done*, she wanted to say.

Turning away, she pretended to study a lottery ticket scratcher in the shape of a finger and heard the man at the cash, who was clearly unsure of what to do next, make a phone call.

Becca remembered how she'd read someplace it was better to let your cry happen so your eyes wouldn't stay puffy, but this was getting ridiculous.

Stop, she told herself. *Stop*. It had zero effect.

She could hear the guy on the phone's voice getting louder. Tenser. She had to go. She grabbed her drink and made for the snack maze, bumping into a bunch of different types of chips, apologizing each time because she hadn't seen them.

Reaching the door, she flipped up her hoodie to hide her face, wondering whether she was legit headed to crazy-town. As she pulled the door open, a happy voice shouted in mechanical sing-song: "Hello! Welcome! Come i-in!"

2
Where Is Gary?

BRENT'S DOG, GARY, HAD been missing for over six hours, and Katherine was getting tired of looking for him. She and Brent had already gone around the entire neighbourhood — twice. They'd put up posters in all the stores, on all the poles and community billboards. They'd talked to every person they'd met, but no one had seen him. The dog had mysteriously disappeared.

Katherine was all for finding him, but she honestly hadn't expected Brent to keep broadening his search area. It was insane to even imagine Gary making it across Dundas West alive. On their way back home, Brent started dragging his heels, like going back in the house was declaring he'd abandoned all hope, which, of course, he hadn't. They'd come to a full stop on the sidewalk near his walkway when Brent began raking his fingers through his hair over and over, as though trying to order his worry into neat rows, but the raking was taking its toll — his brown hair swooped high above his head like a question mark. He was starting to look like a Troll doll — oddly sweet yet slightly pathetic.

"Okay," she said. "We need to take a break."

Brent stared at her crazy-eyed, as if she was speaking to him in a foreign language. Katherine understood he was out of his mind with worry, but he was sort of being self-centred. She needed to pee.

"Brent?" she said, pointing toward the house. "We're going in."

He nodded.

Jesus. Finally, she thought. But just as she started up the narrow walkway to Brent's place, he darted across the street, waving a poster of Gary to a couple returning from a shopping trip. They were the standoffish people who lived at number 47.

The people at 47 were notorious recluses. They didn't trade in hellos or bother with social niceties. All anyone knew about them was that they were excessive leaf blowers.

Noticing Brent's approach, Mrs. 47 bolted from the car and retreated into the house, leaving her husband to fend for himself. Katherine watched Mr. 47 awkwardly shift his grocery bags from one hand to the other as Brent waved his arms around effusively, describing his dog in great detail, despite the fact its photograph was already on the poster.

It was astonishing how Brent's charm often made people want to help him. He used everything he had going for him: his politeness, his crazy hair, his warm tone of voice. People often bought in. Strangers gave him cigarettes. Students shared their lunches. New acquaintances volunteered to drive him places. Katherine herself had felt compelled to offer Brent a comp ticket to a play she'd been holding for someone else. He was just so damned earnest and decent and eager, it felt monstrous to turn him down.

But he was wasting his charm on Mr. 47.

Katherine saw Brent point to where she was standing, presumably to show his neighbour where he and Gary lived. She sighed, dutifully pasted a smile on her face, and gave a little wave. Mr. 47 stiffly raised one of his shopping bags in return. She could tell he couldn't place her even though she'd said hello to him a half-dozen times over the past few months. "Fucker," she mumbled, her face still fixed in a smile.

She heard a gate scrape behind her and turned quickly, a bit startled.

Brent's neighbour, an older man, possibly Portuguese, with white hair coming out of his ears like miniature clutches of baby's breath, stepped out of his front yard carrying hedge clippers.

Katherine had never seen him up close before. She remembered Brent had told her he was a widower, so she smiled. His eyes hardened.

He stood territorially by his hedge, as if guarding his property. Everything about the way he stood said he wanted her to go away. It was crazy how she could feel him not trusting her. Katherine smiled harder and fumbled with a roll of tape and a utility knife to retrieve a lost dog poster from the envelope she was carrying to show him what she was doing there.

She moved toward him, holding the poster out. He stayed completely still, waiting for her to come to him, like he was playing some strange power game.

"We've lost our dog," said Katherine. "Have you seen it?"

The old man's glance broke off. His look wandered back across the street toward Brent, still talking to Mr. 47. He scratched his chest. His fingers looked like meat hooks.

"The dog's name is Gary," she said.

His dark gaze drifted back toward her, but he said nothing. Maybe English wasn't his first language.

"He's usually in the back," she said, pointing to Brent's yard. "He's blind?" she added, strongly resisting the impulse to point to her eyes. "Maybe you could check your yard? Or inside your shed in case he wandered in?" Katherine waited a few seconds. "Because he'd be confused," she explained. "He wouldn't be able to find his way out." She was starting to lose all confidence in words. "I could go look for you if it's too much trouble?" Jesus. This man gave back nothing. Not even so much as a head nod.

And then she smelled it. Rancid and greasy and all too human: pant crotch.

A wave of nausea hit her. This was why she'd dropped out of social work.

Details of the old man's clothing started to pop out at her like pustules: the grungy red, grey, and tan wool sweater that was so pilled she could hardly make out the pattern, the frayed T-shirt collar tamped down with gunge and sweat. The caked work pants that needed to be burned.

"Did ... did you want to keep a poster?" she asked, trying not to breathe him in.

The man raised his clippers and coarsely hacked at the top of his hedge. She'd been dismissed.

"Okay. Very helpful," she muttered, breathing through her mouth. She didn't give a crap if he'd heard her. She was done being nice to people.

Katherine walked past Brent, who now stood on the walkway waiting for her.

"Did he say he saw Gary?"

"What do *you* think?" she answered.

3

The Unsaid

EVERY SINGLE PERSON IN the waiting room could be seen from the street while the clinic door was open. People *had* to know that. And *still*, the patients of the Wellness Centre kept stopping in the doorway like douche-flutes, one after another, to check their messages.

Becca had covered and uncovered her face so many times, she felt like she was playing peekaboo with the ficus, but no one from school could know she was in therapy. Her life was already a gigantic sucking wound. Thankfully, her embarrassing dog poster meltdown was fading ...

Becca started to flip through the March issue of *Parenting* magazine when the inner office door opened. A lady in pink yoga pants came out, slipping dark sunglasses over her red eyes, and made her way to the crepe-skinned receptionist to book another appointment.

Doctor Schofield appeared at the door a few moments behind her. "Becca?"

Becca wished he wouldn't use her real name. She rose to her feet, pulling her backpack over her shoulder, and walked toward his office, trying not to think about how the whole waiting room now knew she was a patient and not just waiting for someone else she knew who had issues. As she brushed past him, Doctor Schofield looked out into the waiting room. "Your mom not come with you today?"

"She had to go to the garden centre. I think your receptionist totally hates me, by the way."

Doctor Schofield followed her in without comment and closed the door.

Becca made a beeline through the warmly lit office toward the fuzzy orange chair across from Doctor Schofield's desk. She liked his space. It felt immediately comfortable, like one of those super casual boutique hotels.

The doctor shrugged off his tailored jacket and set it on the back of an extra chair. As he walked back to his desk, he rolled up his shirtsleeves.

"Does she like gardening? Your mother?"

"Not really. She's just being super weird today." She sighed. Her mom was not into flowers. Becca tugged her hoodie sleeves down over her hands.

Doctor Schofield looked slightly perplexed but nodded as he sat down. He switched gears and flipped open Becca's file to read over his notes.

From what Becca could see, some of the pages were typed, but others were loose-leaf and covered with the inky scribbles he'd made the last time they'd talked. Those were the pages Becca liked best. The round sound of his writing was weirdly soothing.

Caroline had said he reminded her of "The Most Interesting Man in the World" from the beer ads. Becca was pretty sure Doctor Schofield had never petted a fox IRL, but he did squeeze his beard while he read, and it was the coolest. So far, though, he had not attempted to dominate her.

On her first visit, Doctor Schofield had asked a bunch of questions. She'd never had therapy before, and she hadn't been sure what she was supposed to say, so she'd sort of shrugged a lot. Then she'd obsessed for days over whether she should have prepared more for her appointment, which was when she'd realized she felt just as inadequate as a patient as she did in real life. Today, she'd told herself she'd say whatever she felt, whatever came to her mind. She would try not to judge herself.

Doctor Schofield picked up his pen. Becca latched on to a fuzzy pillow.

"So, Becca, when you were here last, we discussed a situation that occurred at school, and we talked about the idea of your beginning a dialogue with your friend ..." His voice trailed off as he shifted through the reams of notes.

He was talking about Leanne.

"Leanne," he said.

Becca nodded. Leanne was the first friend Becca had made at her new school. She was a popular girl with almost perfect hair, and they had become best friends really fast. Like, in the space of a week. They'd hung out and laughed. They went to each other's houses. Tried on each other's stuff. Texted whatever they were thinking, whenever they were thinking it. For the first time ever, Becca had felt she could say anything, because whatever else the world thought, she and Leanne were bound to think the same. It was amazing. And then this random girl had suddenly walked up to her at school and said, "Congratulations, Baskin-Robbins. You're the flavour of the week."

Becca hadn't understood what the girl was talking about then, but she did now.

By Friday, not only was Leanne hanging out with a new best friend, but lots of kids at school seemed to know Becca's most embarrassing secrets — like how she still cried over One Direction's breakup. Still, Becca missed her ex-BFF because when Leanne liked you, you really felt liked, which, by extension, made you likeable to others. Her rejection had triggered a friend pyramid scheme collapse.

"Did you try to talk to her? How did it go?" Schofield locked his eyes on Becca.

"She called me a loser to my face. And on Instagram."

Schofield nodded. Jotted down a few notes. "What else?"

"She got me on Twitter too."

"She sounds thorough."

She was. And when she'd asked Leanne why she was being so mean, Leanne had called her arrogant for thinking anyone actually wanted to talk about her.

"Relationships are partnerships we cannot control," Doctor Schofield said. "They are only pleasant when both people's needs are balanced."

Whatever that meant.

"Now that you've asked the question," said Doctor Schofield, "you've learned that the worst that can happen is someone says, 'No, you can't be my friend.' No gaping wounds, no blood. You survived. Right?" He looked at her, expecting a response.

Becca shrugged.

"Did you start keeping a journal for me?" he asked.

Becca nodded.

"May I see it?" he asked.

She pulled her notebook from her backpack and handed it to him, feeling a bit conflicted about giving him access to something that proved her lameness.

He pointed at the notebook's cover art. "You like anime?"

Becca nodded. She'd specifically picked that notebook because it had Yozora from *Haganai* on the cover. Yozora had zero friends at school even though she was pretty, and everybody thought she didn't care about not having friends, but really she did.

"I like the characters," Becca explained.

"Mmhmm," said Doctor Schofield, nodding as he started to flip through her journal. She had drawn a few different Yozoras on the bottom of some of the pages where she felt it was most relevant, but he didn't say anything about them. Maybe he was taking them in.

"How did you feel about this journalling exercise? Was it useful? Did you make any discoveries?"

Becca wasn't convinced that writing about how much her life sucked could actually make it better. "No?"

"Well," he answered, "that may change." He started to read her entries. It was boring to watch. At one point, Doctor Schofield frowned and started clicking his pen.

"Mm-hmm. You've been crying, you say? Is it more than usua—?"

"Yes," she said too quickly. He started writing. Becca glanced out the window while she waited for him to finish.

Doctor Schofield's pen sounded different than before. It was faster and less round, more scratchy. She really hadn't wanted to talk about sadness. If she was going to survive whatever was going on with her and not have meltdowns in front of random cashiers, she needed to Ice Queen the emotional stuff. She wanted to stop feeling.

"How sad do you feel? On a scale between one and ten, ten being the absolute most sad."

Becca sighed, pulled her thumbs back into her sleeves, and considered. "Four. Maybe five." She heard him scribble and then decided she could be more exact. "Six," she said.

He nodded but didn't seem to revise his notes. Maybe he'd written down a range.

Not that she knew how to give sadness a number. Like, was it just about the amount of crying? Was sobbing more sad when it was done out loud? Could sadness involve more complicated feelings too? Recognizing the dog in the poster had confused things even more.

"This dog?" she said out loud without meaning to.

Doctor Schofield looked up quickly like she'd startled him. She hadn't meant for her voice to come out so strangled and weird.

"I don't know him," she said, "but I know him to see him. And the poster said he'd been lost."

She could tell right away that just talking about the dog was a problem. She could feel something inside her start falling, trying to break away. It was as if her insides were built out of sand. "It's making me really, really emotional. I don't know why."

"Well, losing a pet is difficult," said Doctor Schofield.

"I didn't lose him. It's not my dog! Who goes around caring about someone else's stupid dog? I don't want to care, all right?"

"Then why are you near tears?"

"I don't know."

Becca suddenly felt tired and wanted Doctor Schofield to shut up. A therapist was just supposed to listen and write big, loopy words that made her feel better.

"Becca," he said, underlining something he'd written twice, "I think the first thing we should talk about is some medication to help with your anxieties, but I think your mother needs to be part of that discussion."

"Oh," she said. She hadn't been expecting pills. Pills seemed way more serious than she felt. Now she felt doubly worried about what this could mean for her.

"Am I going to spontaneously start wanting to cut my own hair and give myself weird bangs?"

"Of course not. If you like, we can talk about impulsive thoughts and discuss ways you can handle them. But we'll get through whatever is happening, I promise you. Between appointments, you can always call the office." He nodded, returning his gaze to her journal. "Yes, definitely keep up with the music. It lifts the soul."

Becca must have looked confused because Schofield pointed to her journal. "Katy Perry," he said. "You mention her several times."

"She's for drowning out sounds."

He wasn't getting it.

"My mother's?"

Becca let him hang a few more seconds, then made an annoyed *duh* face.

That, he understood.

He quickly returned to her journal, this time studying the pages more closely, flipping back and forth between entries.

"Can we talk about crying too? Because I don't understand why I cried so hard over a dog. Is that normal? Do people do that? Cry in front of —"

"Becca, just give me a moment, will you?" said Doctor Schofield.

Becca nodded, a bit confused, sank slowly back into her fuzzy orange chair, and clutched her fuzzy pillow tighter. She had been ready to talk about everything, but the doctor had stopped listening.

4

Truth Will Out

BRENT STARTED OFF SUNDAY by following up on the reports of Gary sightings that had been received overnight, but all the leads were fruitless. Unsure what to do next, Kate suggested they do another loop around the neighbourhood to poster further and alert more people about his missing dog. As they returned to his place for a regroup, Brent could hear faint church bells ringing far in the distance, harkening back to simpler, happier times.

"Your neighbours are assholes," Kate called back to him as she walked into the washroom.

She was referring to their earlier encounter with the woman who lived in the house with the dirty windows, a corpulent mother of two with a wide, flat face that communicated it had seen its share of rejection. The woman had been leading her brood into Trinity Bellwoods Park when he and Kate had intercepted her. It took the woman a moment to recognize Brent as they'd never formally spoken, just exchanged head bobs. She had never struck him as being particularly jovial or energetic, but she seemed a much livelier sort when she wore lipstick.

Kate had handed her a poster of Gary, and as she'd laid eyes on it, her face lit up. "If you're looking for a dog to walk," she'd said to him, "mine is around. She needs a lot more exercise than we can give her."

It was a preposterous thing to say, of course, but instead of taking it in stride, Kate had said, "Excuse me?!" rather loudly and remarked that something might be wrong with the woman, leaving him to make the necessary apologies. It had been awkward.

Brent was touched by Kate's efforts to find Gary and happily forgave her brutish moodiness. It was only natural. She was, after all, entirely to blame.

Having enjoyed a sound sleep on Friday night in a cool room under a heavy duvet and awoken on Saturday morning with delicious languor, Brent had cuddled with Katherine, whispering whatnots into her hair, which made her smile. When she'd leaned back and squirmed against him, Brent had realized he'd struck lucky.

Sex with Katherine felt like breathing rarefied air. It was an unspoken rule that whenever she was on, "it" was on. But just as the sexual tension had been building, Kate had spotted Gary sitting at the foot of the bed.

The dog had been doing absolutely nothing other than panting and wearing that wide, foolish pit bull grin on its face, but for some reason Kate had taken exception to him and demanded Brent put him somewhere else.

Her issue was one of modesty, which was positively baffling as theatre folk were purported to be more relaxed about those things. He'd reminded her that the dog was blind, but at that point, she'd become so fixated on Gary's panting she couldn't shake the idea that he was in the bedroom in some sort of voyeuristic capacity. Ergo, Brent had dressed, found his shoes, and put Gary out in the yard. He'd scratched the old boy's ears and promised him a long walk for his patience and forbearance before dashing back up the stairs. Gary seemed to have understood.

And now Gary was gone.

Brent could not stop reproaching himself for not having checked that the yard gate was latched one last time or taken a moment to round up a few of his dog's favourite toys. He knew how Gary hated to be left alone, but all that had mattered to him was getting back inside to ravish Kate.

He'd rushed up to the bedroom, stripping off his clothes and shoes, but by the time he'd leapt into bed, Katherine's mood had waned.

BRENT WISHED HIS DOG would just reappear, amble up the hall, and slip his big, wet nose into the palm of his hand to signal it was time for a good scratch. His gaze fell on Gary's chewed leash on the hall table. He felt a tug at his heart. *There is no greater sorrow than to recall in misery the time when we were happy*, Dante had written. The situation was unbearable. He had to come up with a new plan of action.

"We have to make the next batch orange," he called out to Kate.

"What?" she called back from the washroom.

The first bunch of posters had been printed on the white paper Brent kept in his home office. When he'd run out of posters, he'd ducked into a cheap copy place on Queen Street, ordering sixty more printed on what he thought was an attention-grabbing cyan. But the moment he saw one taped to a lamppost, Brent suspected he'd made a grave error. GARY IS MISSING in cyan could not hold a candle to the competing yellow, orange, or lime announcements for animation festivals and garage sales. His new poster would be invisible come nightfall. He had to act now.

Brent moved closer to the washroom door. "I said, I think we should make next bunch of posters orange so people can really see them."

Inside the washroom, Katherine rolled her eyes.

"Whatever you want," she said.

What Katherine really wanted was for Brent to stop sharing the decisions he was making as he was making them. She sat quietly in the washroom and picked at a cuticle to give him a moment to walk away. Peeing was private. Besides, there had already been too much talk about the poster — the colour, which of Gary's pictures to use, and whether the headline should read "Lost Dog" or "Gary." Especially when Katherine knew damn well that none of it mattered. That dog was not coming back.

"Gary loved orange tennis balls," Brent mumbled into the doorjamb. "When he could see." She heard a light thump against the door, then a scratching sound. She was pretty sure he had just rested his head against it.

"Jesus," she sighed.

Her cuticle had started to bleed. Katherine tore a piece of toilet paper and set it atop her thumb. The blood wicked up through the tissue.

She didn't resent helping Brent, but the constant need to buoy his spirits was starting to wear thin. For some reason, she always ended up being the one who had to stay calm in a crisis, the one who had to be strong for others. She was constantly forced to play this role, which was why some people called her cold and heartless. Part of her would have loved to let herself melt down — to feel what it was like to let others pick up *her* pieces. But someone had to be rational in a crisis.

She could hear that Brent was still resting his head against the door. Clearly, her pee would have to wait. Katherine sighed as she stood, pulling up her pants, hoping she wouldn't get a UTI but not willing to make a fuss because clearly, none of today was about her. She realized how remaining quiet simply enabled Brent's neediness, but wasn't that what relationships were about? Enduring one another — to a point?

She flung open the door.

Brent's hair looked like it had gone through batteries of tests in a wind tunnel.

"What the hell good am I, Kate?" he moaned. "I can't even keep a blind dog in a gated yard." His brown eyes were full of sexy misery.

Katherine slipped her arms around his waist and pressed her body into his as though she might be able to dislodge his sadness if she displayed enough conviction. She would have fucked him all the way to happy, but Brent only messed around when he felt jazzed. It was such a waste of emotional catharsis.

"Come on," she said, "I'll make you a sandwich."

Brent mumbled something about not being hungry but followed her into the kitchen like a child.

"I latched the gate," he said.

"Honestly, it's no good beating yourself up."

"I'm trying to understand how, Kate. How did he manage to slip out? He's a dog with no sense of direction. The only way Gary could have escaped the yard was if someone helped him."

"Exactly," answered Katherine. She tugged the refrigerator door open.

Brent's eyes grew wide. "You don't really think ..."

She shrugged. "It's not impossible, is it? If someone was annoyed enough ..."

"Annoyed?"

Katherine briefly considered how to phrase her comment, but since there was no better way of saying it, she just did: "Your dog barks. It's a barky dog."

"It's how Gary lets you know he wants something."

"Yeah, I know ... Bark, bark, bark. I want in. Bark, bark, bark. I want out. The truth of it is, some days, Gary's got a little too much to say."

As expected, the comment cratered him. Brent looked around wildly for something or someone to anchor him and reached for his hair. "This isn't personal, Brent," Katherine said. "It's not an attack. I'm only suggesting maybe one of your neighbours got fed up."

It was clear from Brent's shocked expression that he believed no one had ever had unpleasant thoughts about him or his dog. Katherine shook her head, amused.

"If you thought Gary'd been abducted," he said, "why didn't you say anything?"

Katherine let the refrigerator door fall shut and crossed back to the counter before she answered. "You seemed like you needed to poster."

She set bread and butter on the counter and returned to the fridge. "And just so we're clear, I never said Gary was abducted. You did. But my gut says that someone let him out."

Brent went pale. He'd probably started thinking of all the dreadful things that could happen to a blind dog. He really needed to step away from the Norman Rockwell version of the world he generally entertained to acknowledge man's capacity for casual irrationality.

Katherine stared into the refrigerator's shelves a minute, vaguely remembering Brent had ordered out a few days earlier.

"Did you finish the Mediterranean chicken?" she asked. He didn't answer.

She glanced over the refrigerator door and saw Brent finger-combing his hair again. People and their fucking pets. *This* was why she hadn't gone to veterinary school.

"I'm making a grilled cheese sandwich. Do you want one?"

Brent didn't answer.

"Well, I'm starving," she muttered and started to pull one together. The grain-rich bread was all wrong, but she had to keep things moving. At some point, this day would end. She set a frying pan onto the front element and unwrapped cheese slices while the pan warmed, but even the noisy plastic film couldn't muffle Brent's silence.

She supposed she needed to say something supportive. Again. Which was when she discovered Brent staring at her in a concentrated way.

"I don't appreciate the way you're looking at me right now," she said calmly. She dropped the sandwich into the hot pan. It sizzled on contact.

"Well, I'm sorry. But it's going to take me a moment to process the deeply disturbing scenario you've just put forward."

"As long as I'm not the bad guy here. You don't have to agree with any of what I'm saying, but your dog barks."

Silence again. It was pissing her off.

"I'm ... I'm ..." Brent's voice trailed off.

"What, Brent?" said Katherine, spinning on him. "What are you?"

"Well ... baffled. I'm baffled, Kate, by all this information you've been withholding. You think my dog's been abducted, but you didn't tell me. You've never once said you thought Gary's barking was excessive, but now I learn it's a feeling the entire neighbourhood shares. What else haven't you told me?"

Katherine stared Brent down. "How about: 'I regret sharing any observations with you and not letting you figure out the neighbourhood dynamics by yourself.' I mean, are you for real right now? Questioning me after I've spent my entire weekend looking for your dog?"

She saw Brent blink and finally knew he'd registered her anger.

After a moment, he nodded as though digesting the information. "You know," he said, "I think I might have a grilled cheese after all."

In Brent's experience, it was best to avoid direct eye contact with Katherine for a few minutes while she was outraged, so he retreated to the bay window to grapple with the facts that had been revealed.

Though he felt stung and embarrassed to learn his neighbours were vexed with Gary and, by extension, him, Kate's abduction theory had been surprisingly sinister. It was as though the more time he spent with her, the less he knew her.

Brent looked out the bay window where he had often written poems and quiet observations about life, his jowly canine by his side. How he envied everyone he thought to be having a carefree Sunday afternoon. His gaze travelled over the items scattered around his neighbour's yard — the misshapen traffic cones, the dilapidated bicycles, the stack of warped screen doors, and the spot where a few rogue tulips bloomed among the cinder blocks every spring — when out of the corner of his eye, he spotted movement. His heart quickened as he zeroed in on a tangle of thorny branches behind the collapsing fence, but it was the Portuguese neighbour, not Gary, who appeared through the thickets and peered about.

"Looks like you got to him, Kate," he said.

Puzzled, Katherine joined Brent by the window and saw the old guy rustling about in his yard. "If you mean I pushed him over the edge," she said, "I think he went over that cliff a long time ago."

"No. He's out there looking for Gary."

The neighbour was parting thorny bushes with his bare hands as though he was tearing apart a soft loaf of bread. Katherine shrugged. "Or maybe he dropped his keys."

"Don't dismiss this, Kate. People aren't as indifferent as you think they are. Yesterday, you appealed to his better nature, and today, he's doing his bit. You have to agree that humanity still has the ability to show its better side. It just has to be engaged."

Katherine remained quiet. She wasn't buying any part of Brent's interpretation.

"You're not agreeing," Brent said.

"Pretty much," she said, pulling her hair back a moment only to instantly let her curls sweep back across her cheeks.

"You could have been a lawyer," said Brent, walking back into the kitchen to check on lunch.

"Yep," Katherine replied, nodding. She certainly could have been.

Even from her excellent vantage point, Katherine could barely pick out the old man from the branches as he rooted around the vines. To some extent, his grungy old sweater was working like camouflage.

He was rough, offensive, and his pant smell was a rancid sensory memory now, whether she wanted it or not. And yet, as Katherine watched him search his yard, she began to wonder whether she'd been too quick to judge him. He'd probably bought his house when the neighbourhood was all rooming houses and labourers. Now he was the last of his kind, a crotchety old guy surrounded by hipsters and marketing influencers rushing around trying to buy experiences. The world as he'd known it was gone. He was an outsider in his own yard.

As though he intuitively felt he was being watched, the neighbour's head swivelled up to the dining room window and locked on to her.

Katherine smiled with embarrassment. Caught.

His expression changed, and she saw something that was not the milk of human kindness. That's when she knew.

"You ... fucker."

5

A New Day

SUNLIGHT SLIPPED THROUGH THE bent slats of the window blinds, disturbing the quiet darkness in Becca's bedroom. The points of light marked the path her once-upon-a-time kitten had taken up the venetians the very first night it had stayed with her. It had been a sweet little orange floof with gold eyes. She'd called it Ella.

One of her mom's contractor friends had found it wandering around a job site, and he'd brought it to her as a gift. She must have been seven at the time, but Becca could still remember staring hard at her mom because she'd wanted the kitten so bad. She recalled that when her mom had finally smiled "yes," she'd felt something explode inside her. How she'd picked up the kitten and carried it up to her room. It had to be one of her top ten happy memories.

But back when she was little, Becca didn't understand that her mother had two smiles and that the one she'd flashed showing all her teeth meant bad news. A few weeks later, her cat went missing, and Caroline explained she'd sent Ella to live on a farm because the kitten was psycho and needed to live in a barn. Becca remembered crying and crying and begging her mother to go visit it, but of course, she'd never seen her cat again. Nothing good ever seemed to stick around.

Like her dad.

He'd told her he'd had to leave because he was a simple man. And all her mom would say was that mistakes were made.

The first year he was gone, her dad had mailed her beer coasters from wherever he was working. They were colourful. Some had funny animal shapes. Sometimes he'd scribble a note on the back like, "Love, Dad." Sometimes there were numbers and lines in shaky pen, but that was normally him figuring out a bid. Becca kept all her coasters in a mini crate beside her bed so her father could see them if he ever came back. He never did. Her mom, Caroline, described them to her friends as a study in regret. Whatever that meant, because it was impossible to know who was regretting what at any given time. Ever.

"Rebecca!"

Caroline's voice cut through the Pink Floyd groove happening in Becca's headphones, so she cranked up the volume and raised her cell phone above her head like a staff. "You shall *not* pass," she commanded. The insides of her ears felt like they were being fried in olive oil, but on the flip side, she couldn't make out a single word her mom was saying.

She'd discovered the band on a playlist called "music for depressed people," and it was perfect. The singer's voice rose through the threads of a trippy drone and then his lyrics dropped into her soul, transfusing his confusion and pain. It was unspeakably good to have found someone else who saw the pointlessness of existence, even if he was in some ancient band only old people remembered. Becca let herself sink deeper and deeper into the darkness until the gurgle of Caroline's blender cut through, and she realized she had fifteen minutes to get ready if she wanted a ride partway to school.

She kicked off her warm grey sheets and sat up, then teetered on the edge of the bed a minute, still feeling its pull. For sure, there were brain magnets in pillows.

She stared at a patch of floor through her long, dirty-blond hair.

The wood looked cold. Her toes curled involuntarily at the thought of coming in contact with it, but her slippers were way over by the closet. She pulled out an earbud to focus. Maybe this was the day it worked.

Come, she said to her slippers in her telepathic mind voice. *Come.*

They didn't budge, confirming she was nothing special and it sucked to be her. Again.

Becca felt around the bedside table and found the lamp switch. The pink walls popped into existence in all their hideous glory. They had been the same terrible colour since she was seven. She'd argued with Caroline that everything about her had changed, but her mom still refused to let her paint her room black.

Becca slipped off the bed and walked toward the clothes piled on the floor. She hadn't quite got around to doing laundry yet. Walking in circles, she kicked through the pants and shirts until she found her favourite bra. As she put it on and was trying to pick out a T-shirt, she caught a glimpse of herself in the mirror and saw her boobs starting to squeeze out the top of the cups. "Fuck," she said, staring at them in the mirror. Just what she needed: more boobage. She hated that they were a big deal to people. They were just things coming out of her. Like arms. Except they were completely useless for carrying stuff.

This one girl at her old school had been so into hers, she'd named them Betty and Veronica. Once that tidbit came out, everyone had gone on a name-your-boobs jag. Everyone except Becca. Her boobs seriously messed her up, so they would remain nameless.

She picked up a dark grey T-shirt that smelled like deodorant, matched it with a pair of cargos, and headed downstairs.

As she reached the landing, Becca heard what sounded like the blender's "end of the road" gurgle. Caroline burned one out every other year. Her mom was hypervigilant about smoothies because she was convinced they would peel years off her face, like bark off a birch tree. What she actually needed was a juicer, but those didn't crush ice, so her mom steadfastly refused to spring for one.

Becca spotted wheat germ, beets, strawberries, and a bunch of green stuff on the kitchen counter. As the blender ground to a stop, she perched herself on a stool at the breakfast bar.

"Good morning, Rebecca!"

"Caroline."

Her mother gave her a sideways look that in mom language meant "I'm not going to react," which was exactly why Becca had called her Caroline.

"Do you want a smoothie?"

"Not with beet leaves, I don't."

"You can't even taste them."

Lies. Becca pulled the "Life and Leisure" section of the paper toward her to look for the sudoku while Caroline peered under the blender lid to judge the consistency of her drink.

"Are you ready to start a great new week?"

It was a classic mom trap. If she answered "yes," Caroline would know it was a lie. If Becca said "no," she'd get a lecture.

"Hey, Mom, do you remember Ella?"

"We're not getting a cat."

"Okay. Whatever. But you remember her?"

Caroline nodded. "I remember you told everyone you were call-ing it Rosie, then you changed its name at least a dozen times, so I came up with my own and at some point, it stuck."

"Ella?"

"No. L.A. Short for Little Asshole. It was such a shit."

L.A. El-la. Becca stared blankly at her mother: another sweet childhood memory destroyed.

"I had no way of knowing the name was going to stick," Caro-line said, checking the time. "Okay. You don't want a smoothie, fine. And toast is definitely out. You can have some low-fat milk and half a grapefruit.

Becca looked up at her mom, confused.

"You're getting a little muffin top," said Caroline, pulling on a perfectly pressed linen jacket.

Horrified, Becca's arms immediately dropped over her stomach. "God! Mo-om!"

"You told me to tell you. I'm telling you."

"Yeah, but not like a minute before school."

There wasn't an ounce of fat on Caroline. Her body had been tanned, tweaked, stretched, exfoliated, and conditioned. She was like an athlete at the top of her game, only there were no Olympics for her event. There was probably a zipper-bag of perfectly young extra skin hidden away in the back of the freezer waiting to be thawed to save Caroline from her golden years.

"You'll feel better about yourself when you're ten pounds lighter. You'll see," Caroline said, straightening out the lacy bits of her bra so they barely peeked out above her camisole. "You going to take the nail polish off before you go to school?"

Becca looked at her hands. She'd painted her nails with her mother's new powder-blue polish on Saturday night.

"Why?"

Caroline licked her spoon and slipped it into the dishwasher. "The colour doesn't do you any favours."

Becca shook her head. "What does that mean?"

Caroline sighed. "You've got your father's hands. The blue polish makes your fingers look short and stubby ... a little masculine."

"Fuck!"

"Rebecca."

"How do you expect me to react, Mom? You just basically told me I have man hands."

Becca shot off her stool and crossed to the junk drawer, trying to remember why she'd let her mother talk her into putting the nail polish on in the first place. She rummaged through stamps, chequebooks, and notepads. "Where's the nail polish remover?"

"If you can't find any, I guess we're out."

"Great. Nice one, Mom! Way to parent."

"I didn't run out on purpose, Rebecca. I'll pick some up tonight."

"What am I supposed to do in the meantime?"

"Stick your hands in your pockets." Caroline shook her head and muttered, "I'm sorry I said anything."

The more Becca stared at her hands, the more they looked wrong. She jammed a finger into her mouth and tried gnawing the polish off, but it wasn't working. "Ugh!" she shrieked. "This sucks!"

"What sucks, Becca? You live in a fantastic home. You have no children to look after. You have food and clothes and everything you need."

Becca spotted a black Sharpie under the newspapers and dug it out.

"Although, I guess I should be thankful or something that at least now you can talk to someone about what's going on, even if it's not me." Caroline's voice trailed off as she walked to the fridge for one of her prepackaged lunches. "I mean, I *wish* you felt you could trust me rather than a therapist with whatever's going on. You obviously don't. But you know, I have feelings too."

"Look," said Becca, proudly holding up her Sharpied thumb. The powder-blue nail polish had disappeared beneath a coat of black ink.

Caroline gave her daughter's brilliant nail colour solution no acknowledgement whatsoever. She hunted through her pockets and found the lipstick that went with her outfit, ravenously bit into the tangerine colour, then lowered the shark-fin shape back into the depths of its silvery tube.

"Okay. Let's go." Caroline jangled her car keys.

"I need five minutes, Mom."

Caroline picked up her tub of baby carrots and her ionized water and started acting like she was already late. "Bring the marker with you."

"I won't be able to put it on straight if the car is moving, Mom. Five minutes. *Please!*" Becca started on her index.

"Sorry. I can't wait. I have a meeting. You're going to have to take the bus."

Becca nodded.

"You really think that's better?" Caroline asked, studying Becca's nails.

"Better than man hands? Ummm … yes?"

And with a rapid series of lipstick air kisses, her mother was gone.

FOR THE NEXT TEN minutes, Becca Sharpied the rest of her nails. They looked not bad, but they weren't drying all that fast, so she decided to wait a few extra minutes before she left for school. She walked into the kitchen blowing on her fingertips and carefully started looking through the cupboards for some actual food.

She wished really hard for a box of frosted cinnamon rolls, but when she flung the cupboard open, she found flaxseed, dried mushrooms, and a package of Wasa Crispbread. Halfheartedly, Becca reached for the crisps. They were Caroline's "sin" food, which was not exactly a ringing endorsement, but the picture on the package, which showed them blanketed with inches of ham and cheese, definitely suggested they were edible.

Becca carefully popped the box open with the tips of her fingers to avoid smudging her nails and shook out a piece of Wasa. She guessed she could technically call it a slice, although it made a polite *clink* sound as it landed on the counter. Naked Wasa looked like brown bread that had been squished flat and dried out. She sniffed it. It had a slightly sweet odour, but so did desserts made with red bean paste, so she wasn't sold on it yet.

She carefully snapped the cracker into a few smaller pieces and popped one into her mouth. Within the space of a few chews, she crossed to the compost bin and spat it out. Being ultra-skinny was so not worth it. As she reluctantly returned to the grapefruit, she discovered her nails were covered in fine specks of crispbread dust.

"Oh nooooo," she said.

She tried blowing the specks off, but they wouldn't budge. She snapped up a tissue and tried to gently coax the dust off, but wispy bits of tissue stuck to her nails.

"Fuck!" Becca shouted. Seriously, OMG! The day was just starting, her fingers smelled like bean paste, and everything sucked ass. Everything.

6

Talking Shop

BEFORE KARL SAW THE call centre, he heard it: keyboards clacking, the soft crinkle of plasticized procedures sheets being flipped, and a hundred choruses of "Can I help you?" All of it devoid of anyone actually giving a shit.

There were no windows in the big room. Instead, a piss-yellow glow from the ceiling fixtures dimly illuminated the desks twenty feet below. Ancient foam baffles clung to the walls. They absorbed not only sounds but all the smells the cramped, overheated space generated. Basically, it was like working at the bottom of a toilet.

Karl skirted the wall and took the ninth row to his workstation. He kept his head bowed in case Ed, his manager, happened to be looking in his direction.

Not that he was late or in any trouble. He just generally disliked drawing attention to himself, especially as AMICO was always looking for reasons to boot people. Serial layoffs kept salaries low and the plebes grateful for their jobs. And Karl, plebe that he was, did not want to lose his job.

His workstation was as cheery as the inside of an early Russian space capsule. There was a phone, a computer, a grimy three-ring procedures binder, and a desk lamp that buzzed when it was on. Of course, he could have taken it upon himself to create a slightly more pleasant atmosphere, but it had never occurred to him he would be at AMICO longer than it had taken SpaceX to develop reusable rockets.

But that was another story.

Employees had to be full-on working by their start time, and Karl had six minutes left before he was on the clock. He sat at his desk, woke up his computer, and started his login, but before he even understood what he'd done, a porn site popped up on his computer. He'd automatically signed in. Jesus. Karl quickly swung his cursor over to the close page button when he spotted the new animation: a chick with stringy hair getting banged, cans shaking, mouth open, saying something. The clip looped. His forebrain started urgently telling him he needed to shut it off, but his reptilian brain was compelling him to watch it again. To study her mouth. Imagine her sounds.

Porn had started off as a "gentleman's pastime" for him, but somewhere along the line it had changed. Now he needed it to get through the day. Because he'd racked up thousands in debt to feed his monkey, he'd had to sell everything and move in to a basement apartment. All he had left to his name was a chair, an Obama-era laptop, and a lumpy mattress, along with whatever Wi-Fi he could steal.

But it turned out losing everything wasn't the worst thing that could happen to him. The more pathetic he became, the more he needed porn. He feared there'd come a day he'd stop wearing pants altogether.

"Hey, Karl!"

Karl's heart shot up into his ears. He hit the space bar. His screen went black.

"Ed!" he said too loudly to sound casual. "What's up?" Karl rolled his chair under the desk to hide his boner as Ed stepped around the divider into his workstation. Classic fucking Ed move.

Ed was fit for a guy in his fifties — muscles strapped onto a barrel kind of deal. You got the sense nothing intimidated him. Probably because he did all the intimidating.

"Something wrong with your screen?" he asked, pointing at Karl's dark monitor.

Ed's hand hovered over the space bar, ready to fix the problem. One tap and the tits would be back in plain sight.

"Nah. I have to reboot. Refresh rate thing? I talked to IT about it." Karl tried to smile, but there wasn't enough spit left in his mouth to make it work.

Ed nodded. "Let me know if they don't get to it fast enough."

"Sure will."

"I have a new employee starting next Monday, but I'll be in a budget meeting at nine when she gets here. Wondering if you could pick her up from HR, make my apologies, and show her the ropes? Get her settled in?"

"Sure thing."

Ed nodded, but he didn't walk away, which was a little strange. Normally, the guy was always on the move. Instead, he looked out across the sea of dividers, then back at Karl. "Another thing," he said with a resigned sigh. "And this is strictly on the QT."

"Sure," said Karl.

"I've been getting reports about … an individual," he said, lowering his voice, "masturbating in the men's washroom. You run into that?"

Karl looked surprised. "No!"

Ed nodded like that was exactly the answer he'd expected to hear. "Well, if you see anything, *hear* anything … you come tell me."

"Absolutely."

Ed straightened up and looked around sharply for slackers, clapping Karl on the shoulder. "Good talk."

Karl's hands were moist, and his skin felt hot. As he went through the motions of a reboot, he did his very best to look like a person who had nothing to hide.

7

Deepfake

LATE SUNDAY NIGHT, BRENT had taken a final look around for Gary in the neighbouring bushes, hedges, and alleyways. Over and over he'd shouted his dog's name into the abyss but heard only night's silence in return.

Feeling despair starting to mushroom, he'd returned home, where he'd discovered eighteen new texts and emails waiting for him. They were mostly from local animal lovers and dog rescue groups, each suggesting new places to post pictures online, providing numbers to call, and offering to help look for his dog. Overwhelmed with gratitude, Brent had followed up with every single person who'd reached out. That very night, he'd acted on every tip, thanked every share, acknowledged each sad-faced emoji, and hearted all "thoughts and prayers" or "poor pupper" comments.

Despite a meagre three hours' sleep, Brent awoke Monday morning feeling optimistic.

He left for work early to tack up fresh a slew of yellow posters, discovering someone had covered many of Gary's posters with the announcement of a yard sale offering "record's" and "antique's." As the dog's owner and an assistant professor of English, Brent felt duty-bound to rectify these breaches of civility by assiduously covering every yard sale poster he encountered with another one of his own. He'd become so absorbed by his task that he was now running late for his ten o'clock class.

He hurried down the limestone steps and strode under the covered walkway toward the faculty offices. He threw a quick, envious glance toward the few students reading at the foot of the centuries-old weeping willows, faces shining in the sun, beginning to weave the fine threads of literary masterpieces they were doomed to struggle with for years.

He followed the red, black, and ochre slate tiles to the English department's administrative offices. Over the summer, its incandescent bulbs had been replaced by energy-efficient CFLs. It had saved the college money but destroyed all of the room's old-world charm. Where before, the departmental office had impressed upon visitors a golden, moody glow of hallowed erudition, the new blast of bright lights revealed tangled cables, outdated monitors, and coffee cup stains. The departmental office now had all the appeal of an airport hotel lobby.

Irene, the departmental secretary, was murmuring on the phone as Brent walked in, her soothing, efficient voice barely registering as sound. She seemed to be fixing something or advising someone. He crossed to his mail cubby and flashed through the paperwork, looking for printouts of his class assignments.

"They're here," said Irene, replacing her receiver. "I printed them just as you were walking in." She collected a packet of sheets from the printer and tapped them square against the front desk.

"Thanks so much," answered Brent. "The darned printer at home runs out of ink at the most inopportune moments." He flashed her a smile and opened his leather satchel, sliding his copies in.

"About your book order," segued Irene.

Which was exactly the conversation Brent had hoped to avoid.

On the surface, choosing a textbook for a new class seemed a straightforward task, but in practice it was always riddled with politics. Picking a book the chair disliked was ill advised, and Brent could not afford to get on anyone's bad side in his make-or-break tenure year. He needed more time to investigate further. He needed to be sure he was making the right choice.

"You've been very patient," he said to Irene.

Irene nodded, because she had. "But that was last week," she said, carefully repositioning her salmon cardigan over the edges of her massive chest to hide her belly. "This week, I am taking charge." She locked her eyes on his. "I'm sending my order in this morning."

Panic hit Brent like a wall. *Deadlines are arbitrary*, he wanted to argue. *This could be my downfall.* He wished he could confess his order paralysis was due to self-doubt and a lack of political insight, but Irene had been sleeping with the departmental chair, and that way madness lay. "To be honest," he said in a slightly overwhelmed voice that he only used in emergencies, "in the whirlwind, I guess I forgot all about it."

Her interest was instantly piqued. "Something happen?"

Brent loathed having to cheapen his personal tragedy, but he needed time. "My dog is missing." The words rose from the depths of his soul like bubbles in a caffeinated drink.

"Oh no," she said, assuming a look of utter devastation. Her brow creased; her eyes softened.

"It's been very traumatic," Brent continued, finding a picture of his dog on his phone and showing it to her. "His name is Gary."

"Oh dear," she said, pressing one hand to the dangly necklace at her throat. "What's wrong with his ...?"

"He's blind."

"Oh dear," she repeated.

"I haven't slept for days, of course. And so the truth is I'm afraid I haven't had a moment to think about this book order."

"Of course you haven't," she rushed to reply. "This is tragic. Absolutely tragic." She handed back his phone. "But the deadline is the deadline."

Brent nodded with understanding, looking ever so miserable. "Of course."

"I could … take a peek," she said, nodding toward the computer on her desk, "get you the same books Professor Jones ordered last year. Would that be helpful?"

Professor Jones was tenured and highly respected. Brent made a mental note to buy Irene flowers.

"If you could, Irene, it would be an absolute relief."

"Leave it with me," she said.

Brent suddenly felt he could breathe again.

"By the by," she added in a quieter voice, "an opportunity might come your way. And if it does, you should be willing to clear your calendar."

"Mysterious," he said, but he nodded in anticipatory agreement. She winked.

Some favours merited reciprocity, and this one clearly fit the bill. He suspected the departmental chair was looking for a prof for a new Regency course called "Romantic Memory" being offered in the summer session.

The course was certainly in his wheelhouse. He'd presented papers on all the players — Shelley, Austen, Ferrier — and written a number of articles: "Fashion Description as Cypher to Moral Value," "The 13 Meanings of 'Fine' in the Works of Jane Austen," and "Weather as Oppressor," to name just a few. However, it was but a tranche — the tip of the Regency iceberg — and he worried that sooner or later, his true ignorance of the subject would come to light and ruin him. He prayed he'd get tenure before that day arrived.

Until then, he would try to keep people's hearts warmly disposed toward him so when the time came, they might find a way to forgive him his numerous scholarly transgressions.

8
Man Problems

"HEY! ACTION-JACKSON," KARL yelled, jingling a bunch of coins in his hand. "I'm buying."

Jackson still wasn't getting his drift.

"Coffee," he clarified.

"Black," answered Jackson.

Not "Thanks." Not "I'll get you next time." A complete ball sack. Karl fed some coins into the coffee machine and turned to the other guy. "Saurav?"

Saurav smiled and waved him off. "No. Thank you very much."

Better. Karl bought himself a regular.

He didn't usually do coffee with new guys — and in the service industry, there were always new guys — but today he felt he needed to do something extra to keep his mind off his dick problems.

He'd spotted Jackson's Cookie Monster T-shirt across the call centre, talked with him a few minutes, then pulled the trigger and invited him to join him for coffee. Jackson brought along Saurav, who was probably going to be dull. His ironed polo shirt and polite smile spoke volumes.

Jackson had grabbed a table in the middle of the cafeteria so he could watch the sports highlights on the muted TVs. Saurav sat down across from him, back straight, palms facing down on the table like he'd been invited to some Barbie tea party and was politely waiting for the scones to arrive.

Karl set the two coffees down on the table and grabbed a seat.

Jackson nodded toward the TV, assuming Karl had been watching the highlights from the vending machine. "I've had it with these guys. This year, I mean it."

Why did every fucking conversation start with hockey? The Leafs wouldn't make it out of the first round. It would all fall apart and everyone would be arguing about what went wrong for months.

"Either of you guys into soccer?" asked Karl.

Saurav shook his head. Jackson did too.

"I can't get my head wrapped around it. All the running around and the long socks." Jackson shrugged, like he didn't need to explain more.

"Hockey players wear long socks," Karl remarked.

"It's not the same," Jackson answered loudly. How it was different, he didn't share. He carefully peeled the lid off his cup and took a short sip, immediately making a face. "I'm sorry. I can't drink this." He pushed the cup away.

"Really? Mine's okay."

"I thought I could drink it black. I guess I need cream and sugar. Saurav, you want it?"

Saurav shook his head.

Karl was a little pissed. "Why didn't you just ask for what you wanted in the first place?"

"This." Jackson sighed, slapping his gut right in the Cookie Monster.

"The girls don't like his belly," Saurav explained, like someone needed to clarify what Jackson had just clarified. Jackson quietly rubbed his beer baby as though the decision to give it up continued to be harrowing.

"I didn't think fat girls were picky," said Karl. It had been meant more as a casual observation, but Jackson puffed up right away.

"I never said I liked fat girls. I like big asses." He looked positively indignant.

"You're splitting hairs. It's the same thing."

"It's not the same thing. Absolutely not." Jackson's face was going red.

"A girl with a fat ass is a fat girl. Even if she had just fat legs or fat arms and the rest of her was skinny, you'd call her fat."

Saurav was smiling like he knew what everyone was talking about. "Personally," he said, "I think beggars can't be choosers."

Jackson snapped. "I don't beg. Okay? I choose."

"Yeah, and from where I'm sitting," Karl said, "it looks like you chose cream and sugar over ass every time."

Saurav burst out laughing.

Jackson hadn't seen any of it coming.

"Fuck you," he growled.

For a fat guy wearing a Cookie Monster T-shirt, he had remarkably little sense of irony.

The rapid-fire clicking of stilettos, like a conductor's baton hitting a music stand, focused everyone's attention. The chatter came to a stop as the guys waited for whoever was coming to appear around the corner.

The first thing Karl spotted were high-heeled turquoise sandals. Turquoise sandals with gold hardware, bare sun-kissed legs, a thick belt cinched over a tailored white shirt, and crazy red hair swept up in a casual style she'd probably spent a lot of time putting together. She was a knockout. Of course, she avoided all eye contact because she was walking into a room full of guys, but Karl kept an eye on her pencil skirt as long as he dared.

Saurav shouted, "Julie!" in a bright, clear voice that wandered into little-girl territory.

Karl caught the expression on Jackson's face. He definitely looked as surprised as Karl felt. Luckily, Saurav was too busy smiling like an asshole to notice their exchange of glances.

Saurav jumped to his feet. "Please," he said, indicating his chair, "would you like to join us?"

Julie looked briefly from Saurav to Karl and back. "I — I'm sorry. I can't today. I have a meeting."

Saurav smiled. "Next time," he playfully scolded.

Julie nodded and left.

Saurav turned to his tablemates, his eyes bright and shiny. "She is very nice. We have gone out two times. To dinner."

"Bullshit," Karl spat out.

"Yeah, you're full of it," echoed Jackson.

"No, no. I can assure you I'm not. She is studying economics, and she says I'm a good catch." Saurav giggled, delighted.

"What are you? New? She's not interested in you. No way." Jackson sounded jealous.

"And yet," Saurav replied, "we are going out for dinner next weekend."

Karl took over. "Okay, let me be straight with you here. She's using you. Obviously."

"I disagree," said Saurav. He smiled even when he was calling you wrong.

"Then she's got a tapeworm, and *it's* using you to get dinner."

Saurav laughed. He was starting to grow on Karl.

"Forget him," said Jackson in a strangled voice. He looked like he was on the edge of tears. "Just follow your heart, man. You gotta follow your heart."

Karl imagined Jackson had a long-winded story about some fat girl he should never have broken up with, but he wasn't sticking around to hear it. Pushing away from the table, he rose to his feet. Jackson looked up at him with surprise.

"Where are you going?" asked Jackson.

"I'm following my heart back to work," Karl muttered.

This break had been garbage. Now he really had to rub one out. Karl tossed out his coffee cup and made tracks.

9

Thoughts and Prayers

ONCE SHE'D DELETED ALL the pictures of her and Leanne from her phone, Becca concluded she had only taken two shots since she'd started at her new school. One was of the dog poster, and the other one was of her crying in a washroom stall. It had been completely unintentional, an out-of-focus snap of her reaching for more TP from her lap. The angle made her nostrils look huge. She hated how she looked, but she couldn't bring herself to delete the photo because it felt like she was telling a lie about herself.

The ugly truth was that if you didn't hook up with a cool group by the time the third week of school rolled around, you were a loner, which meant you told yourself you were deep while you ate your lunch in the bathroom. And Becca was currently a loner.

Since Leanne's rejection, she had started having serious doubts that anything about her personality was okay. She failed all the time, and she never knew she was failing until it was too late.

At her old school, there had been these girls who'd invited her to hang out with them during her free period, so Becca had. They'd asked her tons of questions about stuff. Who she listened to. Who she hated. Becca figured it had gone well because they'd invited her to go car hopping. She'd agreed without hesitation because for sure it was a test.

The stuff they found in the cars was sort of a yawn, mostly phone chargers and earbuds with earwax. Chantelle ended up scoring some Gucci sunglasses she found stuffed up over a visor which she really, *really* wanted Becca to have because Guccis slimmed down round faces, and she thought Becca needed that.

And that's when Becca knew she'd been accepted by the girls, and she suddenly felt one hundred percent awesome.

She wore her Guccis everywhere, even though they were prescription lenses and gave her wicked headaches. She never complained because she felt super grateful that Chantelle wanted her to have them, especially after she'd said nice things about a girl she didn't realize everyone hated.

But it turned out everyone knew about the lenses, and they were laughing at her whenever she rubbed her eyes. And then one person started going on about SKDs. And then so did everyone else. Everything started to be rated SKD or not SKD, and Becca didn't get it until she clued in they were talking about her. She was a skid — a stain left behind by people who were eating life.

Mary the Immaculate was supposed to be her fresh start, but changing schools hadn't solved her problem, because the problem was clearly her.

TUESDAYS AND THURSDAYS, BECCA had Advanced French with Madame Hervé, whose real name was Mrs. Harvey. There had been a rumour about her barfing into a wastepaper basket on Monday morning. No one had seen her since.

All the Catholic kids had started praying for a free period. Hopes were running high until the substitute teacher walked in and ruined it.

"French Two?"

A mostly male groan rippled through the classroom, but the girls' chatter had cut out clean. The boys hadn't quite caught on to what was happening, but the girls' body language had shifted to the vocabulary of hair flips, gel pen clicks, and lip gloss applications, because Monsieur Gaillou was hot. Like, classic vampire hot.

He was slightly pale but looked seriously intense and deadly mysterious. He wrote his name on the board and barely said it out loud. Instead, he just tossed a weird, skinny brown briefcase on the desk like he didn't care if anyone remembered him. His jaw was angular and set. He spoke with a slightly bored sneer. You could barely see his eyes through the wisps of straight, lustrous black hair that refused to obey his hand, which kept brushing it back. But he was watching. Everyone. He clearly had his own way of being and thinking and teaching. Becca decided he looked sad and haunted, which suggested to her that he might have loved someone intensely who'd died. He could probably be forgiven anything.

Monsieur Gaillou snatched up a folder on the desk and read through it, nodding, then came around his desk, annoyed with the growing din.

"*Allez, allez. Calmez-vous, s'il vous plaît. SILENCE.*"

Becca was pretty sure he wanted a cigarette. Like a real one. Without a filter. So it could dangle from his fingers while he gesticulated toward the board, right up until it was time to flick the butt out a window. *They really should let teachers smoke*, she thought. Especially when they were foreign. Schools should also have windows that opened out.

"Okay. So grade ten French, we are doing *conjugaisons, oui*?

"No," everybody mumbled, shaking their heads because everybody hated conjugating verbs. But Gaillou's piercing intellect immediately saw right through them.

"*Alors, Madame Hervé souhaite* — wishes — *elle souhaite que nous parlions du passé.* So, we will speak about something using the past tense. Let's talk about what we did this weekend. Anyone? What did you do?"

Students were avoiding his gaze, so he picked up a class plan. "Rébecca. What did you do?"

Becca blushed and shook her head. "*Rien*. Definitely *rien*." She looked down, her gaze falling on her Sharpied nails, the Wasa crumbs still in full evidence; she hid her fingertips in her palms.

Gaillou drew nearer. "*Allez, allez*. One thing."

He was chiding her like a child. The look in his eyes was growing more intense as he got closer. "You have to set the example for the others. *Une chose. Dites-moi d'une seule chose.*" He was asking for her help. His voice was soft and smoky. She could feel herself sinking into it like a thick, velvety blanket.

As he waited for Becca to formulate her answer, Gaillou turned to the other students and warned them, "Everybody will speak today." The volume in the classroom blew up. Gaillou's voice rose over the din and masterfully brought the room back to order. "*Tout le monde. On écoute Rébecca. Qu'avez-vous fait ce weekend dernier?*"

Becca nodded as her mind raced through the events of the last few days: man hands, therapy, Katy Perry music, muffin tops ...

Becca settled on a half lie. "*J'ai pris un photo.*"

"*Comment?*"

"*Avec mon* cell phone?"

"*Un appareil mobile*," he corrected.

"Yeah, that," Becca said.

The class laughed. She hadn't said it to be a smart-ass, but it was a mouthful of vowels wrapped around a spitty "r," not a word. But Monsieur Gaillou was not letting her get away with anything. He wagged his finger at her like he was scolding her in a cartoon. Very European.

"*Un appareil mobile*," he said. Becca could feel herself blush as she leaned forward to watch his lips articulate the French language's most sensuous words: "*Répétez: un appareil mobile.*"

Becca wished she had a better word to repeat. Something prettier sounding. She tried her best. "Un apparoyl mobell," she said.

Gaillou grimaced.

"I can say it better," she said.

But Gaillou was no longer listening.

"Rébecca will practise at home," he announced. "Someone else can speak." He checked the seating assignment. "*Nelson? Où est Nelson?*"

A thick-necked, thick-armed boy tossed up his hand and immediately volunteered, "*J'ai pris photo* with a *apparell mobeel* of my girlfriend."

He'd piggybacked on Becca's signature word, but Gaillou hadn't noticed.

"Nelson, explain to the class how you took a picture of your girlfriend with your *appareil mobile* in the past tense."

Gaillou plunked his butt on the edge of his desk and listened, an amused smile on his face.

"*Premier, je levé* my phone. *Avec le bras.*"

Gaillou nodded deeply. "Correction: *j'ai levé.*"

"Okay. *Après, j'ai regardé dans mon appareil* for *un* shot."

"*Une prise.* A shot is *une prise.*"

The teacher was nodding encouragingly. Every sentence Nelson spoke seemed to be wiping Becca from Gaillou's short-term memory.

"And *click. Et je baisé mon appreil.*"

Monsieur Gaillou smiled. Carefully. "*Baisser.* It's *baisser.* Soft 's.' *Baisser* is to lower. But *baiser?*" He shook his finger emphatically, first at Nelson, then at everyone else. "It's not a word I am teaching you."

A buzz circulated through class. Someone beside Becca was looking it up on their phone. "Boning … it's boning. *Baiser* is …"

Nelson turned to the guy sitting behind Becca. "French guys *beaucoup baiser!*"

"Okay. Okay. We're going to focus now." Gaillou clapped his hands. "Christiana?"

A girl with a pixie cut, vintage tee, and skateboarder cargos lifted her hand.

10

Destiny Calling

KATHERINE CHECKED THEODORE'S PULSE and carefully set his limp arm back onto the bed. "He's gone," she announced gravely to his family, gathered around. They all hung their heads in shocked silence.

"Good!" called out Jason from behind the director's table. "Great."

This pronouncement was followed by a collective exhale as the actors were released from the effort of concentration.

"I felt like everybody was very present," said Jason. "Very in the ..."

Whatever, thought Katherine, crossing back toward her prompt book. She needed to jot down the new blocking while it was fresh in her mind. She hovered over the script, looking for the relevant scene. The page flips made a lovely crinkly sound. It was glue cracking, but still, it had a magical quality, like she was consulting a great book of knowledge.

"Instead of turning in to myself at the end," said Amanda, who played the hard-hearted wife, "I was feeling like I really needed the pain to open up *more*. Did anybody else feel that?" The actors shook their heads, including Theodore, the deceased.

"I can't open up more," he said. Like it hadn't been obvious.

"We'll try what you're suggesting next time through and see, okay?" said Jason.

Amanda beamed. If there was anything she loved, it was exploring opportunities for upstaging.

"Is this a good time to take a break?" Jason asked Katherine as she drew nearer to their shared worktable.

"Sure. Fifteen minutes, everyone," Katherine hollered over her shoulder. She glanced at her watch. "Back at three on the dot."

The actors raced out of the rehearsal room for their herbal teas, homeopathic drops, and quick cigarettes. Theodore followed them, a few feet behind, his tattered script in hand. He'd curled and uncurled it throughout the entire coma scene. It had been a little off-putting.

"For a guy who hangs on to his script so much, it's remarkable how few lines he actually knows," Jason observed.

Katherine nodded. "I was just thinking the same thing."

She found a pencil and added the new blocking to her prompt script. She'd come up with it on the fly while she was standing in for a missing cast member. Of course, nothing was wrong with the old blocking, but as a character on stage, Katherine had just known it would be more organic to go stage left, check the IV, then push aside Theodore's food tray while reacting to his distress.

Jason had been quite complimentary about it. Probably because it solved his sight line problems. Katherine had chalked up the inspiration to her *Grey's Anatomy* marathons.

"That was good," said Jason.

"Yep. It's getting there." One had to be noncommittal when talking to directors. They were generally insecure.

She could feel Jason watching her, so she snatched up her phone for something to do and discovered Brent had called several times. She immediately deleted his messages without listening to them. If she'd wanted someone needy, she'd have pursued an early childhood education certificate. Maybe it was time to end it with him.

"After the break, let's run the first act," said Jason.

Katherine nodded. "I'll do a reset."

She returned to the makeshift hospital set she'd pulled together for rehearsal. It consisted mostly of wooden cubes and a sturdy coffee table subbing in as a bed. The masking tape lines on the floor were where walls and doors would eventually be on the real set. She'd scored a tray of medical instruments to give the situation a little *veritas*, but it was an absolute mess. Actors had to touch everything like little children. The forceps were in the gauze, and the fake scalpels were mixed in with the real ones. It was a disaster waiting to happen.

"— standing in."

Jason had been jabbering at her.

"Pardon?" said Katherine. She'd become so absorbed by her task, she'd zoned out, and now Jason was standing beside her, an empty coffee mug in hand.

"I said thanks for standing in. As the nurse," he repeated. "I've put out a casting call to replace Mindy because it's shingles, so she's not coming back."

"Right." He wasn't letting her concentrate, so she smiled at him. "I hear those hurt."

"Terribly."

She could feel him staring at her again. It definitely wasn't sexual. They'd worked together before on another show and nothing had happened, not even when they both got loaded.

"You want to do it?" he said like he'd read her mind.

Katherine felt her cheeks flush. "Excuse me?"

"The part?"

Katherine let her long, wavy hair fall over her face to hide her confusion. "I don't know if you've noticed, but I already kind of have a job on this show." She tucked a strand of hair behind an ear. She decided she wasn't going to explore the idea because there had to be a punch line. A "ha ha ha — got you" sort of exchange. Instead, Jason remained quiet.

"Are you kidding me? You're kidding, right?" She tried to sound as casual as possible, to give him every opportunity to back out before she listened to what her heart was telling her — that she sort of wanted to do it.

"You're perfect. Seriously. It's a small part, but it's like it was made for you."

"Huh," she said, thinking about it. Her eyes suddenly narrowed suspiciously. "Are we broke? Is that it?"

Jason laughed. "No! We have money. I happen to think you're perfect. Be the nurse."

"What about calling the show?"

"I'll make sure it doesn't conflict with any cues. And hey! You get a sexy white uniform and an opportunity to ram a thermometer up Theodore's ass every time he drops a line."

"Tempting."

"Think about it, okay? Only not too long." On Katherine's nod, Jason walked out toward the kitchen.

Normally, she'd have declined straight away. Katherine could say no to anyone. But in this case, she hadn't, which was interesting. She'd never considered acting as a career, but something about playing this nurse character felt right. Maybe it was because she'd taken a healing crystals course at the Resonance Centre. People told her she was a natural healer, and she had definitely been drawing on that energy earlier in the day, although this role called for something different.

It would be an experience. She couldn't think of herself as an actress. Obviously. That would be making too much out of it. It was only one line. Her family would be furious. They didn't appreciate public attention. So that was a plus. Katherine bit down a smile. And when she could no longer ignore her excitement, she grabbed her cell and called Brent, grinning from ear to ear. There was something honestly thrilling about being "discovered."

Her call went straight to voice mail.

Katherine hung up and tossed her phone in her bag, her good mood evaporating. She'd spent the weekend searching for Brent's dog, offering emotional support, a fresh postering strategy — she'd even made lunch! And now that *she* had something to talk over, he "wasn't available." So gender-typical.

Unless Brent wasn't answering because he had decided to dump her. He'd been outraged she'd suspected the neighbour had abducted his dog. Katherine stopped herself from exploring the fallout further, surprised where doubt was taking her.

BY THE TIME HER streetcar crossed Shaw, she was obsessively fishing her phone out of her pocket every few minutes to reconfirm Brent hadn't called. And every time she acknowledged he hadn't, her anger ratcheted up a notch.

Fucker, she thought. *Fucking motherfucker*.

This was hardly a surprise. In her experience, whenever one person was happy in a relationship, the other was getting royally screwed.

A woman in a fuzzy orange hat spun her head toward her and stared. Katherine realized she might have been speaking out loud. It happened sometimes when she got angry.

"It's for a part," she announced haughtily, upset to be feeling self-conscious. She was not accountable to women in orange hats. Not by a long shot. She hit the stop request button and elbowed her way to the back doors.

She needed some air.

11

Turned Away

FROM HER CHAIR IN the vice-principal's office, Becca could see her substitute French teacher talking with the principal. He looked even paler and more beautiful than before in the quad. He paced around the office explaining something with vitality, his eyes flashing with anger. Becca noticed how he vainly tried to brush away that one strand of hair that kept demanding attention as he spoke. So European. Gaillou spotted her from across the office and fell quiet. For a few seconds, Becca thought about waving to him, but he slammed the office door shut before she did.

It had been a really confusing day.

The better part of fourth period passed before Becca began to understand why she'd been pulled out of class and escorted to the vice-principal's office.

She'd spotted Gaillou earlier in the quad, surrounded by guys from her French class. It had looked like a game of soccer was imminent.

All she'd wanted was another chance to prove she could say *appareil mobile*, but she'd been too self-conscious to try in front of so many people. She'd proposed to Gaillou that they could go somewhere private where she could show him she'd been practising. He'd locked eyes on her a moment, then refused.

Becca felt a bit annoyed and a lot judged. He needed to get over himself.

"I just need to be alone with you five minutes to show you how good I can do it."

Everyone around them went quiet. Gaillou looked mortified. And Becca started to worry she'd spoken too loud.

It turned out people had misinterpreted what she'd said, and everyone was asking if she had a relationship with her French teacher. It was flattering that people could see them together, but it would never happen. He was a rude, self-important Frenchman.

The VP started asking weird, vaguely sinister questions about Monsieur Gaillou, like something creepy had happened, only Becca didn't know about it. It bothered her when people thought she was clueless, but it was possible she hadn't exactly understood what was going on because she often seemed to be missing a layer of information when it came to relationships. By the time she got home, Becca was in a full-on panic about not being able to remember horrible things that might or might not have happened. She needed to call her therapist.

"Doctor Schofield said to call if I had to. He said!" Becca pleaded.

"I understand," the receptionist answered, pretending she couldn't hear it was important.

"Please," said Becca. "I have to talk to him. I'm fourteen, and I'm totally freaking out." Becca thought she heard the receptionist sigh.

"What was your name again?"

She'd given it to her twice. "Becca ... Rebecca Chalmers."

"Hold on a minute." There was a click, and the hold song came on. It started halfway through and went on for a bit, but right before it finished, it started over again. Only not from the beginning. It started in the middle. And then it did it again. Playing from not quite the beginning to not quite the end. The longer she listened, the more Becca's dread grew as she realized she was reaching the not-quite-the-end point again. Mercifully, there was a click, and the receptionist came back on.

"Becky? Doctor Schofield has asked me to refer you to another doctor. Doctor Jimenez. I'll give you her number. Do you have a pen?"

Becca stayed quiet. She wasn't quite sure what was going on.

The receptionist explained. "Doctor Schofield thinks Doctor Jimenez is ..." She was looking for the words. "... better suited to oversee your mental health requirements."

Her words hit Becca like a slap. She struggled to deal with the blow.

"Why doesn't he want to talk to me?" Becca could hear tears starting to pool in her voice.

"Becky, have you found a pen?"

"Why can't I talk to him?"

"What if I ask Doctor Jimenez's office to get in touch with you? How would that be?"

"Did I do something wrong?"

"No, of course you didn't —"

"Could you please tell Doctor Schofield I'm sorry. Please!" Becca had never begged so hard.

"This isn't right. This isn't my job. What am I supposed to say?"

"I don't know."

The doctor's voice cut in as if he'd been standing beside the receptionist all along. "Becca, this is Doctor Schofield."

"What did I do?"

"You've done nothing. This is my fault."

Caroline walked into the kitchen, tossing her keys down on the counter with a clatter. Startled, Becca spun toward the noise then turned away for privacy.

"Why can't I see you?" she asked.

Caroline moved toward her. "Who is it?" she whispered.

Becca moved away, but Caroline followed.

"I'm not going to get into that with you," said Doctor Schofield. "Rebecca, I'm very sorry, but this is the way it is. I assumed — that is — I was led to believe your issues had something to do with your parents' divorce. I didn't grasp the extent of your trust issues until I looked through your journal the other day, and then I realized ..." His voice trailed off for a moment. "I'm sorry, Becca, but this is the best course of action. Doctor Jimenez is an excellent doctor. You will like her. You must go and talk with her."

"I don't want another doctor. I picked you."

Caroline peered down at her phone. There were several text messages. She read them quickly.

"I'm between a rock and a hard place, Becca." Doctor Schofield's voice was starting to sound sharper. "I have a clear conflict of interest, and for this, I am sorry. Now please accept my apology and let it go."

"But I —" Becca exclaimed.

Caroline made a decisive grab for Becca's phone, and Becca let it go. The fight had drained out of her.

"Sherman? It's Caroline. What's up? Yeah. So? Uh-huh. Uh-huh." She rolled her eyes and didn't look impressed. "You're making too much of it." She listened a moment then wanted it to stop. "Well, I *thought* ..."

Doctor Schofield went on. As Caroline listened, she cocked her head to the side, her eyes widening with surprise. "Excuse me?" she roared and ended the call, tossing the phone on the counter.

"Nooo!" Becca shrieked in utter disbelief. She lunged for the phone and heard silence. "What did you do?"

"I told you you'd be wasting your time on that man. He's an asshole, Rebecca. You don't need a man like that."

Becca didn't reply. She was too busy thinking of her imminent doom. She hadn't felt happier after her sessions with Doctor Schofield, but at least she'd felt like something could eventually change.

"Okay. You need to stop wallowing in despair. It's time to make lemonade." Caroline peered into the refrigerator and considered dinner options, tapping the side of the door with her powder-blue nails.

Unbidden, pieces of Saturday evening suddenly reassembled in Becca's mind.

While lots of mothers and daughters shared memories of hair streaks and summer sandals, moments of closeness were rare in the Chalmers-LeFever household. Mostly because the mother-daughter activities Caroline proposed were like bikini waxes and colonic irrigations. Caroline's invitation to a home manicure had seemed uncharacteristically noninvasive. As they'd both concentrated on painting their nails, her mom had nudged her for details about her session with Doctor Schofield. "Did he ask you about me?" and "What did you say?" followed by "What did he say?" Becca had expected a few questions, but there'd been something about her mother's questions. Something familiar ...

And suddenly, she knew!

"Did you ...?" she asked. Becca's voice was shaking.

Caroline stayed silent.

Becca snatched her mother's phone and glanced at the messages. Three were from Doctor Schofield.

"You *did*!"

Caroline peered over the refrigerator door. Becca stared at her accusingly until Caroline made her "get over it" face.

"OMG, Mom! O-M-fucking-G!"

"I didn't plan this. I went to meet him to see if I trusted him. We were talking about you and your dad and the divorce. And it sort of evolved from there. It happened, and I'm sorry. I'm sorry, he's sorry — we're *all* sorry, Rebecca. Let's move on."

"Couldn't you act responsibly just this once?" shouted Becca.

"Sherman and I were positive you'd talk to him once and never see him again. It's your MO, Becca. Guitar, karate, tap lessons. One and you're done."

"Do not —"

"Okay. I might have picked the wrong time to behave like a human being instead of a parent. But this is on you too. Did I or did I not ask you to see someone else?" charged Caroline. "The answer is yes, I did. The universe was practically flinging itself in your path to stop you from going to that appointment, and still you made the decision to ignore it."

"What?!"

"Remember the big detour we had to take when I drove you downtown? How the clinic's front door was accidentally locked? How my credit card was declined? Three times? Did you think those were coincidences?"

"Are you really blaming me for your decision to sleep with my therapist?"

Caroline emerged from the fridge holding several unappealing vegetables. "Becca, I'm officially done eating humble pie. You've gotten all the *sorry* you're getting from me."

"You ruined my therapy, Mom! What am I supposed to do now?!"

Caroline set the beets down on the counter like it was a line she was daring Becca to cross. But Becca had lost the will to fight.

12

Cold Comfort

BRENT HAD SERIOUSLY UNDERESTIMATED the weather. Every block or so, he'd switch his briefcase from his right to his left hand and jam his icy fingers deep among the warm coins and paper clips in his pants pocket, remembering how that very morning he'd stared into the closet, right past a cardigan, and picked out a linen shirt.

Kate had once jokingly remarked that he dressed like a professor in the movies. He'd chuckled with her, but the truth was that dressing the part gave him the professorial confidence he sorely lacked. At some point in his graduate years, he'd learned that in the right shirt, he could stand in front of a classroom and make undergrads understand how decolonizing postcolonial literature was not only interesting but vital.

It had launched his academic career.

Consequently, Brent had built up a professorial wardrobe that paired clothing with subjects. The houndstooth blazer and denim shirt were for casual lectures and talks on early-twentieth-century poetry. His cashmere pullover was reserved for more elegant affairs such as book launches and introductions on symbolism in Chaucer. Linen was for discussing texts charged with social commentary, et cetera, et cetera. It was just his bad luck to hit the Jane Austen module as the temperature decided to take an icy plunge.

The brisk, cold wind pierced his loosely woven shirt and swirled about his torso and arms. He began to imagine how tea bags felt.

"'Blow, blow, thou winter wind,'" he muttered under his breath, then fell silent as he caught sight of one of Gary's posters fluttering on a nearby phone pole. The wind had ripped the poster under Gary's nose, making Gary's eyes flap around the pole, returning again and again in a sightless "J'accuse." Brent's mood darkened as he silently finished the quote: *Thou art not so unkind, As man's ingratitude.*

Who but an oaf would consider personal comfort while his old dog was still missing? Starving, thirsty, perhaps injured? A fresh gust of wind blew bits of hard earth and sand into Brent's face, stinging his cheeks. He turned in to the gale and accepted the discomfort as punishment. He should have been using his time to call the shelters, tack up more posters, and search the hedges instead of dredging up quips.

By the time Brent reached home, his face was numb.

He followed the path he normally took with Gary, over the flagstones, through the latched gate into the private side yard to his door. The neighbour's fence listed into Brent's yard. Its gentle collapse had begun before he'd moved in to his apartment, but for the first time, Brent noticed a small gap between two sections of fence. He gently shook the post, and a larger opening wobbled into existence. Still, it was highly unlikely Gary could have discovered a way through it.

Gary's plastic chew toys lay scattered around the yard, covered with pale grey tooth marks. They no longer spoke of a dog's enriched playtime. Instead, the scuffed squeaky steak suggested that Gary had deserved much more.

Brent decided on the spot that he would write Gary an elegy.

As he unlocked the door, a few lines started to take shape in his mind. He hurried inside.

Brent set his keys on the hall table, instantly remarking his apartment's heavy silence. He strode into the living room, turned on the TV, and found the Weather Network. It was currently thirteen degrees.

Gary's disappearance had forced Brent to acknowledge his uneasiness with solitude. Caring for his dog had given his life a shape. Certainly, work imposed a schedule, but Gary had connected all the moments of his day, from morning walks to the coffee shop to the tug-of-war rope games after supper. Now all times felt the same. The hours slipped away without barks or the jingling of a collar or reminders to enjoy the day.

There was no point calling Katherine to distract himself. She rigorously restricted their encounters to specific days and activities. Brent had tried on numerous occasions to get her to bend the rules, but Kate maintained that she was a private person and had a right to that privacy under sections 7 and 8 of the Canadian Charter of Rights and Freedoms. And if Brent had a problem with that, he could walk away.

She was a complex creature. Combative yet vulnerable. Meek with sharp edges. A renegade spirit. An *enfant terrible*. She was Shakespeare's Kate and Saint-Exupéry's little fox, but he would tame her.

Brent found some string mozzarella in the refrigerator and crossed the living room to the bay window, looking for distraction as he tore his snack into long, thin laces. He spotted his neighbour rooting around in the garden and slipped behind the curtains to watch him. He was robust and looked as though he'd sprouted up from a soil bed, dishevelled and dirty, a species of hostile, greasy fungus feasting on decaying roots. It was impossible to believe he had been married once.

Neighbours said his wife had been the gardener. That she'd been warm and compassionate, though she'd only been able to speak a few words of English. When she died, he'd withdrawn from the world, and his social skills had withered. Now he was more like a vacant house succumbing to spiders and mould than a man.

It was eleven degrees Celsius.

Brent pulled on a sweater and decided it was time to crack the nut that would become Gary's elegy. He collected pen, paper, and bourbon and was about to start writing when he noticed he'd received a voice mail.

"This is Miriam Mitchell," the voice said. "I'm the fiction editor for *New Fort Yorker*. We've had the opportunity to review the first five pages of your short story 'Inert' and would be interested in reading the remainder of the story for our next issue. Could you please give me a call at your earliest convenience?" Then came a number, which she repeated. Twice. Brent could hear the commas and the quotation marks in her voice.

"Dear God," he said, setting down his pen, and played the message once again.

13

Catch Up

AS SHE REACHED THE bottom landing, her cell phone started to ring.

Katherine sighed and turned back. She rushed back upstairs, taking the creaky stairs two by two to her apartment, her unbuttoned coat falling open behind her. She refused to be one of those people who spoke loudly in hallways on their phones as though their private affairs were fascinating. Events in her life would not be subjects of discussion in the laundry room.

She unlocked the door and walked in, answering on the fourth ring. She was slightly winded. "Hello?"

"Kate. It's Brent."

She didn't immediately return his greeting, partially to catch her breath but mostly to give him a chance to figure out what he'd done. After all, it was Wednesday.

"Oh, gosh. It's your yoga night, isn't it?"

Katherine breathed crisply and silently hung her yoga mat by the door.

"I'm terribly sorry. I forgot." Brent was babbling. "Why don't I call back?"

"I don't know what the point would be. I mean, I've missed my streetcar, right?" Katherine precisely timed her arrival at class to avoid unnecessary chatter. She threw her keys on the hall table with a sharp sigh. "Are you calling me because I called you? Because you shouldn't have bothered."

"No, I — I didn't realize you'd tried to get in touch. My phone has been swamped with calls about Gary." He sounded concerned. "Did you leave a message?"

She hadn't. Which completely undermined the angry response she'd planned, the one about having to share her stellar acting news with a barista who'd drawn a star on the side of her cup. "Never mind," she said. "Did you find Gary?"

She heard a silence.

"No," he finally said. "There's been no news on that front." By the time he'd reached the end of his sentence, his volume had completely extinguished.

"So you checked next door?" she asked, knowing full well he hadn't.

"Kate, I can't just search the neighbour's yard because you suspect something."

"I never said I suspected something. I called him a psycho."

Obviously, Brent wanted her to search the neighbour's yard with him. "Look, if you don't think Gary is worth confronting your neighbour about, don't. But own it and move on. It makes no difference to me."

"Now you're making it sound as if you don't care Gary is missing. Surely that can't be the case?" said Brent.

She paused. "I care that you care," she said carefully.

And heard silence. As she waited for him to respond, she could feel he was judging her. She picked up a pen and started an angry scribble on a corner of the grocery flyer until she got fed up and slammed her pen on the counter. "Okay. If you don't say something in the next thirty seconds, I'm hanging up."

"I'm — I'm *processing*, Kate. I assumed you liked Gary."

"Well, I'm not a dog person, okay?" she said. "And I would have told you if you'd bothered to ask. I mean, I really tried to like him, but it never organically happened. Then he got that cough, and it kept looking like he was on the verge of dying, so what was the point of saying anything?"

"Jesus," said Brent.

"I wasn't expecting a miraculous recovery. And you know, a lot of people don't like dogs," said Katherine. "Priests. Judges. Home ec. teachers." She did not have to explain herself, but she was. "Mothers. My mother doesn't like dogs. I mean, just because you like something doesn't mean everybody else does. It's not a crime." She sounded weak. She hated sounding weak.

Brent had gone quiet again.

"So is this it?" she asked, pushing her pen deep into a brown banana on the counter. "Are you breaking up with me because of what I said about your dog?" She studied the hole she'd made. "Because I'm not taking anything back."

"Of course not."

Katherine wasn't sure he was being perfectly honest with her, but without proof she had to let it go. "Fine. Look, my family is having a dinner party next Thursday. Someone got a promotion. Do you want to come?"

"Your family?"

He sounded incredulous.

"Yes, family. You know, mother, father —"

"I know what a family is, Kate. I just didn't realize you had one."

"Of course I have a family, Brent. Did you think I was hatched?"

"I meant to say, I thought they'd passed on or that you were estranged."

"I never said that."

"No, but you've never talked about them either, so I assumed ..."

It was like he was intentionally trying to annoy her. "Do you want to have dinner with my family or not?"

"I — yes. Of course." He fell silent again. It was getting on her nerves.

Katherine waited, tapping her pen on the counter a few times, then realized she'd gotten disgusting banana gunk all over her hands. She was ending this call. "Brent?"

"I'm trying to figure out how to go on," he declared.

"Sorry?"

"How can I be happy while Gary is still missing? It feels entirely wrong to allow myself to enjoy success."

"I don't understand. What success?" She tossed her pen into the sink.

"I may be getting a story published. But I don't know how I'd even be able to manage to sit at a computer ..."

Brent had begged her a half-dozen times to read his short stories. She hadn't because she didn't feel the need to be disappointed by another artist.

"Okay. *Clearly*, you're looking for permission to work on your story instead of looking for your dog."

"It's not as simple —"

"Yes," she said. "It is."

"No. I'll call the magazine. I can't —"

"Are you being serious right now?" Katherine dropped her cell phone as she reached for the roll of paper towels but didn't apologize for the clatter because she'd snatched the phone back up within seconds. "Brent, let me put this into perspective for you, okay? Gary is a dog. A dog." She repeated the word *dog* slowly, like she was talking to someone who didn't speak English.

"I unders—"

"Pit Bulls live like, what? Nine years? At best, you had another year with him. Either way, Gary was going to die, right?"

"We don't know that Gary's dead now."

"Ninety percent sure, Brent. Ninety." He said nothing. Katherine continued. "Did you steal this story from Gary? No. Is not publishing the story going to help you find him? No. Could publishing the story help you get tenure next year? Maybe. There is no issue here. It's a non-issue. And to be honest, I'm not sure any of this was worth missing a yoga class for, but anyway ..." Her voice trailed off. "Do it. End of discussion."

Katherine hung up.

Questions upon questions. Navel-gazing introspective garbage. This was why she'd dropped out of psychology.

14

Next Steps

IT WAS CLOSE TO midnight. Brent had been standing on the sidewalk in front of the neighbour's house for over thirty minutes, trying to convince himself to go up the walk, slip into the yard, and take a quick look around. But his feet would not obey.

He'd get caught.

Definitely. No matter how early or late he tried his luck. He'd never been stealthy. He imagined the instant he got through the gate, he'd be staring directly into his neighbour's angry face, and he'd be forced to reveal his girlfriend had been pushing him to trespass because she was convinced he was a dog killer. Brent had always been a terrible liar, even if his professional career consisted of a tissue of lies.

The sidewalk was as far as he could go.

Walking back to his house, he shouted Gary's name at the neighbour's property dozens of times. He whistled for his dog over the fence again and again until he retreated inside. He was a coward, but he'd done what he could. And that was the truth.

Brent walked into his house overwhelmed with shame. Intellectually, he knew the likelihood of Gary being in the neighbour's yard was microscopic, but his failure to overcome his personal misgivings to search for him confirmed he'd failed his dog, a creature who'd loved him without reserve.

Clearly, an elegy to Gary was insufficient.

He would dedicate his first publication credit to his faithful writing companion.

15

Forward

IT WAS THE DAY the school janitor waxed the floors with some product that made them smell like sweetened vomit. So incredibly gross.

Becca walked through the halls, hoodie up, head down, trying not to breathe or draw too much attention to herself — all of which was necessary on account of *"Baiser beaucoup,"* which the entire school was saying now.

When she reached the hall near the career counselling offices, Becca looked around to see whether anyone was hanging out, watching.

She needed to replace Doctor Schofield, and she'd had this idea. In her old high school, there'd been this girl whose name might have been Nadia. She remembered how people had said she had regular appointments with a career counsellor, *except* they didn't talk about extra language credits — they spent the entire time discussing how she felt. Of course, people found out about it eventually, and she'd vanished. No one ever knew whether she'd killed herself or her folks had moved. But ... lesson learned. Which was why Becca had been observing the office and the counsellors during her free period all week to see whether anyone was keeping track of students coming and going.

Straight away, Becca spotted something new pinned to the

bulletin board outside the office. It was a poster of grade twelves walking out of school, like at last bell. The kids were super dweeby — obviously — and they all looked excited. All except for this one guy who was off by himself, looking up and going, "Hmmm." Right above his hair was a thought bubble that said, "How Does the Future Look?"

Lame, thought Becca, shaking her head. *Empty* and *meaningless* also came to mind. The only kids who cared about the future were from immigrant families. And that was because their parents brainwashed them when they were little to get excited about crap topics like math and physics.

All Becca wanted to know was how to pull out of the tailspin her life was in, but everything at home was too strange now. Normally after a fight, Becca could forget she'd ever been angry. But this time, it was different. She wasn't sure about her mom on a whole new level.

She glanced toward the AV lockup and saw that the tall, gangly guy who checked out equipment was there, peering over his half door at the world. There was something slightly freakish about him. Maybe it was the eyeliner. He saw her looking at him and quickly looked elsewhere.

"Can I help you with something?"

Startled, Becca spun around and saw Greeley walking straight toward her.

Two people worked in the counselling office. One counsellor was young and pretty. Her name was Marietta. She dressed so supercool, she could have worked in a mall. Becca had watched her a lot. They'd smiled but never talked. Despite that, she'd imagined them hanging out and becoming friends and going for cocktails. The other counsellor was Greeley. She was old.

Greeley was definitely not her first pick, but as Greeley's eyes searched hers, Becca started to feel something. Like crying, maybe.

Becca spun back toward the poster and locked on to "How

Does the Future Look?," telling herself she was not allowed to lose it. Not in the hallway. Not with Greeley.

"I, umm ..." Becca swallowed hard. "I was wondering how tough it was ... to become a ... an ... astronaut?" God. So stupid. "If that was even possible."

"Huh," said Greeley, reflecting. "This is the very first time anyone's ever asked me that particular question." She smiled pleasantly without a whiff of judgment, revealing a tooth with a filling that was whiter than the rest of her teeth. "Let's see what we can find out online." She marched ahead toward a computer desk. Becca trailed behind, forced to follow through.

Greeley wore hideous black wedge lace-up shoes. Her skirt looked like it was made out of stiff chair fabric. She'd sat on it wrong, so one flap at the back was folded straight up. Around Becca's house, wrinkles were called mediocrity statements. Greeley would qualify as a mediocrity proclamation. Maybe even a mediocrity manifesto.

"I may be wrong," Greeley said, "but I imagine making it into the Canadian Space Agency is pretty competitive." She dropped into a chair in front of a computer desk and gestured vaguely toward a bunch of chairs across the room. "Bring one of those over."

Becca walked toward a few racks of photocopied pamphlets and saw two small offices where talking in private probably happened. The hip counsellor was still nowhere in sight.

She dragged one of the chairs across the carpet back toward Greeley, picking up small shocks off the chrome all the back way to the computer desk.

"What's your name?"

"Becca?"

"Becca," Greeley repeated, shaking the mouse to wake up the monitor. "I don't think I've seen you around before."

"I just transferred from another school."

"Really. Isn't that great for us. What do you think of Mary the Immaculate?"

Becca shrugged. It seemed exactly like her other school: polished floors, shiny trophy cases, lame oatmeal muffins, dusty mineral samples.

Greeley read her look. "Not sold, huh? I think it'll grow on you once you make some friends. There's a Pokémon Club and a Reach for the Top group that meets on Wednesday nights, I think."

Becca could not make herself fake any enthusiasm whatsoever, which Greeley noted as she started typing. Eventually, she hit "enter" with a lot of enthusiasm, and all this text popped up. Greeley started to speed-scroll, her eyes darting all over the monitor like crazy.

"I think astronauts," said Greeley calmly, still searching, "usually start off with a Bachelor of Science or something in advanced engineering. What are your grades like?"

Becca sat. "Mostly A-minuses. A few B-pluses."

The counsellor crinkled her nose like something didn't smell good but she wasn't going to say so. She clicked through a few web pages. "Why do you want to be an astronaut?"

"To be alone."

Greeley paused for a moment, considering, then shook her head. "Such an interesting answer. But I don't get the sense you're actually alone in space," she said. "Normally, astronauts work with a big team of people on earth who are responsible for keeping them alive and safe." Her eyes searched Becca's face for signs of comprehension, which was when Becca started to feel upset again.

Greeley must have straight away noticed Becca's change of expression because she backtracked, like she was trying to fix wrecked icing on a cake.

"If working alone is your goal, there are plenty of other jobs you could do. But maybe not at the Canadian Space Agency."

"No. I don't think so."

"Oh, dear," said Greeley. "I didn't mean to discourage you, but you know, it would be a shame to put in all those years of study and then not have things turn out the way you want."

Becca nodded. "I just want to go away," she admitted. It was the closest Becca had ever come to telling someone she didn't want to be part of the world anymore. It felt like she could trust Greeley.

Greeley frowned. "Do you mean travel tourism?" She peered at Becca, waiting for confirmation. "Because it's an iffy job market for travel agents right now."

Becca shook her head. Telling people what she wanted never seemed to work. She'd thought she'd come right out and said it. She stood up. "I have to get to class now," she muttered.

Greeley stood up with her, which surprised Becca. She walked alongside her toward the exit, still puzzling out her problem. "Becca, I think we should set up a real appointment for you," she said. "We could figure out what you want to do together. I have an aptitude test you could take. Would you like that?"

Becca knew Greeley was trying to help, but she was over both the conversation she'd started and her lame inability to make it stop. "Oh, look!" she said too enthusiastically, snatching up a few pamphlets on a table. "This is exactly what I came in for."

Too late, she noticed it was information about herpes.

"This has been really helpful, thank you," she muttered and hurried out before Greeley could ask her any more questions she couldn't answer.

16

Working Girls

THE SURFACE OF THE small table Katherine had snagged at The New Leaf was crowded with tea, salad, a notebook, and a sharp pencil. She'd decided to dig in to some medical research over lunch because something about Theodore's performance had started to ring false in rehearsals.

At the top of the second act, Theodore's character had landed in intensive care after he was beaten up at a strike meeting. But despite his serious physical state, he jabbered in his hospital bed near death's door for over twenty-five pages until he lapsed into a coma. It was preposterous — opera minus the deathbed aria. And yet, not a single cast member had spoken up for the importance of truth in art, or even raised a concern.

"Hey, *you!*"

Katherine plastered on a smile before she could see who was talking to her. Then she had to struggle not to let her expression change. It was a cast member.

"Amanda," Katherine remarked simply. Amanda was the worst paraphraser. Katherine could already tell that getting her off-book would be a monumental feat.

"I spotted you through the window," said the actress, "and I thought *why* haven't I checked this place out?"

Amanda was gushing. There really was no reason to. She was also hovering. It occurred to Katherine that she might be expecting an invitation to join her at her table, but she wasn't inclined to change her plans as she'd only just started tucking in to a list of precursor symptoms to comas. Katherine smiled and glanced back at her iPad.

"Is this where you get all your *yummy* salads at lunch?" Amanda asked. Her eyes were huge. If she'd been talking about meat, it would have been disturbing.

Katherine nodded and dug into her salad.

"I ordered the teriyaki edamame. Is it good?"

Katherine nodded and finished chewing so she could swallow. "They're pretty much all good." She could feel there was something weird on her lip. She had some dressing on it or something. God, she hated talking and eating. She reached for a napkin.

Amanda pointed to the empty chair. "Do you mind?"

Katherine was about to say she had some reading to do when Amanda threw off her coat and waved toward the food counter. "Can I have it for here, please?" She turned back toward Katherine. "Theo and I have been going to that other restaurant by the bus stop? The one with all the pigeons over the door? It's a little *drab*."

As Amanda launched into a long, unnecessary description of a mediocre Greek salad, Katherine could see her hunting for a spot to set down her Slurpee-sized coffee. Katherine made no effort to accommodate her, but soon enough, Amanda's gaze was returning again and again to her phone, like a pointer showing the hunter where to find the duck. Obviously, it was where her coffee was destined to land.

Katherine slipped her phone into her purse. Immediately, Amanda's coffee went down in its place.

"Oh my *God*!" she said, leaning in for a good look at Katherine's potato and kale salad. "What is *that*?"

Katherine's answer was lost in an explosion of scarves, sweaters, and bags that settled in and around Amanda like an entourage.

"So, this is nice!" said Amanda, presumably about them having lunch together.

"It is. It is."

"We always see you rush off at lunch, and we wonder, where does she go?"

Katherine frowned. "Really? I didn't realize I was that interesting."

"Oh, Katherine, *definitely*. You're positively *mysterious*."

It was impossible to have an actual conversation with someone who shat compliments for the inanest stuff. "Well, there's nothing much to me. I basically just write emails and make lists until it's time to go." Katherine saw the waitress approaching with Amanda's salad and tucked her iPad into her bag.

The waitress immediately spotted Amanda's coffee. "No outside drinks allowed," she said. Her voice was flat. She meant it.

"I know. But I bought it before I knew I was coming in," Amanda explained.

"It's on the door." The waitress was stone-faced.

"I'm so sorry." Amanda looked like she was wincing from the pain she was causing her hostess, but she made no attempt to make the coffee disappear. Shaking her head, the waitress marched back to the counter without letting her off the hook.

"It won't happen again," Amanda called after her. The moment she was out of earshot, Amanda turned to Katherine. "Wow, right? I mean: *wow*."

Katherine shrugged. "I think she's saying the problem is that you're not buying her coffee."

"Well, if *she's* drinking it, and it makes her like *that*, she can *keep* her coffee."

Amanda speared a few edamame beans on her fork. She'd barely nibbled a second when her eyes widened again. "Oh my God. *So* good! I'm going to have to come here every day for lunch. The pigeons will survive without me, right?" She laughed at her own joke. "So," she said, gathering up items for another bite, "what do you think of working with Jason?"

At last, Amanda's real agenda. Katherine knew to be careful. Actors were the worst gossips. "I honestly don't have an opinion. Why? How do you find him?"

Here, Amanda tilted her head back as though she were considering the matter for the very first time. "Well, I feel like he's hands-on. With *character*, you know? I was put off by it at first, but I'm really starting to *accept* how he articulates what he needs." She frowned and shook her head. "I think the problem is I can't get a reading on whether he likes what I'm doing. At *all*."

"Well, I'm sure he'd tell you if he had a problem."

Amanda nodded vigorously, waiting for Katherine to continue.

Great, thought Katherine, trying to think of pleasant things Jason might have said but not really finding the will to dig too deep. "Well, he's never said anything negative about your work."

Bingo. Amanda's face lit up like it was Christmas. She pressed her hand to her heart, like she'd been blessed or humbled or needed to resuscitate herself, and squeezed her eyes closed. "If you only knew how much I needed to hear that." Her eyes were twinkling as she opened them. "*Thank you*, Katherine. Thank you."

Katherine wondered whether Amanda's need for validation was part of some sort of histrionic personality disorder. Another thing to look up. She checked her watch and started to pack up her lunch. Somehow, Amanda managed to notice.

"Wait. You're going?"

"Yes. I need to set up for the third act."

"Oh. Should I come back with you? Do you need help?"

"No, I'm fine, thanks," answered Katherine. "You finish your lunch."

"Won't it be great when Jason finds someone to play the nurse?

Not like you don't have enough to do for your actual job, right?"
Amanda winked.

"Oh, it's fine," answered Katherine. "I just have to wear a
costume to call the show." Amanda was looking confused. Katherine had to start over. "I'm going to play the nurse. For real. Jason
asked me."

"Oh!" Amanda fake-dug in to her salad with her fork, gathering
more greens than she could ever stuff in her mouth. "When did he
decide that?"

"He asked me the other day."

"But do you *want* to do it? Because I have this friend who's been
trying to get her foot in the door forever. I talked to Jason about
her, but he must have forgotten."

"I don't think your friend is missing out on some great opportunity if that's what you're thinking. It's only a walk-on."

"You know, there are no small parts." Her face was all serious
now.

"Come on. It's one line."

"No. It's an old theatre saying, Katherine. 'There are no small
parts.' It means it's what you *do* with your opportunities that
makes you an actor."

Katherine understood Amanda was pissed at Jason and not
her, but she refused to be schooled by ignorant people. It felt too
much like reality TV. "Actually," she replied, barely keeping the
bristle out of her voice, "it's a quote of Stanislavski's. 'There are
no small parts, only small actors.' It's less about opportunity and
more about how every actor, in their own little sphere, is the lead.
But yeah. Point taken."

Amanda's mouth had dropped open.

Katherine had always followed her natural curiosity. She'd done
deep dives into ants, lace-making, flora, and protein chains, to
name just a few topics. It was preposterous *not* to know things,

when information was available everywhere. Especially when you were supposed to love your professional field and the opportunity to deepen your knowledge of it.

As she walked back to the rehearsal hall, Katherine could feel her determination kick in. She would succeed with acting like she did with everything she loved.

17

Kindred Spirits

BECCA HAD GIVEN UP painting Ari ten minutes into class, but everybody else was still trying to finish up their portraits, sighing dramatically, shouting out things like "Stop!" and "Fuck's sakes!" over and over and over.

Ari was hyper or whatever, so he couldn't sit still. Especially not while he was posing, which was what he was supposed to be doing. Every five minutes, the need to move would start winding him up. He'd inevitably leap to his feet and jiggle around. By the time he sat back down, he'd have forgotten how he'd posed.

Miss Nash, who was usually pretty chill as grade ten art teachers went, was getting sick of the class's howls of indignation, so she'd been shouting random stuff like "Art is flux" and "Don't panic, explore" to make the students calm down. It sounded helpful but it wasn't.

Becca had decided to draw freestyle, and the first thing that had come to mind was a skull. She probably should have roughed it out in pencil before she'd jumped to the inking part because the eye sockets weren't lining up. Death looked sort of winky.

She'd used a really skinny marker to do some linework — dots and details — and then she'd put a fat, juicy black line all around the outside of the skull to give it a graphic pop like a logo on a skateboard. It drew attention away from the wonky stuff going on inside. The fat line was sort of protective, preventing meanness from getting in.

"Oh. My. God! So lifelike. Really fucking cheery, Becs" Leanne squawked, looking over Becca's shoulder at her drawing. A few students glanced over to see what Leanne was on about, but Becca already knew it was nothing good.

"Basically just need to bury it at this point," Leanne said. Then she rolled her eyes so everybody could see she was being an arch, ironic bitch. Becca capped her pen and quietly slipped her drawing back into her sketchbook. She said nothing back. First, because it was more dignified, but mostly because she could never come up with stuff on the spur of the moment. Luckily, it was almost the end of the period. Miss Nash walked quietly into the middle of the classroom and spun around, assessing what students were doing.

"Everybody?" Miss Nash said in her gentlest voice to allow her budding artists to take a few final minutes to enjoy a few final brushstrokes. "It's time to start thinking about clean—"

Almost all the chairs scraped back at once. Ari leapt off the riser, and all the students raced toward the sinks.

Miss Nash looked disappointed. She always did.

"I want to remind you another time," she said, her voice trying to rise above the din, "that shoes, backpacks, and lunches are not acceptable objects to bring in for your still life assignment." If you didn't bring items for your still life project, you had to strike a pose for the class that revealed the "essence of yourself." Ari had nailed it. "This is important, people," Miss Nash shouted, clapping her hands for attention. "The subject you choose for your still life must represent who you are as an artist. What you choose to paint is deeply personal, and it should tell me immediately not only who you are but how you *personally* look at the world around you. Josh, it's your turn next week. Becca, it's yours the week aft—"

The period bell rang. Whatever Miss Nash said next was lost in the mass exodus. Miss Nash threw her hands in the air and started the long walk around the tables gathering forgotten paint bottles to return to the cupboards. Becca waited for the tide of people to retreat from the sinks to wash her paintbrushes in solitude.

The deep stainless steel sinks were covered in fresh gobs of acrylic paint and gouache. Becca turned on the cold water tap and leaned over to watch the paint blobs burst like vivid fireworks: oranges and blues, mauves and white. As the blobs thinned, what remained of the colours became ghosts, reaching out with long, spindly arms to the edges of the sink as though they were trying to hang on to something that no longer existed. On and on it went until the water ran clear and Becca couldn't remember the last colour she'd seen.

"Hey."

It was the guy from the AV room. He was older than her. Probably grade eleven. Up close, his eyeliner didn't look as mysterious as it did ghoulish. It sort of bled out all over his eyelids and smudged under his eyes.

"Oh. Um … hey. Are you in this class?" she asked. It was conceivable. Becca wasn't in the habit of doing a lot of looking around at people. Eye contact just created problems.

"Nah," he said, "I'm working on an independent project back there." He nodded to a table behind a divider. "Nash lets me hang."

He'd dyed his hair black. It was growing back in a pale brown and made his skin look *über* white and his freckles translucent.

"I saw you were drawing. Can I see?"

Becca hesitated. Nobody ever asked her to see her drawings unless they were going to make fun of them. She walked over to her sketchbook and pulled the page she'd hidden from Leanne out of her book. "It's not finished," she said, handing it to him. He studied it really, really seriously for a long time. Mysteriously, Becca felt naked and exposed.

"Nice line work."

Becca could feel her cheeks flushing. She dropped her head and felt her hair slide over her face. "One of the eye sockets is bigger than the other," she admitted. She knew it wasn't perfect, and she wanted him to know that she knew.

He flashed a warm smile. "It'll probably be the most cool part about it when it's done." He peered up at her from over the page. "The girl who trashed this drawing before really doesn't know shit. There's no rule people have to draw things that make other people feel good. Art is a state of mind."

He held her drawing out in his gigantic hand. She took it and hid it in her book. "What's your name?" he asked.

"Rebecca," she answered, surprised to hear herself using her full name rather than her mom's diminutive.

"I go by Raven Shadow pretty much everywhere online, but at school it's Dylan." He pulled his black shoulder-length hair out of his eyes to talk more intimately. "I've seen you around the AV room by the counselling office." He lowered his voice, made it all quiet like he was concerned. "I don't know you, so this is completely out of line, but … you seem, like, bummed out?"

Becca stared silently into Dylan's ringed eyes. She was not going to answer him, but he nodded slowly as though she had. "Thought so," he said.

Becca wasn't sure whether he meant he could see her slipping off the deep end or that he could tell she was depressed because he was depressed too.

"We could talk if you want," he said, nodding toward the hall.

Becca considered. The hallway was full of bullies, prying eyes, and sharp tongues. She picked up her markers and books and clutched them tightly to her chest.

"I don't think so," she said, brushing past him.

Dylan looked surprised, but the last thing Becca needed right now was to get cornered into talking to a lonely freak.

18

View from the Bottom

KARL WAS ON DAVENPORT Road, stopped for a light, sweat free-falling from his face. People under thirty who said cycling was a great way to get to work were assholes.

Pedalling up the hill was hard at the best of times, but today it looked ominous. He hadn't started the week and already he felt beat. Part of it was that he hadn't slept much because he was worried about losing his job. He'd also had to jack off a few times before he left to delay getting a pull in at work for as long as possible. At least until lunch. Karl was taking all precautions.

He really had to get his shit together, get back into coding, get his dick on track. He was getting too old to still be living in an illegal basement suite.

He looked up Bathurst again. The hill loomed large. "Son of a bitch," he sighed. He really missed the car he'd had to sell.

From a dead stop, he'd have to peddle like a bastard for nearly two minutes just to crest the first part of the hill. He was almost tempted to walk his bike. But that wasn't going to cut it. Walking was for tools. That goddamned hill would not win.

When the traffic light was on the verge of going green, he edged his way out in front of a black Subaru. As it turned, he jumped on the pedals. He rode hard all the way up, making traffic go around him, telling himself whatever lies he needed to hear to get through the ride to work.

Thirty minutes later, Karl's front wheel jumped the curb and coasted to the bike racks. They were jammed to the tits as usual. He was technically late, so he locked his bike to someone's back wheel and headed for the entrance. He'd deal with the repercussions later.

On the outside, AMICO was a smoky glass monolith with all the warmth of a pair of reflective aviator sunglasses. Inside was no better. As Karl hit the cool lobby air, he spotted Jackson coming up out of the stairwell from the cafeteria, carrying a coffee with so many creamers stacked on the lid he looked like he was going to play fort.

"How's the diet going?" Karl asked.

Jackson didn't get the jab. Then he did. "Fuck you."

Jackson's gaze dropped to something on Karl's shirt: "Hot?"

Karl checked himself out in the mirrored lobby wall. "No," he answered matter-of-factly, wiping his face with the back of his forearm and flashing Jackson a big, wet pit.

"Some woman was looking for you. She's waiting in HR. Not my type," Jackson threw in, walking away.

"That's a relief," Karl answered. "I don't like your type."

Karl had completely forgotten he'd promised Ed to show the newbie the ropes. He ran into the john, splashed some water on his face, finger-combed his hair, and dried his pits under the hand dryer. Some jerk-off came in for a piss while he was mid ablution and gave him a look. The company had seriously lost its human edge.

He walked through the HR offices, looking for the guy who staffed his division, a man who habitually made absolutely no impression on anyone. He was like having an extra beige task chair in the office. Everything about him was soft and blurry: his clothing, his hair, his expression. His voice seldom rose above the volume of a private conversation, and he reacted to all jokes with a pained smile, as though he were afraid of offending the Newfies, the Frogs, and the Jews in bars and rowboats everywhere.

Luckily, Karl didn't have to describe who he was looking for because Beige spotted him first.

"We all seem to be running late this morning," Beige said. He paused, obviously leaving room for an apology Karl wasn't about to make.

"Is she here?" Karl asked.

"Yes," Beige answered. He waited another moment. "I'll go get her, shall I?"

Karl nodded. "Sounds like a plan."

Beige headed toward a small conference room, and the new employee followed him back out. She was wearing slacks and a baby-pink polo shirt, but she wasn't what you'd call "a girl." More like centre ice with boobs. Karl held out his hand.

"Karl Reynolds."

"Nicole Wilkins." She took his hand and gave it a squeeze.

"You got a real grip there, Nicole. Softball?"

Nicole smiled. Karl suspected they were batting for the same team.

He gave Nicole the five-dollar tour, taking her to the mail room, the boardroom, the cafeteria. He even showed her where the john was. "I don't mean to seem ungrateful," she said at one point, "but where's the women's?" She was all right.

Karl led Nicole across the call centre and herded her back to his desk. All the kiddies in the pit were gawking at them like they'd never seen two people walking together before. Karl pulled a chair out from an empty desk and rolled it up the aisle for her. Someone yelled out, asking if Nicole was his replacement.

"Eat it," he yelled back.

Karl couldn't see Ed anywhere, so maybe he'd gotten away being twenty-five minutes late. But Ed had his spies.

Karl flicked on his PC and monitors and started rummaging around in a drawer for a second headset. He caught Nicole checking out his spartan workspace.

"Did you just start here?" she asked.

"I've been here seven years."

"Holy shit. *Seven?!*" she said, rather loudly. "Years?" Then, trying to lower her voice: "That's a really long time."

Karl plugged in his headset. This fucking morning …

"I'm sorry," she said. "Honestly, I'm not usually this much of a twit on my first day. It normally takes a lot longer for it to become obvious to everyone."

Nicole held his gaze. No bullshit. She was sorry. Karl nodded.

"What do you know about call centres?" he asked.

"I used to work a hotline for a pharmaceutical company. Mostly calls from hysterical people about the side effects of weight loss drugs that may or may not have been killing them." She shook her head. "I had to quit. After a year and a half, I didn't know which side of the equation I was rooting for anymore, if you know what I mean."

"Well, there's nothing life-or-death here," said Karl. "The only thing you have to remember at all times is that Ed, your boss, is an asshole."

She looked at him a few moments, her clear grey eyes assessing the information until she nodded. "Got it."

"He'll listen to your calls for no reason. He might clap you on the shoulder, tell you you're doing a great job, but he's going to listen to your calls. When you hear a long beep in your headset, that's him, listening. And *he* knows you know he's listening. It's a mind game. Do *not* let it get to you."

"Okay."

"You get bonuses based on your call load. That's the time you're on the phone plus your after-call time multiplied by your call volume. The magic number you're looking for is one-five-oh. Anything higher than that is gravy. You're going to get yelled at. Every day. Figure out how to let it roll off your back or you'll burn out in four months. You rep AMICO, therefore you are a corporate stooge. Whatever you say or do, that's how you'll be perceived. People call to get help, but we only make money if we get rid of them fast. Don't look for sense. It's just the way it works."

Nicole held up her hand. "I don't mean to interrupt, but I have to. This job sounds terrible. How could you possibly do it for seven years?"

"This is no one's final destination," Karl explained. "Every single person in this room is on their way to someplace else, or thinks they are, whether they remember the destination or not."

"This is like having a conversation with Buddha and Dr. Phil at the same time."

Karl smiled. She was all right.

"Okay: What do you know about high-speed internet?"

Nicole flashed him a smile. "It's really, really fast?"

19

Portrait of an Artist

IT WAS 10:00 A.M., and Brent's hair had never looked wilder.

He'd spent the entire evening and early morning searching for "Inert," his short story, through hard drives and old random thumb drives he'd dug out of his desk drawer. His last hope was to do a file-by-file review.

It was an impossible task.

Years ago, a young author, now of note, had impressed upon him that the key to cracking a first publication credit was a solid title, an impactful first line, and a stirring description of rain. To this day, he revised his short story titles obsessively, but rarely did he accord the same diligence to his file names. Now everything was a wretched mess. The only good that had come from his laborious search was the discovery that the word *inert* figured far too prominently in both his fictional and his academic writing.

Brent poured two fingers of Scotch over his last three ice cubes. He had office hours at eleven-thirty. He'd have to switch to coffee soon.

It was possible, though not probable, that a hard copy of "Inert" was buried among the reams of papers stacked on the floor beside his desk, but he hadn't found the courage to begin sifting through them. Each document contained the humble beginnings of ideas he'd intended to pursue or revisit, but hadn't. The pages had been trundled from printer to briefcase, from coffee shop to office, and, inevitably, back to his study, where the title pages had progressively become covered with phone numbers, book titles, coffee cup rings, and grocery lists — the literary equivalent of tree moss.

Brent took a deep swig of his drink, trying to remember the gist of his story, wondering if he could perhaps reconstruct it.

He dipped a finger deep into his tumbler, pulled out a piece of ice, and thought back. He could remember feeling pleased with the first line because it set everything up — the world, the tension, the themes. He popped the ice cube into his mouth and gently cracked it between his molars, draining the last of the Scotch through it.

He seemed to recall a groundskeeper at the centre of the story, stumbling into a room to fix some shutters. An image popped into his head of a woman, whom no one seemed to notice except the groundskeeper. She was sitting on a chair, trembling ever so slightly. He began to recall the story was set amid sun, sand, and linen.

It had to have been a story inspired by Jane. Lovely woman. Long blond hair, strong calves, a fierce, independent spirit. She had a bit of a temper, but she could just as easily be sweetly disposed.

Their relationship had been a few months young when Jane had invited him to spend a week in Cuba, which Brent had readily accepted. During their first few days in Eden, they'd had giddy sex and sweaty sex and the type of sex that borders on nervous exhaustion. Aside from learning about Jane's peccadilloes — she had a fondness for stealing little bottles of shampoo from the maids' carts — the beginning of the trip had been quite heavenly. But despite all their best intentions, their paradise was lost.

The fallout had occurred around the middle of their stay, when they'd decided to leave their room. Brent still remembered wearing his casual linen trousers for a day trip to the market.

Over breakfast, he and Jane had gone through some of the tourist brochures and decided to take a bus into *Habana* for some sightseeing. Naturally, Brent's thoughts had turned to *The Old Man and the Sea.* He could imagine Hemingway writing in his large office at Finca Vigia, windows thrown open, shirt cast off to receive an errant breeze, a cold drink and a six-toed cat by his side. And, dammit, inspiration had struck him — the way inspiration does — at the most inopportune moment.

Brent had started to tuck in to his breakfast of *arepas* when the threads of a new short story began to take shape in his mind. It was going to be a metaphor for social divisiveness or some such thing. His thoughts had been so fully engaged with it he'd neglected to try the complimentary fruit salad.

As he and Jane had been about to board the bus, Brent had confessed that his story had become bigger than the both of them and that he needed to stay at the hotel to see it through. In spite of his effusive apologies, Jane hadn't taken kindly to the abandonment. She'd announced they were over.

Brent had retreated to the resort's bar, where he'd lost himself in pineapple, coconut, and strong rum. He recalled now he'd decided to pour his feelings into a new story, the tale of a simple man besotted with a distant woman. He'd jotted down the broader points in a flurry of inspiration, using coasters and menus until mercifully, a bartender had rented him a laptop.

Once he'd found his first sentence, the words had followed one another like pearls on a string. It had been a thrilling, surreal experience: a fleeting moment of direct connection to his creativity he'd tried to recapture every day since.

When Jane had returned from her day trip, shopping bags stuffed with coconut monkeys and bottles of Havana Club rum, she'd had her belongings moved to a separate room. For the remainder of their stay, she'd refused all attempts at communication or reconciliation.

Brent had soon learned from hotel staff that Jane had hooked up with a local man who seemed to live on the public beach. He had understandably been devastated by the news, but when they'd crossed paths in the lobby, he'd thought it best to wish her well. She'd called him an idiot.

Brent had spent the remainder of his vacation in the company of Javier, the kind bartender who'd rented him the laptop. It was at his urging that Brent had printed the first few pages of his story, bought a Cuban stamp from the front desk, and mailed the pages to the editor of the *New Fort Yorker*. Typically, Brent hung on to his work and severely revised it to withstand editorial scrutiny. This story must have been fabulous. No other publisher had ever called to read his work before. Ever. And he couldn't figure out where he'd saved the whole thing, or remember a damn word of it.

All that emotional and narrative upheaval. All for naught. Every word lost.

Suddenly realizing that he'd spent the entire morning following his story instead of going out to look for Gary, Brent lurched to his feet. Which was precisely when he remembered where his story was.

20

Big Brother

FIRST THERE WAS A flat, quiet tone, then the pre-recorded voice announcing the call transfer. Three seconds later, the next caller was patched through.

Nicole adjusted her headset and looked eagerly toward Karl like he was about to share a secret.

"Thank you for calling AMICO. This is Karl speaking, how may I help you?"

"Hello, Karl. I'm in a bit of a bind. I'm looking for an email account? And I, ahh — I can't seem to find it. I created it while I was on vacation, and I wrote this thing. It's the only copy in existence. But I can't for the life of me recall the —"

"Are you in front of your computer?"

"Yes."

"Could you shut it down for me, please?"

There was a brief silence. Karl thought he could hear the Weather Network in the background. "Karl, you see my —"

"Let me know when it boots up again." Karl glanced at Nicole, who raised an eyebrow, surprised by his assertiveness.

"Let me put you on hold for a moment while I pull up your file." The caller started saying something just as Karl hit the mute button. He turned to Nicole, who was listening, pen and paper in hand. "Rule number one: every person who calls in thinks they know what's wrong. They don't."

"I think you cut him off."

"Doesn't matter. He has nothing to say that's of any importance. If you went by what most people told you, you'd have to believe that someone physically stole the internet last night." Karl opened a large blue AMICO binder filled with plasticized pages. "This is the procedures bible. It's a true/false tree that helps you eliminate problems so you can zero in on what's wrong. You start from the beginning, and you work your way through until either you find a resolution or you pass the call on to another department. You may not, for any reason, skip any part of the process because that's a surefire way to screw up the entire diagnosis."

Karl flipped to the middle of the procedures bible. He smiled. "But seven years as CSR says it's his router." He clicked off the mute and returned to his caller.

"Thank you for holding. Has the computer booted up yet?"

"Yes. But I don't think you've —"

"Can you try opening your email account?"

There was a slight pause. "You know, I don't think you understand what the problem is. Maybe I haven't explained —"

Karl hit the mute button. "He's resisting me. Can you hear it?"

Nicole nodded. "Amazing."

"Yeah. You can tell it's going to be impossible to convince him I'm right. So, from this point on, whatever a client says, I don't agree or disagree — I redirect."

Karl unlocked the mute button. The caller was still talking. Nicole rolled her eyes.

"… and if I can't send my story by the end of this week, it may not get published."

"I understand your frustration. Fortunately, AMICO has a troubleshooting process in place to address this exact problem. Let's go through the necessary steps, and we'll resolve the issue in no time."

"As long as you understand —"

Karl hit the mute button again. "Another thing you're supposed to do is smile while you're on the phone. The company believes customers can hear the difference. I have personally mastered the art of the smiling sneer. You'll find your own way."

He deactivated the mute button, which was exactly when Karl and Nicole heard a long beep. Nicole looked over at Karl quizzically.

Karl drew a sphincter symbol (*) on a Post-it note and pasted it up on his workstation wall for others to see. Ed was listening.

"Thank you for your patience," Karl said in his most unctuous voice.

From that point on, Karl talked his client through every step. He made him disconnect from his network. Run some commands. Ping. Change some settings. Disconnect. Bypass the router. Find a different cable. Try it all again. The client was getting testy, but Karl stayed as sweet as an apple.

"What do you see?"

"Nothing."

"I've identified your problem as being your router." Karl flipped the procedures book shut followed by a long beep. Ed had finally hung up.

"It's not the router that's the —"

Nicole hit the mute button. "Ed was listening *that* whole time? Why? What possible reason could he have to sit on the other end of the line for an entire hour?"

"Exactly. Welcome to AMICO." Karl returned to his caller. "Sir, our records show you do not currently own an AMICO router. Could I interest you in purchasing one at this time?"

"No. You could not interest me in purchasing one. My router is fine. All I'm missing is an email account. That's it. Now I've done everything you've asked me to do, and you've totally screwed all my settings." The caller's voice was clipped and his words enunciated. He was definitely pissed. "I demand you send someone over to my house to fix this mess, now."

Karl put on his best smile. "I can certainly put in a technical assistance request, but you should know that if the router is the problem, you *will* be required to pay a minimal service charge of four hundred and ten dollars. If you had an AMICO router, this service would, of course, be free of charge."

"You guys are ... unbelievable."

"Is there anything else I can do for you?"

"Oh, no. I'd say you've done quite enough, Karl. Wouldn't you?" He hit the K in Karl's name with clear contempt.

"In that case, thank you for dealing with AMICO: communication with a friendly sm—"

The caller had hung up.

"This fucking day," said Karl, switching his station to aftercall mode.

"Wow. That was intense. Now what do we do? Hit the bar?" asked Nicole, peeling off her headset.

"We have to go through the paperwork. Let's take a break before we start on that. Back at one?"

Nicole stood up. "Don't have to tell me twice," she said, tugging down her polo shirt.

"Actually, make it five to one. Early is on time."

She nodded and took off down the aisle, didn't even suggest she needed to hold his hand for her first break. She was all right.

Karl was peeling the sphincter Post-it off his workstation when Jackson popped up over his partition. "Ed found out you came in late."

Karl sighed. Just what he needed.

Jackson chuckled. "Speaking of earfuls, wouldn't it be hilarious if Ed turned out to be the Moaner?"

"The ...?"

"The bathroom guy? The guy that jacks off all day? Makes a racket."

Karl suddenly started to feel sick. "Yeah. I've been meaning to tell you to stop that shit," he said. "It's upsetting the youths."

"Screw you," said Jackson. He wasn't subtle, but his comebacks were consistent.

Karl stood up. "I gotta get out of here and get some air."

Karl was standing behind the large dumpster at the back of the AMICO building, jerking off by the paper bins. Overnight, his bathroom "issue" had gone from top secret to viral. From now on, anyone who heard anything in a bathroom stall would hang around to nab him for bragging rights. He'd be fired on the spot.

The stress and anxiety he felt couldn't be ignored. No fucking way.

As he started getting closer to coming, the pressures of his dingy basement apartment, his shitty job, and his credit card debt started to fall away. His breathing got lighter and shallower until his cock relayed the signal it was on a one-way road to go town. Karl could feel all his frustrations on the verge of being washed away, but just as he was about to close his eyes to succumb, he spotted the new security camera mounted on the side of the building and realized he was well and truly fucked.

21

When to Say When

RESISTING ONE'S IMPULSES WAS exhausting.

Becca had resolved that whatever she thought of saying, she shouldn't. Ever. But by that same token, it was hard to keep fighting who she was and how she felt.

The last thing she needed was to feel worse, so she decided to skip Canadian history. She couldn't handle any more downer stories about bitter cold, starving settlers, religious zealots, or the gross treatment of First Nations. There seemed to be zero happy moments recorded in history. Anywhere. No parties. No stories about people goofing around. The past was just one miserable moment stacked on top of another, usually at someone else's expense. A massive stack of downer pancakes.

Becca snuck out of school the back way, crossing the overgrown field to the bus stop. She sidestepped all the turd piles like a boss, although at one point, she skidded on a condom and freaked out about dead sperm being on her foot for several minutes, which was basically why she missed the 12:10.

The next bus was due in twenty minutes, which meant thirty in real time.

She had never thought much about busses before this year. When she'd picked Mary the Immaculate, she hadn't even considered how far it was from her home. She'd wanted to change schools so badly.

Now the only difference between the new school and the old one was that she had to travel further to experience the suckage.

She decided to kill a few minutes in the tiny plaza across the road. It had a covered walkway with wavy red roof tiles so the old people who shopped there could pretend they were buying their half-price bananas in Spain.

There weren't more than a dozen stores in the plaza. Becca walked past a sub shop, a Tan Lines salon with an orange receptionist, and The Clothes Closet, where the world's ugliest cardigan had been on the sale rack for two weeks, and walked straight into the drugstore where they didn't like students. Sometimes, staff followed them around the store, up and down the aisles like in *Centipede*.

Becca went to the cosmetics department to find nail polish remover because Caroline had forgotten to buy some. The Sharpie had worn off in spots, letting patches of baby blue appear here and there on her nails like the promise of a new day that would probably never come. Looking at her hands reminded her of how she felt like her mom's failed DIY project.

It turned out there were lots of different nail polish removers. Becca sniffed every brand, trying to determine which one smelled least toxic. It took her a full five minutes of comparing before she settled on one.

On the way back to the cash, she realized she was feeling wobbly. Alarmed, she picked up a bottle of Vitaminwater. In case.

The cashier punched in her items and held out his hand: "Ten forty-nine."

Becca was silent a moment. "I only have ten," she said.

The cashier stayed silent, making everything super awkward.

"Can I owe you?" she asked.

The cashier gave her a stony stare and kept his hand out. Using the other, he waved the next customer toward his cash.

"But I *need* this Vitaminwater," Becca said, lowering her voice.

"Something is wrong. I'm dizzy. I might be anemic."

The cashier waved the next customer forward again. This time, the line advanced. Becca stared at the cashier in disbelief. "Fine," she said. "Just the nail polish remover." She paid and walked out, secretly hoping she'd pass out in front of his store so he could feel bad for being so shitty.

All the benches had been removed from the plaza because of the threat of skateboards or bombs, so Becca sat on a concrete parking divider, trying to wrap her head around the fact there had literally been no concern shown for her. Everybody was so hyper focused on getting through their day even if it meant walking over her dead body to get cashed out.

Luckily, she was starting to feel less wobbly than before. She unscrewed the cap on her bottle of nail polish remover and dripped some onto her finger. The exposed blue nail polish came off. The Sharpie hung on.

"Hey."

She followed the voice, looked up into the sun. It was Dylan or Raven Claw or whatever. She quickly hid her hands inside her hoodie cuffs.

"You have a spare now too?"

"Not exactly," Becca said, knowing she probably looked guilty.

"Oh," he said.

Becca could tell from his voice he didn't think much of her skipping. Maybe he was just a rebel on the outside.

"Why are you in the AV room, like, all the time? Is it detention?" Becca said.

"No. It's Intro to Business. I get half a credit if I work during one of my spares. My folks are basically forcing me to become an accountant. It's not who I am, and it sucks immensely."

"Brutal," she agreed.

He shrugged, tousling his shaggy hair into his eyes, then fell silent.

"Yeah. My mom wrecks my life too. She slept with this guy I was seeing," Becca said.

"Oh," said Dylan, looking a bit confused. His gaze dropped down to the patterned toes of his clumpy black boots for a moment, then back up at her. "That's definitely messed up."

"Why are you talking to me?"

He half smiled. "You seem interesting in a complicated sort of way." Dylan looked at her for as long as he dared, then set his sights on something far away, like he could see a mountain ridge. "I should get going."

Becca nodded.

And that was it. He turned and walked back toward school.

Becca marvelled at how he seemed so sure of himself and his weirdness, deciding for himself what was cool. As he reached the edge of the parking lot, the wind kicked up. His black coat snapped and popped in the gust like a flag. A few small tufts of black hair curled up like neck feathers. For a few seconds, she could imagine him as an actual raven. Then some traffic went by and he was gone.

Becca stuffed the nail polish remover back in her bag and walked back to her bus stop, one whizzing right past just as she was about to cross the street. She spotted a kid from math class in the back of the bus. He pretended not to see her.

How did people figure out who was too lame to acknowledge? It seemed like everyone in the world was playing a game she was supposed to be playing too, only no one had given her the rules. No matter what move she made, she lost. Like, all the time.

Over the summer, Caroline had told Becca she needed to stop overthinking her decisions. To let go of having to have every answer. Her mom had said she should leap into things once in a while — to see what happened. She was sure Becca would be able to deal with whatever situation she was in. All she needed was to listen to her instincts more. Her instincts knew what she wanted, she'd said.

Just then, Becca spotted a middle-aged guy sitting in a Sentra, waiting for the light to turn green. He was looking at her. He smiled as he bopped his head to some tune. She heard something deep inside her telling her to go with it.

So she did.

Becca walked up to his car, her heart pounding in her ears. He lowered the window. She heard herself say, "Which way are you going?"

22

Wayfinding

BECCA'S DOUBTS ABOUT HER intuition quadrupled in the five seconds it took her to get a closer look inside the car and recognize Lil Wayne on the car radio, telling all the hoes how he was single.

The driver must have noticed she was reassessing because he flew into a frenzy picking up the demolished Taco Bell wrappers on the passenger seat and turfing them on the floor in the back.

Becca got into the car and struggled with her seatbelt. She was slightly freaked out. Here she was, not planning, not questioning. Just doing. It took two tries. When she was buckled in, she said, "Hi," but it was just as the light turned green, and the man started to shift. She said, "Hi" again. This time, the man noticed she was trying to chat, and then *he* tried to say something and realized the music was loud, but he had to shift again. They were not hearing each other when Becca suddenly realized she hadn't really thought through that being in a car meant they'd be going somewhere.

The guy stopped shifting and swiped at the volume knob. Suddenly, everything was too quiet and awkward, like when the lights come up at the end of a dance and everyone can see how much you've been sweating. Except for the traffic sounds. She guessed it was weird because it was her first time being alone with a guy in a car who wasn't a relative or an Uber driver.

Anyway.

She could really smell his shampoo.

He looked younger than her dad. More like store manager age because she could totally imagine him dealing with her mom returning a faulty paper shredder. His hair was brushed back all the way in a straight line, like the sports guys did on TV. His eyes were bright and shiny. It was like he was really happy to see her. He kept looking over at her, smiling. Expecting her to say something, but she wasn't sure what to talk about. Eventually he said, "Where are we going?"

Becca had been heading home, but it occurred to her she didn't want to tell him where she lived, so she decided to be vague. "Um. Downtown?" she said.

He nodded deeply like he understood.

"I'm going east," he said. He wasn't being an asshole about it. It was more, "Sorry, not sorry."

"Oh. Okay," said Becca. "That's totally fine," she said. She wasn't going to put him out. Because she was still getting a ride. And it was closer to home. Somewhat.

"I have to see a client."

"Oh. Like a sales call thing?" Becca asked. She'd heard her mom say that a bunch of times on the phone.

"Exactly," he said, staring at her.

"Yeah. That's what I thought," she said. She smoothed down her shirt the way she'd seen Caroline smooth down hers and saw he was smiling weird at her again.

"So, this is a little crazy," he said, laughing. "Like, you in my car? I mean, women don't normally just jump in."

She shrugged like it was normal for her, but she also didn't want to come off as strange. "I really hate the bus," she said. "Like, so much," she sighed.

He nodded like he understood how much busses sucked.

"Someday, I'm going to buy a Tesla," Becca said. She rubbed her hand over the upholstery. "Is this leather?"

"No."

"Yeah. I didn't think so," she said.

He stared at her a moment longer, then he bumped the volume button with his thumb. It was a song that sounded like a robot singing about other dimensions. The rap part started as the car merged onto the expressway. It felt like everything was taking off. Becca had no clue where she was going, but she hoped the music would get better.

23

Dumb Move

JESUS. JESUS, JESUS, JESUS, thought Karl, speed-walking around the building looking for a way to make himself disappear. He'd been such an idiot to not look for a camera.

Karl reached for the door but thankfully stopped himself from tapping the reader with his fob. He spun and walked away. Better to use a different door to go back inside. Better yet, use someone else's fob. It would be stupid to record his movements. Because he'd already been stupid enough.

Within a few minutes, a chunky guy in a tapered shirt carrying takeout tapped the door open with his fob. Karl walked in right behind him and got a dirty look for spooning, which was probably well deserved.

He scanned the corridors ahead for cameras as he hurried toward the main hall. As he passed them, he called up every Jason Bourne trick he'd ever seen to keep his idiot face obscured. He had fifteen minutes to get back to the call centre but he felt untethered. His head was swimming with the consequences of his not-so-private wank. He needed to get his thoughts together first. Make a plan. Not panic.

Karl ducked into a washroom and went straight for the sinks. His reflection revealed how rattled he felt. He looked like an angry jerk-off. He jammed his hands under the faucet and vigorously started splashing water everywhere — on his hands, his face — checking the stalls to see whether he was alone. Two cubicles were occupied.

Goddammit!

He wanted to smash something. Hadn't he seen the security company installing cameras everywhere? Hadn't he been the guy making jokes about the Eye of Sauron? Of course there were cameras outside! He was so fucked. He could see life getting ready to give him a good swift kick to the curb. Karl wondered how much time he had before security managed to track him down, before someone figured it out.

What if he quit before that happened? The tantalizing hope of escape hung in the air a few moments before it burst into flames. And go where? Do what?

Stay cool, he told himself. He rapped his knuckles against the sink counter a few times to focus. He was smarter than this moment.

He walked out of the washroom shitting confidence, but he still couldn't hide his relief when he saw there wasn't a security team waiting to haul him away. He needed to get back to his desk like nothing had happened.

"Karl."

Karl felt the blood drain out of his face as he spun around. It was Ed, wearing his "let me have a word with you" expression. There was no telling whether it was good or bad.

"Hey," Karl answered meekly.

Ed shook his head, wincing like he was being hit with a migraine. "Goddamn it," he said. "If this GM doesn't start dealing with reality and admit his blueprint isn't working, we're looking at a repeat of last year." He chewed a thin wad of gum with vigour a few times. "It's time for a tear down."

Karl nodded, ever so grateful he wasn't having a conversation about his dick with his boss.

"Oh, right," said Ed, sounding more bothered than disappointed. "You don't follow hockey, do you?"

"No," said Karl.

"You lose your trainee?" Straight back to business.

"We broke for lunch. Just heading back now."

Ed nodded and glanced at his watch like the fucking bastard he was. Checking whether Karl was running late. He wasn't.

"How is she doing? Nicole?"

It was an ongoing game they played where Karl did things like training and scheduling and Ed got to pretend like he'd eventually help Karl up the ladder instead of keeping him in the pit with all the other schmoes.

"Good."

"You're killing me here. Give me a little more. She's good how?"

"She seems smart, quick. Holds on to information. Doubtful she'll piss anyone off. She'll probably outrank Marsh in a few weeks."

The news seemed to please Ed. Marsh was top five in the numbers game.

"A little competition would be good for that guy," said Ed. "He's getting smug."

Karl smiled. But only barely. Ed hadn't said what he'd said for Karl's amusement. Ed was planning on making Marsh sweat.

"Speaking of replacements," Ed went on, "I heard you were late this morning and made me look like an asshole with HR."

"It couldn't be helped."

"It could have if you'd left home earlier."

"I got a flat at the bottom of the hill."

"Tires don't get flats like they used to," said Ed. "Did you know that?"

"Yeah," answered Karl, keeping his eyes steady. "That's why it took me by surprise."

Ed looked at him.

Normally, when Karl was trying to convince people to buy in to half truths, he'd keep talking. A barrage of sound. But he recalled his dad's number one piece of advice for getting out of sticky situations, and it seemed right for the occasion. He said nothing. "Nobody likes a shit cake," his father had once counselled. "Layering bull on top of bull turns everything into full-on crap, and people will only stomach so much."

Karl glanced toward the call centre. "I should go."

Ed held his look a moment longer, more to feel his power over Karl than anything else. Then he nodded. Karl was off the hook.

When he reached the call centre, Karl spotted Nicole wandering through the aisles trying to find his cubicle. He got her attention and pointed. She started to move in the right direction.

He spotted Marsh coming back from lunch and wondered if he should give him a heads-up about Ed wanting Nicole to take him down a few pegs. But then his dad's second bit of advice came to mind: "Keep your eyes on your own pecker."

Truer words were never spoken.

He turned up the ninth row and got back to work.

24

A Hot Date

THERE WERE DEAD FLIES on the windowsill. Beyond that, the patched asphalt of the motel parking lot. And beyond that, a bunch of sandwich boards huddled together on the sidewalk that no one could ever read from a moving car.

Becca let the stiff motel curtain fall back into place.

She wasn't sure why she'd asked to go to a motel. She had no idea what she'd expected the man to do when they got there. All she knew was that she felt gravely disappointed by how it had turned out.

The man had fallen asleep wearing only his tie and socks. He was planted face down, lightly snoring on a flowery nylon bedspread that was covered by so many cigarette burns the big orange chrysanthemums looked like they were infested with aphids. Becca had been sitting in the chair next to the bed, waiting for him to wake up to find out what happened next.

She had never been in a dive motel before. It was rank and dank and fascinating with shit-stained carpets and a smell like moist gym clothes. No one was pretending it was a home away from home. It was just a room for sleeping and fucking in, and if you didn't like it, you could go someplace else.

Becca noticed that someone had peeled off a strip of simulated oak veneer on the bedside table and exposed the layers of plastic and woodchips and glue. She felt like she was seeing the grunged-out sedimentation of desperate affairs and poorly planned road trips to Wonderland.

The room's naked truth was oddly liberating. Becca needed something to remind her of her experience before she lost the feeling. She stood up and looked around for something to take. There was a print by the door, a sun-bleached landscape of a grassy field that was somewhere between yellow and brown, between life and death, but it had been screwed to the wall. She was starting to wonder how hard it would be to shatter the Plexiglas when she spotted a crushed pack of matches on the dresser. It had almost slipped under the TV set, but she managed to fish it out with a stir stick.

The matchbook was white. It was crumpled and had a strip of gritty stuff on the back cover that was scuffed with pale marks. Becca quickly stuffed the pack into her front jeans pocket. She didn't want the man to see her taking them or to think she was being immature.

Becca turned around, set to walk back to her chair, when she stepped on the man's pants. They were still on the floor where he'd dropped them by the edge of the bed. As she picked them up, his wallet fell out, landing on the carpet with a soft plop. It was leather, but dull and worn. The stitches were nearly worn through around the edges.

The man's ID and credit cards spilled out, so she picked them up. They were slightly warm to the touch, which grossed her out because technically, that heat had come off his ass, and Becca wanted very little to do with it.

The driver's licence informed her that his name was Wayne Jennings of 1024 Pinecrest Crescent. The picture made him look like a much calmer person than he was in real life because in real life, Wayne Jennings had lost his shit when Becca had told him she was fourteen. He'd shouted and paced and sat down on the bed, wringing his hands, saying how his life was ruined.

Becca had felt bad for him, so she'd taken off her shirt to let him look at her boobs, and he'd come. Almost immediately. Without touching her. Or himself. It had been a whole lot of noise about nothing, really, as far as she could see. As he'd started falling asleep, he'd thanked her, and she'd answered he was welcome, although upon further reflection, she wasn't sure it had been necessary to be polite back.

Becca was tucking Wayne's cards back into his wallet when she discovered a picture stuck to the back of an insurance card. It was Wayne, looking like he'd been stuffed into a suit like a cannelloni. His arm was around a woman wearing a shiny green gown that hugged her rolls of fat. She looked like a pupa that was about to rip open and turn into something else, only you could tell this woman wasn't going to turn into anything good.

It wasn't that Becca was being mean about the way the woman looked, or that she thought she was better. She could just tell. Her mom had taught her all about how secret pockets of fat hid below shoulder blades and over knees. How they accumulated like snow packs, waiting for the right conditions to send fat down to the rest of the body. The pupa had a fat avalanche coming her way.

Becca suspected she was being weirdly jealous about a guy she'd only known for forty minutes. Maybe the pupa was Wayne's sister. Or his neighbour or some cousin. If she was his girlfriend, it couldn't matter. She needed to be an adult, rise above her hurt feelings, and do the right thing.

Becca carried Wayne's suit and underpants into the bathroom to hang them.

She knew how to be a hostess. About a month after her dad had moved out, Caroline had sat her down at the kitchen table and told her they would have to pull together to get through the tough times. It turned out that meant Becca had to clean stuff around the house, hang coats, and make cocktails — rye and sevens, screw-drivers, white Russians, gin and tonics.

Whenever her mother had company, Becca had to carry tinkling drinks on a round bar tray into the living room along with some peanuts she wasn't allowed to eat in a little turquoise dish. Once she got to be eleven, she graduated to blender drinks: lime margaritas, daiquiris, Pimm's cups, and mojitos. Those were served with oven-baked corn chips no one ever ate except by mistake.

It was around this time Becca had started to notice all her mother's guests were men. It wasn't much later after that, when she got her boobs, that her delivery services were no longer required. She'd continued to hang the coats and make the drinks, but things with Caroline had started feeling different. And then one day, poof! Everything she knew and felt about her mom had changed. From one day to the next, depending on what they were doing or who was around, it felt like she and her mom were on the same but opposite sides. And she didn't understand why it was happening. It was like knowing you were walking into dangerous territory, only all the land mines had moved.

There were no hooks in the washroom on which to hang Wayne's suit, only a canted rack for scratchy towels, so Becca decided to just lay his clothes out in the tub. She started with Wayne's shirt, which she tucked into his pants, then she laid his jacket over everything, folding the arms. She wasn't quite sure what to do with the wallet, so she set it on top of all the clothes.

Becca flipped up the toilet seat with her foot and checked underneath like Caroline had told her, but she had literally no clue what she was looking for. It was just another incomplete set of instructions she had rattling around in her brain. What if she'd found something? What if she'd found something but she really needed to pee? Why didn't people explain things properly? Like Doctor Schofield asking her questions about the dog poster but not telling her what to do with the answers she gave him.

She let the toilet seat drop and pushed down her pants along with her panties. A row of almost invisible lines popped up high on her thigh. They looked weirdly three-dimensional in the harsh fluorescent light, like those ancient messages left for aliens in the Nazca Desert. She'd made the marks a million years ago and had no idea what they meant anymore.

Becca wondered how often people had died in this motel. She'd seen enough TV shows and movies to know that kind of thing happened. Once, she'd imagined taking a bunch of pills and sleeping until … whatever happened. Like some tragic Ophelia on a bed of nasty flowers. The thought of Wayne waking up and finding her dead body beside him was hilarious. He would so completely lose it.

Caroline would have to get in her car and fight traffic to ID her body. The coroner would fling back the sheet, and she'd be there, on a cold metal table. Caroline would be all dramatic. Not accepting it. And not just because Becca had died in a bad motel. And then the coroner would tell her mom it was tragic to lose someone so young who wanted help but obviously couldn't find a therapist. Then Caroline would break down and say she was sorry. But Becca would be dead. And Caroline would have to wear that. Forever.

Becca flushed.

She was going full dark again. She had to think of something else. She hopped up onto the vanity and pulled out her matches. She decided she would light one and focus on the flame instead of the negative stuff.

She scratched the match across the rough brown stripe, and a tiny baby flame rose up, but she didn't really have time to look at it because she got absorbed by her ugly man hands. Becca tossed the match and tried another. It didn't light. The third one sparked. She focused in on it and watched clear liquid run down the cardboard match stalk to feed the flame. Helping it.

It was weird how sometimes the match sparked and sometimes it didn't. She wondered whether people were like matches. Whether they randomly lit up in the world or they didn't. Becca struck more matches and watched how some burned brightly while others went out the instant they landed. It didn't seem to make any difference how she lit them. The matches just did what they did.

Becca spotted a thin plume of smoke rising up from the tub and hopped off the vanity to have a look. There was a small, almost invisible flame in Wayne's suit jacket, sputtering and weak. She watched it dim then brighten along one edge of Wayne's wallet. It was sort of mesmerizing to watch, not knowing whether it was going to fully spark or fail. A second small flame shot up from between some shirt buttons. And then smoke appeared, and Becca realized the situation had spiralled a little out of control. She rushed to the sink for a glass of water and noticed the bathroom was starting to fill with black smoke. Becca dumped the water into the tub. It didn't help with the smoke situation. She flipped on the exhaust fan but it was noisy and worked like crap, and she was coughing, so she had to get out.

She quickly drew the bathroom door shut behind her, pretty confident the fire would go out on its own.

Wayne was still asleep so she quietly picked up her schoolbag. She hovered at the foot of the bed a moment, shifting her bag from shoulder to shoulder, wondering if she should wake him up and say something. Then she thought no. It was probably more grown-up just to go.

Becca crossed the motel parking lot to the traffic light, then crossed again toward a bus stop, realizing she felt not only disappointed but also a bit concerned. She wasn't exactly sure what had just happened. She'd let her intuition lead her like she was supposed to, but she was left wondering what her intuition knew about her that she didn't.

The bus arrived a few minutes later. Someone got on with a baby stroller and blocked the lane so everyone had to stand by the front doors. Becca saw the driver look over at her a couple times. She checked herself. She was pretty much behind the yellow line. She saw the driver crinkle his nose.

"Smells like a campfire," he said.

Bus drivers were freaks.

As the bus pulled away from the curb, Becca jammed in her earphones. She glanced over at the motel one last time. She saw people stumble out of their rooms and the motel manager come out of Wayne's room, carrying an extinguisher. Everybody looked pissed.

Becca felt bad about everything and wondered how long Wayne would be mad at her for burning his pants.

The bus turned south.

25

The Third Wheel

SHE CAME OUT OF the subway station wrestling a feeling she couldn't shake: something wasn't right. Becca kept coming back to the idea that something that was supposed to happen hadn't. Not sex, because Wayne was old and gross, but something else.

Halfway down Constance Street, Becca spotted a big, blue pickup truck parked in the laneway at her house. The trucks were always massive and shiny. The only thing that changed was the logo on the driver's side door and the wheel rims.

Becca debated waiting for whoever it was to leave, but she needed to eat her feelings more. She went around the back way and let herself into the kitchen through the patio doors. She slipped the frozen Pizza Pocket she'd bought at the gas station into the microwave. She'd stop it before it beeped.

Becca could hear Caroline entertaining in the living room. No distinct words were audible, but her mother's voice was definitely flirty enough to inform Becca it was game on. Her volume always rose with jokes and dipped when she talked "sexy" so only select ears could hear. The pickup truck guy laughed loudly — either because he was shocked by what she'd said or because he liked it. Either way, it was TMI.

Her dad always liked to tell people that Caroline was one step short of white trash. When she was little, Becca thought that meant someone in their family drove garbage trucks, but what it really meant was that her mom had grown up like her dad — sort of wild. When they'd moved to the city together, Caroline had become good at rewriting events from her past to make them more palatable. She called it making lemonade. Becca's dad called it lying. It was basically why they couldn't be together anymore. Her dad could never let go of where they'd come from, and her mom always needed him to.

Too late, Becca heard the clacking of mules on the Mexican tile floor. The kitchen door swung open, and the smile slipped off Caroline's face like cheese off a cracker.

"Oh. You're here. Why?"

"… I live here?"

"No. I thought you had a …" She paused and looked for the word. "… a thing tonight," she said, checking her watch as if she'd find Becca's schedule on her perfect, slender wrist.

"I'm not hanging out with someone who calls me a skank."

"Right," Caroline sighed. "Right." She shook her head. "Do you want to come out and meet …"

"Ray?" offered Becca. She'd seen his name on the truck door.

"Ray," repeated Caroline, like she was testing it out. She'd probably been calling him "Reg" or "Larry."

"No."

"I know!" her mom said suddenly inspired. "Why don't you make us some of your famous frozen lime daiquiris?" *Clack-clack-clack*. Caroline crossed to the refrigerator.

The fridge was always stocked with things that went into drinks. It was the reason Becca had learned to appreciate olives at an early age.

"Mom, I don't feel like it. Besides, the blender is busted and doesn't chip ice anymore."

It was a setback to be sure, but once a blender drink was an option, Caroline rarely let it go. She grabbed an ice cube tray from the freezer and dumped it into a clean tea towel. "Get the limes," she prompted.

Becca didn't move. Caroline didn't notice.

"I don't understand what's going on with you. You do nothing but hide here. You haven't gone to any parties or joined a single club at school. You're home all the time."

Becca was not a failed teenager. "I do plenty of stuff, okay?"

"Like what?

"Things!"

"Uh-huh."

"You know, I'm in school, Mom. I have homework."

But it was as if Caroline hadn't heard a word she'd said. "You have no idea how many kids would kill for the freedom I give you. You should count yourself lucky you don't have to shimmy out a window like I had to."

Becca had had enough. "For your information, I did something, Mom. I cut loose, and I did something bad."

Her mother looked at her like she was finally taking her seriously. But then she said, "Wowwwww" like she was super amazed. It was the voice moms used when they were pretending whatever their two-year-old was babbling was incredibly deep.

"No, I mean it! I did something extra stupid. You and dad would have been especially proud."

Caroline looked at her more carefully. "Bullshit."

The microwave timer beeped.

Caroline's eyes narrowed. She looked hard at Becca and walked to the microwave. Clack-clack-clack.

"Mom, focus! For one second."

But Caroline had already put her hand on the door. She paused dramatically, like she didn't want to look, but she knew she had to. She tugged the door open and pulled out the Pizza Pocket with the gravity of a parent who's discovered a kilo of heroin in her child's schoolbag.

"Mom, can we —"

Caroline held up her hand for silence as she moved to the window, mules clacking, to squint at the nutritional information on the back of the paper wrapper. Her eyes shifted back to Becca with disappointment. "Nine grams of fat, Rebecca," she said in an accusing tone. "Nine. In my house." Caroline tossed the pastry onto the counter. "We've talked about this. You agreed you'd start respecting your body."

"I'm not happy, Mom."

"Well, I'm not the one who put the fat in cheese, Rebecca."

"No, I mean for real. All the t—"

Whatever Becca tried to say after that was drowned out by the sound of Caroline angrily pounding the ice cubes with a knife handle.

"Know what?" Caroline said, shaking her head. "I'm not happy either. You keep complaining that your life is hard, but you never take a single step to change anything. Nine grams." Caroline peeked at the ice under her tea towel and shook her head. "You have everything you need. Clothes. Food. You have *no* children to look after. You live in a fantastic home. You have nothing to complain about."

"I got into some random guy's car today, Mom."

"Tch," Caroline said. She yanked open a drawer and pulled out a meat tenderizing mallet.

"I'm pretty sure I wanted him to do something to me. Something bad."

Caroline gave no reaction. There was no sign of an impact. It made Becca feel like her heart had stopped beating. "Did you hear what I said?!"

"Definitely. I used to like telling my mother that I was pregnant," said Caroline, giving the ice another whack. She glanced at Becca. "This isn't my first time at the rodeo, little girl. You're trying to make me choose between you and … my guest in there. No dice."

"Ray, Mom. His name is Ray."

"You want my attention? Try acting like an adult. Now get the limes."

Becca shook her head and walked away, abandoning Caroline to her citrus drinks. She retreated to her room, furious and confused and humiliated by her spontaneous confession about Wayne.

When she'd said she'd wanted Wayne to do something bad, had she just been using words as something pointy to jab her mom with, or had she really meant it? She didn't have the answer, but it was clear to her that any crisis that was happening to her would always be treated as baby drama, especially when compared to her mom's epic tales of underage driving to Halifax to catch a Green Day concert and crabs. She had to find a way to make her mom care. To make Caroline understand she needed help, using methods her mother respected. Something that would force Caroline to realize her daughter's life struggles were more important than nine grams of fat or a guy whose name might be Ray.

26

Friends and Foes

IT WAS ONE OF those rare Tuesday nights when interesting stuff was happening. A maintenance worker had dropped off an incident report, but the night shift supervisor had forgotten to assign the investigation to the day shift like he normally did, so Roy had decided he and Doug would crack the case.

Roy was off the clock and working through a mouthful of kung pao chicken, but he was itching to get started. "Okay," he said, waving at the security monitors with his chopsticks. "So ... so which cameras cover the north side of the building?"

Roy couldn't name the camera numbers off the top of his head because they were all new, but Doug had walked the building perimeter a few days ago and made a detailed, comprehensive map in blue marker, which he'd put in a plastic sleeve and took home at the end of his shifts. Doug's hunch that the information had value had been correct because normally, Roy never asked him shit.

While Roy dug his sticks back into his takeout container and fished around for some bamboo shoots, Doug tugged his map out and read: "North view, far west side entry and parking, cameras 12 to 14. Service entrance, cameras 15 to 17. Bay doors one to three are on camera 18. Loading dock interior is on 21. And 22 and 23 have eyes on the maintenance bins."

"What about 19 and 20?"

"Fucked if I know. I couldn't find them."

Roy nodded and sucked some garlic out from between his teeth. "Okay. So that ... that doesn't help us. That's too many cameras. Can you imagine us looking through that much footage?" He mimed pushing an imaginary play button over and over and looking at a screen like a zombie. "Right?" Roy hit the bottom of his kung pao container and smiled. There was a bunch of nuts.

He chewed thoughtfully for a moment. "Did any trucks pull in for deliveries between twelve and fifteen hundred hours?"

"Which day?"

"Monday. Whichever date that is."

"Hang on."

Doug set down his onion rings, licked the fingers on his right hand clean, and grabbed a clipboard. "Shredding truck came eleven-forty a.m. on Monday and parked in bay one all day." He set the clipboard aside. "Yeah, I remember that. I was covering for Rick. My second double."

"Sweet."

"It wasn't those guys, if that's what you're thinking. They went straight up to seven, and I had to keep letting them in and out all day because we were out of visitor passes. It was a real pain."

"Did the guy —? What's his name — the guy who reported it."

"Whitehead."

"Yeah. Did he write a statement? Maybe we should read it."

Doug pulled up the report and read the statement out loud. He read stiffly, at the pace old guys walked when they first got up from their chairs. "On Monday, October twenty, I came out with third floor's recycles. There was strange sounds behind the green bins." Doug interrupted himself. "Green bins. Does he mean the waste bins?"

Roy nodded. "What else?"

Doug read on: "… strange sounds from behind the bins … like someone got hurt."

Roy stopped him. "Oh, man! Do you know what this is? This is the Moaner. Has to be. Has to be." The pieces were falling together. He crunched the remaining nuts, his mind racing fast.

Doug's eyes widened. "Jesus Christ," he said, the sense of Roy's words fully descending upon him. "I'll bet it's the Moaner."

Roy balled up a napkin and wiped it across his lips. "Okay. Did he see him?"

"Ummm," Doug said as he skipped through the rest of the statement. "No. No description." There was a lull. "This guy happened to tell the story to a friend of mine who told him he needed to fill out an incident report. He wouldn't have written one if my friend hadn't told him to."

Roy shook his head. "That's … that's exactly why there's procedures. Don't think: just do it. Do the procedure."

Roy tossed his empty kung pao container in the garbage can then dragged his chair over to the camera playback area. "Okay. I say we find the son of a bitch."

Doug nodded and pulled up the footage from camera 22.

27

Setting the Scene

BECCA WALKED STRAIGHT PAST the kitchen where Caroline was turning her antioxidants into a sludge. She hollered she was leaving from the front door. It was important to give her mom zero chances to talk to her. Like her dad used to say, her mother could smell a lie like some dogs smell cadavers.

It was a good day for an abduction. Becca had the beginning of a plan. If it worked, it would forever change the way her mother saw her. But she had to thoroughly prepare.

She walked into High Park on the Howard Park trail. It was early enough to watch the morning joggers handing off the paths to the dog walkers, who would eventually cede them to families and then to old people.

She found a bench on one of the quieter paths, stuffed her hands into her coat pockets, and stared at a big maple, trying to work out why its branches had come out so twisted. It was one of the first trees to change colour in the park and it really stood out. Near the top, a cluster of electric-pink leaves waved and rustled without the slightest provocation. It looked added on, like someone had come around overnight and tagged it with spray paint. "This tree belongs to the Five Point Generalz."

The wind kicked up a little, and the leaves rubbed against one another in a frenzy. They seemed like they were trying to warm up or maybe spread the pink gang tag around. Becca closed her eyes and listened to the leaves. It sounded like applause. Or a deep fryer. Either way, it was the best sound.

By 9:30 a.m., Becca had roughed-out a plan. Now she had to do research. Since rush hour was over, it was probably safe to walk home. She took the long way back, going up Algonquin instead of Garden and then down the other side of Indian to encounter the least amount of people who might recognize her or notice her.

She quickly unlocked the door and slipped into the house. She felt a hush as she walked in, like she'd just interrupted a huge party and the furniture was being quiet until she left. She weirded herself out for a minute thinking about it until she told herself to move on.

She strode into the living room, toward the sofa, automatically releasing the top button of her jeans. Once again, she'd been talked into getting clothes that were one size too small. Caroline had sworn they would be incentive to lose weight; instead, they'd become a reason to do laundry.

Becca tossed the vintage gold velvet throw pillows onto the rug, then wearily dropped onto the sofa. The cushions had wood buttons, which were pretty useless and not comfortable. She couldn't understand why Caroline had bought them.

Her mom was forever buying new lamps and rugs to make their furniture look "modern" and "relevant," but lately, the stuff she'd been buying looked like all the things her grandparents had tried to pawn off on them when they'd sold their home and moved to Florida. Caroline had refused to accept anything, which was why Becca had named the look "ironic retro."

The strangest thing Caroline had bought was a gigantic paint-by-number someone had already done of a German shepherd. Whoever painted it had done a really shitty job. You could see the paint colour numbers and blue lines through a lot of spots, and her

mom had paid $450 for it! Becca had actually seen Caroline look-
ing at it. She stared at it for hours. For sure it meant something, but
she never talked about it. Becca never asked.

The phone rang. Becca answered.

"This is Mary the Immaculate High School. Mrs. Chalmers?"

Fuck. Because of course. She'd answered automatically. OMG,
she hated landlines so bad right now. "Yes?"

"We're calling about Rebecca. Are you aware she's not in school
today?"

"Yes?" she said, trying not to say more because she sucked so
hard at off-the-cuff stuff. But the caller was silent. She might need
to give the school more details.

"She's barfing, so I said to stay home." Silence. "As her guardian."

"Is this you, Rebecca?"

She thought about hanging up when the voice on the other end
of the phone said, "It's Dylan. Raven. Whatever."

Becca got a little creeped out and defensive. "Umm, how did you
get this number?"

"I work in the school office for extra credits. Becca, what are
you doing? Why are you pretending you're your mom?"

Becca briefly wondered if she really needed to answer and how
much she should spill, but she needn't have bothered. It all came
out in a big information dump. "Okay, I'm not sick, but I have
to stay home to do this thing, and my mom one hundred percent
can't know I'm here. It's really important, and I'm not even joking.
Can you mark me confirmed sick?" She heard Dylan groan, which
meant he was at least thinking about it. "Please?"

Dylan sighed. "Are you going to do something stupid?" he asked.
"Wait. Let me rephrase that." He lowered his voice even more,
presumably so the school secretaries couldn't hear their conversation. "Are you going to hurt yourself?"

Becca thought about his question. "No," she answered truthfully. Then she realized with amazement that if the answer had been yes, she would probably have said so.

"Fine. Just this once," he said. "But I'm giving you my cell number. You have to text me if you need something or if something happens because I'm probably legally responsible now." He lowered his voice again and had to repeat his number three times because he was talking so quietly.

BECCA DID A BUTTLOAD of research on the internet until it was time to set the scene.

She'd decided she'd walked in on a robbery. That she'd been forced to go with the thieves in their car so she couldn't call the cops. And that as the car had slowed to get onto an on-ramp, she'd seen her chance for escape, pushed the door open, and jumped. She'd gone over it multiple times. That part all made sense.

She still needed to flesh out how many robbers, how they were dressed, and what kind of car they were driving. She also thought she should come up with some strange factoid — like the back of the car smelled like vinegar — because she'd seen a movie where an undercover cop convinced the bad guys he was legit by creating the right amount of detail. She'd liked the film until it got too gross to watch, but she imagined the strategy had worked.

A YouTuber who was either an ex-con or an ex-cop explained that robbers usually got into homes through doors or windows that were hidden from view. Becca decided it would be the patio doors. But as she walked into the kitchen, she spotted the pipe Caroline laid across the door's bottom tracks and realized all the video tutorials she'd watched that morning had been completely useless. Except for the one on French braiding. There was no way to legitimately pop the door out of the frame. That left her with no choice except to act drastically.

For around ten minutes, Becca stood in front of the patio doors working up her nerve, wishing hard that someone would show up and break the glass for her.

When that didn't happen, she decided to square off. She tried to give the door a lame sideways martial arts kick. She even yelled, "Heee-yah!" but she couldn't commit. She was too scared of hurting herself. What if this was the one time safety glass didn't crumble into little cubes and went full shard?

Becca needed something to smash into the door. And she found it on the kitchen counter: the blender.

Her first throw was admittedly tentative, but OMG the sound it made was so loud. It *sort of* hit the door but mostly landed on the floor. Becca unscrewed the pitcher and tried again, this time bashing just the blender base against the door. *Bam*! Her heart beating, she drew closer to inspect the damage. Fine, spidery cracks like fireworks appeared where the blender had made contact with the door. Her aim was balls, but it would work. She just needed to smash harder.

Becca went for it, pounding the blender into the glass, tracking the cracks as they spread. She smashed the door again and again, each blow making her realize how much she hated the blender for making her smell like coconut since she was eleven. It was exhausting in a liberating sort of way she could never have anticipated.

Becca backed up a few steps, catching her breath. She was so close. She was tired, but she had to finish what she'd started. Balancing the blender on her shoulder like a shot-putter, she ran toward the door. A primal scream ripped out of her throat as she hurled the blender through the glass.

Cool autumn air rushed in.

Half laughing, half crying, she pushed out the rest of the glass. Screw frozen piña coladas forever.

Next, she needed to set up a scene her mother would decode. Things torn out of cupboards in the search for valuables. Becca's interruption. Signs of a scuffle in the wheatgrass and a trail of scattered pencils. She waffled on leaving some study notes behind then decided that was overkill.

She wasn't sure she had done the right thing. But then again, if all she had was a choice between positively knowing that she could count on her mom caring for her and dying ...

Becca left through the back door to regain her hiding spot and wait until her mother's return.

28

Theatre of the Mind

NO ONE HAD CHECKED their tire pressure, which was a lucky thing because Becca had no idea what she'd have said if she'd been discovered hiding in the thicket by the air pumps behind Petro-Canada.

She stood under a six-foot-tall reedy tree with long, spindly leaves that fanned out like a droopy parasol. The leaves had trapped some of the midday warmth, which was good because the air was turning cool, but it also concentrated the smells of dank concrete and pee, so Becca tried not to go in too far under the branches.

She realized she didn't know what kind of tree it was because her teachers had never taught the name of this kind in school, even though they seemed to grow around gas stations. She was looking it up on her phone, wondering what else school hadn't taught her, when she spotted her mom's Lexus. Early.

Fuck!

Not part of the plan.

Becca grabbed her backpack and ran to the crosswalk. She was supposed to be hiding in the neighbour's yard when her mom got home so she could watch her discover the break-in and deduce she'd been abducted. She needed to see Caroline break down to know her con had worked. Now she'd have to guess.

Darkness hadn't been part of her plan either. Of course, Becca had known night was coming. She'd actually intended to use the darkness to hide and watch Caroline unravel. But as Becca walked up and down Hewitt Avenue, trying to figure out which house's yard backed on to hers, she understood its disadvantage. Without ever having seen the front of their rear neighbour's house, and without being able to see her own house in relation to it, she wasn't exactly sure which yard to walk into.

Luckily, Becca spotted a Halloween scarecrow and a row of small, mangled pumpkins lined up across the front stoop of one place and remembered how Caroline had called the neighbours avid breeders. It had to be the right house.

Becca took a deep breath, flipped up her hoodie like Elliot on *Mr. Robot*, and quietly started down the dark driveway toward the backyard. Nice and easy, like she was supposed to be there.

There were lights on inside the house. Becca spotted the whole family in the living room, watching TV together, which totally blew her away because who did that *Little House on the Prairie* stuff?

She'd never considered the neighbours would be home, that they might see her or prevent her from going into their yard. Her doubts began to expand. Becca wondered what other details she'd failed to consider. Like garbage bin night. And motion detector lights. And just as she paused to reconsider her plans, she heard a tinkling, like a chain. Then a low, ominous growl.

Becca froze.

The sound had come from behind the house and rose from the dark. A warning. It appeared. Its black eyes were glassy and unreadable. Its lips were pulled back in a snarl, and its jaw was shoved forward all the way so all its teeth could be seen.

"Shh-shh-shh," said Becca, holding out her hands in front of her. She had no idea what she was doing. "Shh-shh-shh."

The dog inched forward, its long growls becoming punctuated by barks.

"No," Becca said firmly, backing up along the driveway. "No."

The Pom kept advancing. It looked taller and puffier and more menacing in the porch light. Becca knew it could totally tell she was scared. It could *feel* her fear. And just as she reached peak anxiety, it lunged.

Becca screamed and bolted. She ran and ran until the barking and the sound of scrambling toes were far behind her.

UNDENIABLY, STUFF WAS GOING wrong. Her biggest mistake was that she'd let herself be intimidated by a Pom. Her other problem was that her phone battery was on its last bar. She wouldn't be able to watch the news and see what was happening, which was crucial. She needed to be able to gauge when she could go back home. Too soon and Caroline's relief at seeing her return would be minimized. Too late and there might be demands for accountability. Becca wished she had a solid Plan B. She needed eyes. She texted Dylan for help, but her phone died before she received a reply.

As she walked into the park, she started to look for places where she could hide until she figured something out. She recalled the patches of long grass near the mountain bike trails but worried they might be full of deer ticks and snakes. Becca stepped off the path to deliberate. She was standing among the trees, out of the way in the dark, and she ended up scaring a lot of people who hadn't realized she was there. She felt bad about it, but whenever she tried to make a noise to reveal her presence, people literally leapt out of their skins. So she started walking again.

What she needed was a place where she could be around people but invisible at the same time. And preferably in close proximity to concrete.

Becca had never been much of an outdoors person, which was strange given that her most vivid memory was of standing in a garden, plucking the heads off flowers with no one stopping her.

She still remembered the feel of the sticky red petals in her hands and how she'd scraped them into a little bucket. So random.

Walking past the playground, she spotted a row of round bushes backing on to a retaining wall. She strolled over and casually squatted down in front of one of them to take a closer look at them while pretending to pull up her Uggs because she couldn't figure out whether the branches went all the way to the ground. It was getting late, and since it seemed there was no way to know for sure, she just went for it.

It was pitch-black inside the bush, but Becca kept moving, using her backpack to push her way through. She could hear leaves and branches sliding over her Gore-Tex coat, making the sound of a thousand zippers as she moved. The further she got in, the more she started to feel panic. What if she was trapped, surrounded by sharp twigs? The branches suddenly thinned out, and a space appeared. There was barely enough room for her to sit. But there was enough.

She flipped herself around and managed to rest her back against the wall. There was one terrible moment when she thought she'd sat on her single-serving Cheetos, but it turned out it was her phone. She'd cracked the screen.

Becca got busy breaking off all the dead branches and leaves in face range. When she'd cleared enough of them, she laid out her Cheetos, leftover licorice, and a few caramels on a plate she'd made out of leaves. She ate slowly and humbly, imagining this was how settlers must have felt when they ate their first dinners in their sod shacks.

As the park emptied out and the lights switched on, Becca's bush became a peaceful, protective cocoon. This was probably what Heartland felt like after the TV crews went home and the horses went to sleep.

But just as she started to drift off, her bush started to shake.

29

Pre-Departure Check

KATHERINE HAD TAKEN A Paxil, drunk a little pinot, and was starting to feel a bit more positive about having dinner with her family.
She would probably have indulged in a Xanax too, but she didn't
want to completely abandon Brent to her siblings. They could be
such assholes to people she brought home. The impulse was sweet
and protective because she was the youngest, but she honestly didn't
need anyone's help.

There'd been a whole slew of guys her family had never met.

Dating was the way Katherine had figured out her true nature.
It had allowed her to explore what she thought and define what
she liked. In her search for self, Katherine had dated extensively.
There'd been actors and anarchists, architects, stockbrokers, ski
instructors, and one nihilist. She'd tried on each of their worldviews
the way a person tries on a vintage coat in Kensington Market —
with great reservation. She'd checked the stitching, moved her arms
around to make sure there was enough room for her moral views,
stared at the stains, and spent a considerable amount of time wondering whether the colour worked with stuff she already owned.

Brent's coat didn't suit her. His naive gentility had eventually
become annoying. He believed that people were decent and would
act for the betterment of their society if given a chance. Ironically,
it had been her persistent attempts to convince Brent the world

was fucked up that had helped Katherine realize she was a pessi-
mist. And for that, she'd always be thankful.

It was 6:45 p.m. and time for a mirror check before going down
to the lobby to wait for Brent. As she started her circuit, Katherine reminded herself not to linger over details and to stick to
her viewing pattern: hair, eyes, teeth, scarf, tits, and a mandatory
fabric accident check, which she'd added five years ago after discovering she'd gone all the way across the Bloor line with the back
of her skirt tucked into her pantyhose. Apparently, the citizenry
of Toronto was paralyzed by the prospect of informing someone
that the world could see their ass. You had to rely on yourself so
much more these days.

With that in mind, Katherine took a deep, cleansing *ujjayi* breath
to accept that she would hate the way she looked and approached
the mirror.

Hair, fine. Eye makeup, okay. Scarf, none. Her neck, of course,
was terrible.

People told her she was imagining things, but her neck was
unusually long — longer than normal. It was abnormal. But she'd
picked a dress with a plunging neckline and then accessorized it
with a dangly necklace that would draw eyes away from her "problem area." The Versace was nothing pretentious — a prêt-à-porter
paisley her mother had sprung for when they'd gone to Switzerland. It felt nice against her skin, and yet it didn't make her feel like
a complete fake for wearing it.

Dressing up was mandatory for family dinners. It seemed a bit
abusive to her, actually. Her brothers could show up wearing the
suits they'd worn at the office, but she had to rush home and shower
and change because she'd spent her day in a filthy rehearsal hall.
Every time she shucked off her Cavallis, she felt forced to acknowledge her gutlessness.

Anyway, she was in the dress and the dress suited her.

Finding something to wear was a constant battle. Clothes could look great in store windows, but they inevitably looked horrid when she slipped them on because her hips were not made for fashion. They weren't round. Or maternal. Nor did they suggest softness, generosity, or femininity in any way, shape, or form. They were narrow. They jutted out in front like bumpers on an old car. She also had absolutely no ass to speak of. The worst thing about her hip situation was that sooner or later people she had sex with saw them. The moment she undressed, she'd often lose all interest in sex because she was one hundred percent evaluating reactions to her hips.

Of course, intellectually, Katherine understood no one would recoil in horror at the sight of her when they were about to have sex. Nevertheless, she suspected most of her boyfriends of being closeted.

It was 6:55 p.m., and Brent was scheduled to pick her up at 7:00 p.m. in an Uber.

Her stomach was churning in earnest now. She was really counting on Brent to bolster her courage if the need arose. Whatever her family's reaction to the announcement of her acting career debut, she vowed to herself she would remain thrilled by the direction her life was taking.

Pulling on her coat, she tugged up her lapels and slid two fingers alongside her collarbone to find her carotid pulse. She'd learned how to locate it in a nursing manual she'd picked up at a garage sale. Actors on TV shows always grabbed the wrist, but it turned out there were literally dozens of places you could check for a pulse, like the stomach, the groin, and the ankle joint. She found something reassuring about being able to find it wherever. In case.

As she reached the front door, Katherine felt strangely calm and confident, as though she innately knew she would be able to overcome any negativity that came her way. She decided to trust her feelings.

30

Revelations

KATHERINE SLIPPED INTO THE rear seat of the cab. The back of her legs felt cool against the dark, slippery upholstery. As Brent came around the other side, she thought she heard the driver ask her a question. She looked up at him. "I'm sorry. What?"

The driver glanced at her in the rearview mirror. He was muttering on his cell phone.

Brent's door opened, and he stepped in with a cool breeze. He turned to her, looked her up and down, and smiled. "You look ravishing this evening, Kate!"

"Really? Thanks." She smiled back. "It's just something I threw on." Patting down the folds of her coat, she began to feel genuinely chuffed. "You are so sweet."

Brent pointed to the driver. "He's asking where we're going."

"What? Oh." Katherine leaned toward the driver and pointed to his Bluetooth earpiece. "Sorry, I thought you were on your ... We're going to Rosedale." There was no point in giving an address. He wouldn't know the street. "Can you cross to University, and I'll give you directions as we get closer."

The driver nodded and pulled into traffic. She could see his eyes lingering on her in the rearview mirror. Then his lips moving. She wasn't sure whether he didn't agree with her route or he'd hopped onto another call, so she leaned toward him again. "It's faster this —"

Nope. He was back on a call.

Katherine turned to Brent. "It's actually much faster this way," she confided, but Brent wasn't listening either. He was staring at her black Valentino boots. She didn't normally wear heels.

"It should take us fifteen minutes. We should be right on time," said Brent. He wasn't really talking. He was babbling so he could meditate on her boots a little longer.

"Actually, we'll be a little late, but it's fine."

Brent frowned. "How could that be possible? I got to your place exactly at seven," he said.

"I miscalculated. No big deal." Which was a lie because Katherine was never late, and her family would definitely notice, but she was setting the tone and the focus for the evening. She wanted to be sure everyone knew she was in control of her life. Not them.

Katherine caught the taxi driver looking at her again. She glanced from his picture back at him a few times to make sure. She leaned in toward Brent.

"It's not the same guy," she said quietly.

"Hmm?"

Katherine pretended to fix her hair. "The guy in the picture is not the guy driving the car. It's a different driver. This is why I wanted an Uber."

"I'm sure it's fine. He probably just forgot to switch the card," Brent said.

Katherine pursed her lips. Brent was welcome to his "everyone is okay" opinion, but he'd obviously never cabbed in Beirut. Some things, you paid attention to. "Could you turn right up here and go through to Yonge?" Katherine pointed. The driver said nothing, but he turned. Then he mumbled. Katherine was about to respond, then didn't. There should have been a light or a sign or something to let people know when cab drivers were talking to them.

"Who will I be meeting tonight?" asked Brent.

"Just my immediate family. My mother and father, my older

sister, Juliette, her second husband, Laurence, and my brothers, Daniel and Joseph."

"Your family sounds very formal."

"I'm sorry? What are you saying?"

"You're calling your siblings by their full names. When my sister Cecile and I hang out, I call her Ceec or Scooch."

Katherine stared at Brent a moment. "I call my siblings by their names," she said plainly. "It's what they're called."

"Yes, but ... I guess I presumed there'd be some informality because it's the sort of thing that happens over time. I mean, your name is Katherine, but I call you Kate."

"And I'd rather you didn't."

Brent's mouth dropped open. "I ... I'm not sure what to say." He was obviously trying to recover. "I never knew. I didn't think — I mean, I hope you realize that when I call you Kate, I mean it with nothing but affection."

"I know," said Katherine. "But it's still not my name." She looked out her window at the rows of little houses and little windows, some of which were sporting Halloween decorations, trying to forget the number of times he'd called her Kate and she'd said nothing.

She felt Brent sink back in the seat beside her. He was shocked and struggling not to touch his hair. They rode the rest of the way in silence except for the few occasions when she gave the cab driver directions. At one point, she raised her cell phone and took a picture of the taxi licence, making sure the driver saw her do it. There were no further incidents.

31

Gobsmacked

KATHERINE, NOT KATE.

For the second time in as many weeks, Brent was stunned, speechless.

Kate had only to provide the tiniest new shred of information about herself, and it radically changed his understanding of who she was every time. It was as though she were a master chef, concealing the key ingredient that would identify the kind of confection she was. Perhaps meeting her family would clear up some of the mysteries, but given how shaken he felt by her latest admission, perhaps he wasn't prepared for the answers.

The cab turned off Yonge Street onto a narrow, winding road lined with giant trees and manicured lawns. They passed a grocery store with valet service, a dry-cleaning home delivery van, and gaggles of nannies waiting to catch a bus home. It was a world within a world Brent had never seen.

Kate pointed ahead, giving final directions. The driver pulled up in front of a dry-stacked stone fence whose rocks had been shaped by craftsmen and kissed with moss. Rising behind the low wall was a large Georgian house. This was Katherine's family home.

The driver pointed at the fare box. Brent paid, barely counting his change. He got out and walked around the cab, feeling increasingly unsteady as he took in the details of the lush grounds he could see through the branches of a gnarled centuries-old oak in the dark. Unable to process the expansiveness of the house, which completely redefined his vision of Kate's childhood, Brent fished around for the cab's door handle. Kate became impatient and cracked the door open herself. He remembered himself and helped her out.

"Kate. Katherine. This is ..." he stuttered.

"Home," she said.

"Palatial," he corrected. The word stuck to his tongue. His mouth was going dry.

Kate appeared puzzled by his remark. She followed his look toward the home with the slate roof and the opulent chandelier glowing through the windows. Peeved, she looked back at him. He was making more of this than he needed to.

"It's just a house, Brent."

"It's bigger than my public school," he answered.

Kate looked back at her home as if needing to check whether they were talking about the same structure.

"You're really overreacting," she said.

Brent's hands travelled up toward his hair. Kate intercepted them.

"Okay, fine," she said. "It's a big house. So what? A lot of people have big houses." She waved toward the other magnificent houses on the street. "It's big, but it's not a mansion. I mean, we don't have butlers or stables or formal gardens."

"What do your folks do?"

"Mom's a food chemist and Dad's a judge."

"A judge?!" Brent's voice came out strangled.

She mock-gasped. "Is that a problem? Are you a convicted felon?" Her eyes narrowed. "That was a joke. You're not laughing."

Brent felt physically incapable of laughter. "This isn't funny, Kate. I'm underdressed, and I am not prepared for this encounter," he said, trying to force his lapels to sit flat.

"You're perfectly dressed for a celebratory family dinner. They'll be overdressed, but try not to let it get to you."

Had Brent only known who and what he was about to face, he'd have found something much more structured to wear. A worsted suit with notch lapels. Something with a waistcoat and a cotton tie that showed he was down-to-earth, principled, and ethical to a fault. Goddamn Atticus Finch in *To Kill a Mockingbird*. That's who he needed to be right now.

"You're going all white," Katherine observed.

"For God's sake, Katherine. What have I got to talk about? With a judge?"

"No one cares about what you're going to say, Brent. I promise. Mother will barely talk to you. She'll just go on about how we all failed to live up to her dreams." Katherine must have realized what she was saying wasn't helping, because she took a different tack. Her voice softened. "You can chat with my sister, Juliette. You'll have loads of things to talk about. She writes, you know."

"Does she?" Brent said, feeling an inkling of relief.

"Well, not write-writes, but she does articles. She recently interviewed Margaret Atwood about something for the *Globe*. You can talk about that."

"Your sister is Juliette Simone?" he said, putting it together.

Katherine flashed him an exasperated look. "Would you stop?! She's a journalist. She's plain people. Nothing special. Like you and me."

Brent was done holding back his hands. They could twist his hair into a Roman candle for all he cared. Maybe his head would explode, and he could be spared the rest of the evening. But Katherine wouldn't have it. She wrestled his hands into hers and looked deeply into his eyes.

"Brent, listen to me. Just because people have more money and more success than you doesn't mean they're better or smarter. Okay?"

He could tell she was waiting for a moment to discern agreement in his eyes, but he couldn't generate it.

She lost patience and let his hands drop. "I've just saved you fourteen years of therapy. The least you could do is say thank you."

Brent was going through his catalogue of amusing anecdotes: the time his family forgot him at Upper Canada Village, the time he'd met Robertson Davies' widow, the time he was chased by a rabid white squirrel in Trinity Bellwoods. Then it occurred to him that Kate had heard all his stories before and how she had absolutely no tolerance for repetition. Dear God, he had to retreat.

Before Brent could formulate an excuse, he realized they'd travelled from the curb to the front door and Katherine's hand was firmly engaged with the door buzzer.

She glanced back at him and smiled reassuringly. "It's just a place where I played hide-and-seek."

She turned toward the door, flipping her hair back over her shoulders as she waited for entry. A perfect little girl's gesture. He could easily imagine young Kate with barrettes, wanting to impress a tutor or a person of authority.

The front door cracked open cautiously, then swung open wide, revealing a svelte older woman with a warm, inviting, and generous smile. There was a touch of silver in her meticulously combed hair. She was dressed simply but elegantly in black and wore one piece of stunning but tasteful jewellery. Her humanity was palpable. Brent felt an instant wave of relief rush over him.

"Hey," Kate said quietly, letting her coat slip off her shoulders into the woman's ready hands. "How are you?"

The woman smiled, lovingly draping Kate's coat over her arm. "Very well, thank you." She approached Brent and smiled, reaching invitingly for his coat.

But introductions were in order. "I'm Brent. I'm so very pleased to meet you." He smiled broadly.

Katherine leaned in. "That's Consuela," she hissed. "Give her your GD coat and come into the living room to meet my parents."

Consuela kept smiling.

32

Clarity

THE TINY LEAVES THAT hung inches away from Becca's face quivered with every movement the bush interloper made. She tried to see who it was, but all detail beyond the branches in front of her face was a slurry of shapes. There was only the interplay of dark and less dark, a form without a profile.

The rustling stopped. Becca remained completely still and waited long enough to decide the danger had passed.

As she was about to tuck into her last piece of licorice, she thought she heard a voice. It was so quiet she wasn't even sure she'd heard it. She replayed the sound in her mind again and again until she persuaded herself that someone had whispered, "I'll get ya."

A shiver ran down her spine. Before she could process what to do with that information, the branches made a hellish cracking noise as though they were being pulled apart like rows of woody stitches. The noise was coming toward her.

Becca drew her knees up to her chest and tried to flatten herself against the retaining wall. The cracking stopped momentarily and was replaced by the sound of fabric rustling.

"Rebecca?"

A flashlight snapped on. She saw a tall purple Doc Martens boot with a painted raven, its wings spread out over the toe.

"Down here," she said, trying to find her voice. Too late —
Dylan was moving again. She saw his hand pass by and grabbed
it, pulling him toward her, leading him down into her tangled laby-
rinth like he was Apollo and she was Daphne about to turn into
a laurel tree as she tried to remember her humanity one last time.

"Ow! Hold on. Stop. *Stop*." Dylan wrenched his hand free. She
watched the ravens fly back through the branches into the night.

Becca waited, wondering what would happen next. As the last
of the warmth from Dylan's hand begin to leave her skin, she heard
him say, "Rebecca, could you please come out?"

It was probably the smart thing to do. "Okay."

She took a final look around her secret space that was tailored
to her. No one would ever know how little she needed to feel safe.
Or that she'd made a plate out of leaves. It was probably for the best.

It was easier getting out of her hiding place than it had been
getting in. Becca flipped her hood over her face, got into a half
squat, and slid up the wall until she was standing, then she walked
straight out of the flower bed toward Dylan, who was waiting for
her under the streetlight.

He was wearing a bomber jacket. It looked good. When she
drew closer, she saw he had a few long scrapes on his face.

"Did I do that?" she asked, pointing.

"What? Is there blood?" His hand came up hesitantly to his
forehead.

She put her hand on his arm to stop him. "Don't," she said,
wondering where all the arm touching stuff was coming from.
"Maybe we should find a washroom."

He nodded and started walking like he knew where he was
going, so she followed.

"I'm so sorry. I saw your hand, and I wanted you to know
where I was."

Dylan seemed miffed. "It would probably have been easier just
to answer me."

"I couldn't hear what you were saying. I didn't know it was you until I saw your boots." Becca decided that it was probably better not to mention the leaves and twigs in his hair.

"This whole thing has been weird," he said.

She could see how it totally had been. "Did you go by my house?"

Dylan nodded. "Your place is huge. You know my whole family lives in a —"

Becca cut him off. "What did you see?"

Dylan's confused expression clearly conveyed he wasn't following. "What did I see?"

She decided to jump ahead. "How many cop cars were parked out front?"

"None. There were none."

Becca's heart sank. "You sure you went to the right place? Indian Road? Not Indian Grove?"

"Totally. Big stone house with a blue door. Your mom came out and everything."

"What?!"

"You texted me to go look at the house, so I was looking at the house, but it wasn't obvious what I was looking for. I was texting you back when she came out. You know your phone is dead."

"Dylan. My mom — what did she say?"

"She asked me what I wanted."

"And what did you say?"

"That we were friends from school." Dylan shrugged like everything had gone fine.

"And then what?"

"She said you weren't home, and I said okay."

"Okay?!"

"It's a legitimate answer. I wasn't going to hang out and wait for you there, right?" Dylan quickly added. "Geez, Rebecca, what the hell is going on?"

Becca's thoughts were racing. Maybe her mother hadn't discovered the busted patio door. Maybe she had, but hadn't noticed the signs of a struggle. Or maybe this was the response she truly feared.

She must have looked cratered, because Dylan took her hands and asked again, "Rebecca, what were you expecting?" His voice was warm and concerned.

"More," she answered and fell silent.

33

Entrances and Exits

HIS MOTHER HAD ALWAYS said the rich were like ordinary people, only with extra pocket change, but sitting among the Radcliffes in a gargantuan living room, on the brocade Chippendale sofa, Brent suspected dinner would be worlds away from family night at Ribby and Wings.

They were spectacular, each Radcliffe more worldly and glorious than the next. Everything about them, from their teeth to their tailoring, attested to old money.

The Radcliffes' ordinary lives were inconceivable experiences for most of humanity. Impromptu weekend getaways to Paris, attendance at the annual yacht club race to Mackinac, organic handcrafted doggy treats for their spaniel, thermal pools in Switzerland. Katherine spoke with ease about horse boarding then debated the merits of owning a plane.

There was nothing he could contribute to the conversation. Brent remained quiet but engaged for the first hour of his visit, nodding with great enthusiasm at both stories and questions in place of providing answers. Mercifully, no one seemed to have noticed.

Still, it was a relief when Consuela appeared in the doorway and Missus Radcliffe announced dinner was served.

PRIME RIB MAGICALLY APPEARED, and Brent tucked in, pleased to have something to do other than nod. As the conversation drifted to the topic of nannies in rehab, Brent allowed himself to fully absorb the minutiae of a life well lived: the starched linen napkins, the tang of the drizzled San Giacomo balsamic on the strawberries, and the Strasbourg-patterned sterling flatware. He simultaneously felt joy to be experiencing these wonderful things and regret, knowing it would make his return to grilled cheese sandwiches and ketchup on Formica a tad difficult.

Brent sensed the table go quiet around him and glanced up from the horseradish spoon he had been admiring. The judge was looking at him expectantly, as were the others. Brent intuited that some sort of response was required, so he lifted the spoon.

"Yummy," he said. He returned the spoon to its dish.

The judge nodded wisely and let his knife sink into his perfect medium-rare prime rib. "Brent, why don't you tell us a bit about what you do," he asked.

Brent cleared this throat to the sound of tinkling cutlery. "Ah." He lightly dabbed his mouth with the linen napkin, hoping he'd left no stain. "I teach," he said, keeping his answer brief and to the point. "English literature."

"Isn't that interesting," the judge commented generally.

Brent wasn't sure whether it was interesting or not, as no one at the table had replied, but Judge Radcliffe continued with incredibly generosity.

"Who's your dean?"

"At the moment, it's —"

"Consuela?" said Katherine's mother. "Could you get Judge Radcliffe more gravy, please? And I need water." She briefly hit her crystal water glass with the tips of her manicured nails. It made the ringing sound of an impatient bell.

The judge, a man obviously used to interruptions, nodded at Brent as he cut into his next slice of beef. "Go on. Your dean?"

"Giselle Radner. She's come to us from Acadia, and she's a wonderful fit." Brent heard Katherine sigh. He was boring her. "I've been with the department a little over five years as assistant professor."

Katherine let her utensils drop with a clank — a warning to wrap it up. The judge's eyes darted momentarily toward his daughter.

Brent quickly delivered the abridged version of his career prospects in three swift strokes. "Hoping for tenure. Old story. Sure you're heard it before."

"Tenure is highly prized. I imagine there's some stiff competition for that kind of job security."

"Yes. Yes, there is—"

"Okay. Blah-blah-blah, blah-blah. But also, Brent's getting a story published," said Kate, cutting to the chase.

There was a collective "oh" and a round of effusive "well dones." Kate's brother Joseph drained his Shiraz and vaguely smiled. Missus Radcliffe thoughtfully centred a two-carat diamond on her finger.

"Nothing of your standard, of course," Brent said, nodding in red-cheeked deference to Juliette Simone. Juliette's second husband, Laurence, smiled thinly as though Brent's comment had been wholly anticipated, but Juliette accepted the compliment with grace and modesty.

"Getting anything published these days is a bit of a miracle," she said.

Joseph held his empty glass out and waited for Consuela to arrive. "Am I the only person who thinks it's funny that Katherine's hooked up with a professor?"

It was assistant professor, but Brent didn't bother correcting him. "Funny? Funny how?"

"Katherine's had a hell of time staying in school," said the judge.

"You're exaggerating. He's exaggerating," Katherine said. "It wasn't that bad."

"High school. She dropped out at least twice," said Joseph. He was a CFO for Greenpeace and apparently good at holding others accountable. "You dropped out of the Gould Academy, then Berkshire ..."

"I didn't drop out. I thought I wanted to study aeronautical science, but once I got into it, I lost interest." Katherine appealed to Brent. "They're really making it sound worse than it was."

"Glasgow, Norway, Austria," added Missus Radcliffe. "The London School of Economics."

Brent visibly reeled with shock and turned to Katherine.

"I audited a few courses. Maybe a semester here and there," she clarified pre-emptively. "Look, I'm sorry, but I'm not going to spend years studying something I'm not interested in to make people happy. That would be crazy. What would be the point? I mean, it's my life, right?"

Missus Radcliffe picked up her butter knife and studied the reflective patterns it cast on the mahogany table. "She's always had to be her ..." Her voice sounded tired, joyless, and far away.

"Katherine's never been engaged by scholastics," explained the judge. "It's not a question of focus. It's a question of interest. This girl can concentrate. I can remember Katherine studying a small fragment of Queen Anne's lace for over three hours." He turned to his wife. "You remember that? She would have been around sixteen."

"Yeah, well, I think that might have been more about the prescription drugs." Katherine turned to Brent, explaining, "I was a little over-medicated in my youth."

Brent laughed out loud. Then he realized no one else was.

For his part, the judge did not acknowledge any awkwardness. "I've always thought arts administration might be a good move for Katherine. What do you think, Brent?"

Brent noted Kate lightly shaking her head. He pinned a smile on his face. "I'm sure Kate is in a better position to answer that."

"Well, I think," said Missus Radcliffe, slowly and thoughtfully, "that Katherine would make a wonderful dental hygienist. She's detailed and has very nice teeth."

"Really, Mom? A dental hygienist?"

"If you don't like my suggestion, Katherine, then by all means, don't feel obliged to take it." Missus Radcliffe set down her butter knife. "Consuela, please clear."

"My parents," said Kate, turning to Brent, "don't seem to expect much from me. Which is sort of weird, isn't it? Given that my entire family has this crazy need to succeed. Mother," she explained, "is a pioneer in nutritional research. Daniel invented a housing system for victims of natural disasters that could be erected in two days when he was seventeen. Juliette, of course, is a celebrated journalist. And when Joseph isn't busy as CFO at Greenpeace, he shoots visual essays of war-torn countries. So ... of course, it should follow that I become a dental hygienist! I mean, that makes perfect sense. While you're all changing peoples' lives, I can stay in town and scrape plaque."

Brent, who hadn't anticipated an outburst, had resumed eating to prevent Consuela from taking his unfinished beef. He nodded supportively while trying not to draw attention to his chewing.

"Would it make it better if I said I was disappointed in all my children equally?" said Missus Radcliffe. She held Katherine's gaze, but her daughter had gone silent, catching up with the emotional blow.

Joseph grabbed his wineglass and drained it.

"Looks as if this is as far as my promotion celebrations go." He stood up.

Missus Radcliffe made a sour face. "Sit down," she said. "I ordered a cake."

Judge Radcliffe never looked up from his water glass. He seemed to be busy contemplating some faraway issues.

"In my opinion, Mother," said Juliette Simone, "we're all doing fine."

Juliette's second husband appeared amused by his wife's off the cuff statement. He casually tugged at his sleeve, awaiting the crocodile's reaction.

Missus Radcliffe looked askance at her daughter, nodding as if in agreement. "You used to write beautiful poetry," she said, "and now you count words. But to each her own."

Juliette Simone pushed away her plate, her appetite quite destroyed, and turned to Katherine. "You do this every time," she stated. "Someone says the slightest thing, and you blame us because you're embarrassed by what you do. It's not our fault you haven't got a career."

"As it turns out," Kate said, "you can all keep your recommendations to yourselves, because next Friday, October 31, I'm having my professional acting debut at the Mustard Extra Space."

Her announcement was followed by the sound of expensive clothing creasing as its wearers shifted uncomfortably on damask-covered chairs.

Missus Radcliffe looked toward her husband, wearing a painfully unimpressed expression.

Brent hesitated only a moment, then charged in. "Brava, Kate! I had no idea."

Katherine forced a laugh. It sounded hollow and dreadful. "It's very exciting!" she said.

"I thought you were stage managing," said Brent.

"I am. But the director thought I also happened to be perfect for a part, and he asked me to do it."

The judge nodded gravely. "You'll have to tell us when we can come see you."

"Yes," echoed Katherine's mother, lagging several moments after the judge. Kate, of course, caught it.

"You can never have any happiness for me. Any joy."

"That's not true, Katherine," her mother replied. "We've supported you all the way."

"Only with money," Katherine answered. "Not in a way that actually matters."

Missus Radcliffe turned to Juliette. "You should write something about Katherine's play."

Juliette Simone did not immediately look enthused.

Missus Radcliffe seemed piqued. "I thought you said you were interested in writing some theatre stories, Juliette," she persisted. It was a statement rather than a question, and it was met with meaningful silence, but Missus Radcliffe either wasn't picking up on it or wasn't having it. "Well, did you or didn't you?"

Silence.

"Juliette?"

Juliette shrugged.

Missus Radcliffe turned to Katherine. "It's settled."

But Kate had already felt the sting of Juliette's rejection. "Please," she spat. "Don't do me any favours."

"Juliette's doing a story on your play, and that is final," said Missus Radcliffe.

"But not for me," said Kate. "For her."

"Oh God," Juliette Simone sighed. She locked eyes with her second husband. Within moments, they seemed to have an entire exchange of long-suffering looks.

Everyone else fell silent, passively watching as Kate's anger took on a life of its own.

"As long as it's not about me," Kate railed. "Because I'm here for everyone else's fucking convenience." She turned to Daniel. "Isn't that right?" Daniel stared blankly at his sister. "How about you, Joseph?" Katherine asked. "Isn't there something I could do with my life to help you out?"

"You could take it down a notch," he said into his glass.

BRENT WAS DESPERATELY TRYING not to judge them, but he was starting to feel like a character in an F. Scott Fitzgerald dinner party. He couldn't understand why no one was defusing the situation. "Perhaps we should have the cake?" he heard himself say.

Katherine spun on him, eyes burning like brimstone. He'd never regretted saying something aloud so much.

"Of course! Let's have the fucking cake," Kate replied. "Because we're such a big, happy family. Right? Can we have it now, Consuela? Please?"

Consuela glanced toward Missus Radcliffe, who ever so slightly shook her head.

"I am so sorr..." Brent fell quiet, mortified.

"No. You're fine. *She's* the one who creates the drama," Katherine said, staring down Missus Radcliffe. "This is all your fault."

Missus Radcliffe casually fiddled with her dessert fork.

"From day one, you've pitted us against each other," Katherine said. She turned to Juliette, "We don't have to play her games. We're better than the way she sees us. We're so much more."

Juliette looked back at her smiling husband, refusing to turn Katherine's monologue into a conversation.

"Perfect. Do nothing. Be complacent," Katherine said. "I'm tired of having to do all the standing up in this family. And I've done it for the last time." She rose to her feet. "Go ahead. Believe everything she tells you. It'll be your loss, not mine." Katherine's napkin slipped off her lap onto the floor. "Dammit," she said. She'd probably meant to throw it on the table.

Consuela stepped forward.

"Do not ..." said Katherine, quivering with self-actualization.

She turned and walked out, leaving Brent unclear as to whether he should follow and console or give her space for solitude.

He heard her bark his name from the hall. "Brent!"

Ah. They were leaving.

Brent rose from his seat, deftly did up the single button on his jacket, set his napkin on his chair, and, for some reason unknown even to himself, bowed deeply, lightly clicking his heels — a count leaving by train for Bratislava.

Which was when Katherine knew their relationship was over.

34

Illusions of Grandeur

THEY'D BEEN WALKING IN silence through Rosedale for almost ten minutes in the brisk night air, she leading, he following, Kate moving at a brisk clip, her boot heels making a sharp *clack-clack-clack* against the damp pavement. Her wrath would not be hushed by the blankets of foliage, nor could it be impeded by the proximity of others. She wanted everyone to know of her indignation.

Over the last few minutes, Brent had noticed her gait change. Initially, he'd hoped it was a sign that her anger was abating, but now he suspected it had something to do with her boots, though she made no mention of discomfort. Still, he could tell by her expression that she was using her pain to gain some distance from her family.

Brent followed silently until his hands got cold. "Darn, I've lost a glove," he remarked, patting down his pockets.

Katherine glanced back at him. "Well, I'm not going back there, if that's what you're suggesting. They've insulted me for the last time. I am *not* a step-child." She pulled her coat closer around her and walked harder.

She was in a fine lather. Even her hair was bouncing with rage. She could not have looked more fierce if she'd been riding a horse in full armour, leading a charge. Once again, Brent felt the urge to de-escalate her anger, but this time, he stopped himself.

While Brent was friction-averse, once Katherine was irked, she did not back down. He remembered one occasion, as they'd been on their way back from a wine bar, discovering himself to be in the middle of an altercation between Kate and a bike courier who had cut her off. Before Brent had even been aware of a slight, Kate's outrage had found its full voice. She'd bellowed, "It's called a side-*walk*, asshole!" The courier, who'd been dismounting, had told her to eff off. Kate had taken to him like a little dog to a mailman.

"Is that supposed to scare me?" she'd asked. "Because don't think I'm intimidated by a guy who's too much of a pussy to ride his bike in traffic."

The courier hadn't been sure he'd heard her correctly, but everyone else within earshot had got the gist of things and started speed-walking past them.

Kate had planted herself directly in front of the courier, preventing him from going into the building, effectively forcing him to deal with her. Brent still remembered the courier turning to him, his face curled into an ugly, hooked smile. "Get your fucking girlfriend outta my face."

Once he'd realized he was implicated, Brent had shouted, "For God's sake, Kate. Let him by!" The courier had scoffed and walked away.

It had not gone well for Brent from that point forward. "I'm sorry," Katherine had said, not sounding sorry at all, "was my standing up for my rights embarrassing you?"

It had been the absolutely wrong thing to do, but he could not, would not, fight.

Brent saw the flash of a map on Katherine's phone and intuited she'd become turned around. "I have a very good app if you're —"

"I have an app," she snapped, pocketing her phone. "It's like my family has this 'We're Awesome' club. Of course, I'm not allowed to be part of it."

She spoke like she was picking up a thread, as though they'd never stopped talking about the Radcliffes, as though attending the dinner to make her anticipated earthshaking announcement hadn't been her idea in the first place.

"My family expects *nothing* from me. Did you see that? Complete disregard for my goals and aspirations because *they* know what's best. A dental hygienist, for God's sake. Of course, whatever I'm working on is irrelevant. My mother is so dismissive ... It must have shocked you."

It had seemed to Brent that Missus Radcliffe had spotted an opportunity to help both her daughters. "To be perfectly hones—"

"— the Rolling fucking Stones rehearsed in the Mustard Extra Space for their fucking Tour of the Americas in the seventies. That's where I'm debuting. Do you think my family could acknowledge the significance of that? Of course not! They're too fucking pretentious. Like all these people." Kate waved at the opulent houses around them. "Every person on this street is so full of themselves, it makes me crazy," she said loudly. "Like money means these people know more."

She pointed to a mansion with a turret and columns on the front. "I mean, what is that? Seriously? Fucking Henry the Eighth meets CEO of fried chicken?"

A sliver of yellow light appeared from behind a heavy curtain as someone peered out.

"Katherine, maybe you should lower your voice a little before someone calls the po—"

Katherine pointed at a Tudor-style home.

"Do you think Henry the fucking Eighth lived here?"

"Of course n—"

"No. But the pretentious assholes who built it want you to know they understand how kings lived, because that's how *they* live. All of this is here so you can be in awe of it. These people are not wise. They're not admirable. All they have is loads of money."

She spun around, looking into the distance.

"I think Yonge is —" Brent said, beginning to point.

"Don't patronize me," said Katherine. "I know exactly where I am."

"I appreciate that the evening didn't go as planned, but —"

"Oh, there were *no* surprises, Brent. It went the way it always does. I say something real, and everybody clams up, so it's just me being loud and ungracious and imagining things."

It had *looked like that*, thought Brent, but it felt wrong to agree. "A lot of terrible things were said," he noted, trying to comment broadly.

"Right?" She turned to him. "What did they say to you?"

"Me? Oh. Nothing specifically ... or nonspecifically. Your family was inclusive, and I appreciated their effort very much."

Kate's face crinkled. "What the hell does that mean?"

"We come from different worlds, Kate. Obviously. I have nothing in common with the people around that table tonight, but we managed to have a pleasant conversation."

"Is that how you feel about me? We have nothing in common?"

"Of course not."

"Because wealth is not who I am, Brent. That's who my family is. Money has nothing to do with me."

She stared at him, expecting immediate agreement, and Brent discovered he couldn't oblige. "I'm sorry, Katherine, but it's hard to believe that if you'd grown up in a blue-collar neighbourhood, called a drive to Niagara Falls a vacation, and had only one shot at a post-secondary degree, you'd still be you."

Katherine's mouth dropped open. Her silence turned into melancholy.

"It's not a reproach," Brent hurried to add.

But she didn't want to hear it. "Everything about this evening has been offensive on so many levels!" she screamed.

A black Tesla S pulled up beside them, and a man with a winning Brad Pitt smile leaned out of the driver's-side window. "Katherine?"

"Thank God," she sighed. The door handle on the passenger side popped out.

"What's going on?" said Brent.

"I called an Uber," she said. "I think it would be better for everyone concerned if you made your own way home tonight."

"Everyone concerned?"

"This conversation is over."

Katherine got into the car, closed the passenger door and spoke with the driver. A moment later, the Tesla slipped silently into the night.

Katherine did not look back.

35

Reflections of Becca

EVERY TIME HE GAVE the car a little gas, the muffler rumbled and the dashboard shook. Which was why Dylan had turned on the radio — to obscure the sounds — but Becca asked him to shut it off. She didn't want to pretend everything was fine. It was time to face a lot of unpleasant reality. Nothing was going to change that.

She tracked the reflections of streetlights sliding over the curves of the car hood, coming closer and closer, only to drop off and leave her in darkness again. Always in darkness. Always in loops. Her return home would not be the joyous event she'd let herself imagine. There would be no deep moment of reconnection. No pop of Instagram colour flashing between warm hugs and happy tears. She would feel more alone. She had no idea what would happen after that.

"Don't take this the wrong way," said Dylan, his eyes never leaving the road, "but this has been, like, a really strange evening."

It had been.

"When you asked me to help you," he continued, "and you said it was important, I came all the way out here to help. I spent like an hour looking for you in the park 'cause your phone died. Which is fine. But I don't get what's going on here, and it's ... sort of ... unsatisfying, you know?"

"Does it have to be satisfying?" Becca asked.

Dylan went silent. He pulled his hair back into a ponytail so he could better see where he was driving. It actually looked okay that way, although she didn't know why she was noticing.

"Okay," he said. "Maybe it doesn't have to be satisfying. I guess what I was really wondering was if maybe there was some other reason you asked me, specifically, to help you?"

Becca thought of all the clever ways Caroline could answer that question that would hook him without any commitment on her part, but when she opened her mouth, all she said was what she felt: "I don't know yet."

If Dylan didn't like her answer, he didn't say so. He just kept looking further out into the distance, like he was trying to see where getting a straight answer might intersect with Becca wrapping her head around her feelings. It must have been way off because he let out a long sigh.

Half a block up from her house, Dylan pulled the car over to the curb where Becca had asked. The idling engine made the fat *glub-glub* sound cars did in old movies — the ones where everyone is waiting for the daredevil girl to drop a flag so all the cars can peel out.

Dylan was waiting.

"Thank you," said Becca, her voice barely audible even to herself.

She slipped out of the car and shut the door behind her. She felt a bit unsteady, but she was trying to hide it because Dylan was watching, trying to gauge whether she'd be okay so he could leave. Becca pushed down her fear.

Dylan raised his hand to wave. Becca nodded but didn't wave back. She watched his car pull away. When the *glub-glub* sound of its engine had completely evaporated from the night, Becca walked the rest of the way home.

As she reached the front door, her stomach tightened unpleasantly. She pushed the feeling aside, reminding herself how she'd put everything on the line to make her mom see that she mattered.

She had hoped her return would nudge Caroline into acting like an actual parent. Instead, it looked like Caroline was about to clarify the one thing Becca had suspected but had never wanted to know: that she didn't care.

"Mom?" she called out. No answer.

Becca spotted a pair of sequined Indian slippers on the edge of the carpet, which meant that Caroline was in the living room, meditating.

Becca was going to call out again but faltered as she walked in. For a few alarming seconds, it seemed like her mother was floating in complete serenity above the rug. She was, in fact, perched on a yoga roll. Caroline had painted her fingernails and toenails gold. She looked like a quiet sunrise, radiating the universe, oneness, and all-knowingness.

"Mom?" Becca said, trying to inject the word with the crazed urgency she needed to sell her abduction story.

Eyes closed, Caroline held up a golden finger to let Becca know she needed one more moment. The mastery of her finger sweep could have made time stand still. It also told her Caroline had never bought in.

Becca's panicked mind raced ahead, losing bits of her prefabricated story in the process: her fears, the conversations she'd overheard; details of the abduction she would never share. Goodbye vinegar smell and Slavic version of Harry Styles. Adieu rusty tan sedan and highway on-ramp near Chinatown.

"Mom, I —"

"Shh-shh-shh."

Caroline took a final deep, cleansing breath and slowly released it. When at last it was time to talk, she hummed her speaking voice into consciousness and opened her eyes. But even before she looked at Becca, her lips had curled into a smile, and her inner reptile awoke.

"I was meditating on what happened here, Rebecca. About what the universe was trying to tell me by giving me this 'experience,'" Caroline said. "Because when I got home, nothing made sense. I wasn't sure where to start, so I thought a while about the concept of 'making sense.' We've talked about how you're supposed to use what you know to make sense of the world to connect to another person, right? And how that process can make both people better?"

Becca barely nodded.

"Well, you and I need to do that. Right now." She interlaced her fingers. "Connection."

Becca felt confused. On some level, it was exactly what she'd wanted, but something about it was wrong and was starting to make her feel queasy again.

"So. Here's what I know," said Caroline. "The glass from the patio door should have landed on the kitchen floor. Not the lawn. Because it's called a break and enter, Rebecca. Not a break and exit." Her voice hardened with extra-crispy clarity, presumably so Becca would hear her mother's words for the rest of eternity.

"It cost seven hundred and fifty-two dollars for an emergency door replacement, and there's also a few hundred dollars in destroyed food. Which you *will* pay back. But what you did to my blender ..." Here, her mother's voice caught. "... was personal and despicable. I don't know what you thought you were going to achieve with this pantomime, and right now, I don't want to hear it. A thousand dollars. We will discuss payment tomorrow."

Other than the mention of the blender, Caroline had spoken with infuriating, controlling, calm. Now she unfurled her long legs like a mantis and rose to her full killer insect height.

"If you just admitted you didn't want me here," said Becca, hating that she was shouting and not pronouncing shit back, "I could go away. I could live somewhere else."

"Oh, you're not going anywhere until you pay me back. You're grounded," said Caroline. "And that handsome boy who dropped by earlier tonight? He's off-limits too." Caroline slipped her golden toes into her slippers. "For now." She smiled.

Becca blinked, trying to understand. And then she did and her gut tightened. By the time Becca reached the washroom:

Love.

Hope.

Regret.

Revenge.

Cheetos, licorice, caramels, and orange Fanta.

Everything had been lost.

36

Awakening of Desire

KATHERINE PAID EXTRA NOT to have to talk with her Uber driver. They'd exchanged just enough banter that she knew he lived in Rosedale and booked fares whenever he had insomnia. The rest remained unsaid.

The drive to the lake was ridiculously expensive, but the journey was warranted. Katherine refused to wear the evening's emotional residue a moment longer than she had to, and water was the only way.

When they got to Cherry Beach, she hopped out of the Tesla and walked toward the water, letting her heels sink into the coarse sand in a bid to connect with the surroundings. *Screw the boots*, she thought. *Screw her feet. Screw all of it.* She needed to breathe deeply, stare at the lapping waves, and find centre. She had no idea why it worked. It just did. Very possibly, she'd survived some childhood trauma in proximity to waves and then forgotten.

A Master Pranic Healer once told her she shouldn't let her anger build up. She had to let it go. But he'd also said that anger was like a chariot you needed to steer. She'd left the ashram a bit confused, wondering whether she was supposed to be letting go or steering. She probably needed to send him an email.

At any rate, spending an hour beside Lake Ontario did the trick.

She concluded that her spiritual happiness had greater value than a career as a dental hygienist.

As soon as Katherine got back home, she strongly felt a *tabula rasa* gesture was in order. She needed to do something that would symbolically destroy the control she'd let her family have over her life. Her new MacBook Air immediately sprang to mind because it was a recent gift from her asshole brother, but she'd just had it set up the way she liked, so that option was off the table. God, she hated herself sometimes.

Katherine committed to defrosting her freezer box.

"Right," she said out loud, tossing her purse onto a nearby chair.

Reminding herself that she could be stronger than all the negativity, Katherine bolted the front door and let her coat slip off her shoulders and drop to the floor behind her. She peeled off her boots, determined not to linger on how her feet looked even though her left brain sent her impressions of "ground beef," then she made straight for the kitchen, deviating only once to pick up the ER manual she'd bought earlier.

Because Katherine's building was under rent control, the refrigerator had probably been in her apartment since the late seventies. It wasn't a weird, terrible colour, but it had an awful freezer box that froze ice cubes, burned meat, and kept ice cream sloppy soft. Over the last six months, it had become a bit more problematic, but it still kept things cool enough. She'd tirelessly debated the ethics of sending a working refrigerator to a landfill versus letting it devour energy like a pig. Obviously, environmental consciousness was not easy. In the intervening time, a lot of frost had built up.

Katherine flipped the front stove burners on high and grabbed some saucepans from under the counter. She set her nursing book open on the counter. It was called *The ABCs of ER Triage*. It was more of a set of automated protocols than medicine, but it was *so* interesting. She'd already memorized a lot of it. Not on purpose, of course. It was the way her mind worked. She loved processes and jargon. The cast would laugh at her if they knew. It was, after all, complete overkill, though it had made Nurse Reeves — that's what she'd secretly named her character — three-dimensional.

"A is for Airway," said Katherine, filling a saucepan with water. "Check for obstructions: tongue, blood, loose teeth, vomit." Whenever a patient was brought into the ER, the first thing a triage team did was to assess whether there'd been trauma to the patient's airways. She could imagine accident victims arriving on gurneys. Everything coming down to that initial assessment. Everyone focused on the line between life and death. She suspected she had an actual affinity for medicine because she could be both very technical about things and also not bothered by people's suffering, unless, of course, it was necessary.

Katherine set both saucepans on the hot elements and heard the strange reverse squeal that cold steel made when it landed on heat. It had to be one of her favourite things.

"B is for Breathing," she recited. "Respiration, chest wall movement, the position of the trachea, one hundred percent oxygen."

It made Katherine realize that sometimes she felt like she was barely drawing breath. She had to stop blaming herself for having abandoned careers. It had more to do with her family's criticisms and the pressure of their successes, than any of her personal choices. That was a fact.

She flung the refrigerator door open and within moments realized that frost had completely creeped over the freezer box's hinges and frozen it shut. But although it was getting close to midnight, Katherine was not willing to abandon her commitment to herself. Everything counted tonight. Symbolic gestures most of all.

She pulled a chef's knife out of the butcher's block and gently tapped the ice with its wooden handle. Small chunks of frost cracked off the box and fell to the floor. Melting would take hours, so Katherine continued to gently tap around the icebox edges as she recited the steps to assessing breathing distress.

Several minutes of tapping didn't produce the results she'd expected. She could barely pry the freezer door open an inch. Besides which, tapping was incredibly tedious. Katherine peered into the frost, wondering what the hell she'd left in there. She gave the door hinges two big thwacks with the knife handle. Ice crackled, and suddenly the door could open wide enough for her to jam in a few fingers and feel around.

Katherine touched plastic. A bag of frozen somethings. She tugged at it gently, but it didn't budge. It was obviously frozen into the ice box. Knowing she'd have to wait until 3:00 a.m. to discover what it was made her feel like screaming — which would have been okay seeing as this was a therapeutic exercise — but there was nothing to gain from straight-up anger.

Except that it was after midnight and she needed to go to bed.

"Okay," she asked herself out loud. "What if a bag of frozen vegetables was the one thing standing between you and the rest of your life?"

It was the incentive she needed. Katherine gave the plastic bag a hard yank. The bag unexpectedly gave way, breaking the freezer door off its hinges, ripping the bag, and sending frozen peas rolling out across the kitchen floor like a miniature green panzer division.

Katherine kicked at them. "Dammit!" she shouted. "God *dammit*!"

She retrieved the ice box door from the floor then let it drop to the ground again, suddenly feeling resolute, acknowledging to herself that she was into this purge all the way. With the door gone, she now had unobstructed access to the contents of her freezer. There were two ice trays trapped in three inches of frost. Holding her chef's knife more like a pick, she jabbed at the ice.

"You. Are. Coming. Out!" she said, punctuating every word with a stab. Ice started to fly.

"C is for Circulation," she said. "Check skin colour. Skin temperature. Blood pressure. Check pulse."

Brent had been barely sentient at dinner. She'd watched him fawn over the horseradish spoon. He had gawked at everything and had seen nothing. He'd just gone on and on about himself. Katherine became conscious her face was burning. It was ice chips. She hadn't noticed her knife hand picking up speed, but now it felt like it was out of control. She saw the motion of the knife as a blur, but her hand was rock steady, precise, deft. She'd never been aware she had this ability, probably because she'd always been too preoccupied with other facets of her life. But there it was. Confidence. Skill.

It felt so good to be good at something. So foreign. So strange.

And finally. It happened.

In the dawn of a new day, she began to see how much more she was than a series of failures. She could see that what she'd been reaching for all these years was well within her grasp.

37

Means to an End

"OHHHH," MOANED KARL. "UHHHHHH."

Jesus Christ, he caught himself thinking. He sounded like he was wounded. Lying in some ditch somewhere, waiting for the end to come.

He really had to stop listening to himself moan or it wasn't going to work.

"Okay. Okay. Okay," he said, working to get his focus back. "Uhhhhhh. Uhhhhhhm. Here we — here we — uhhhhhhahh. Ahh. Ahhhh. Ssssssss. Mmmmn. Mmm. Mm. Mm. Mm. Ah, fuck. Haaaaaaaah. Haaaaaahhh. Hahhh."

He breathed deeply, savouring the final nanoseconds of his release, the tension still draining, the moment when he had perfect clarity. It was just him and whatever was going on in his balls.

But almost immediately, the world reappeared. It rose up like dirty water in a basement, bringing with it issues of crappy work and failed dreams. Then the high-pitched volume of the HVAC reminded him that he was in a semi-public place and had to get his shit together to leave.

Karl fumbled and zipped as he started his circuitous route out of the mechanical room. He hoped it would stay accessible for the next little while, because he didn't know what he was going to do once it got cooler. Over the years, he'd jerked off in less than stellar places: cars and parking garages, the absolute worst location being the Royal Agricultural Winter Fair. The steady stares of the sheep had stayed with him.

Karl had found the electrical room by accident. He'd actually been looking for the place where AMICO kept its security tapes, in the hopes of recovering the video evidence against him. Thanks to the cop shows he favoured, he'd imagined a dingy closet filled with dusty decks, but the truth was far more soul-crushing. Footage was kept in a high-tech control centre, guarded by cameras and secured behind a thick *Mission: Impossible* sheet of glass to keep it all clean and untouchable. The end was imminent. He had to get another job before AMICO discovered he was the Moaner.

When he'd initially learned his nickname, he'd thought people were reactive assholes. It was just the sound he made when he came. A sound, by the way, he couldn't control any more than people could control the volume of their farts or the stupid way they sneezed. But now that he'd heard himself, he was just grateful there was a machine loud enough to cover his noise.

Karl cracked open the electrical room's door into a secondary hallway and listened a moment. It was the tail end of the lunch hour. There was a trickle of foot traffic here but a substantial one in the main hall, so his reappearance would probably not be too noticeable.

When he was sure traffic was low, he swung the electrical room door open and walked out like he belonged. He'd almost reached the main corridor when a familiar voice behind him said, "Why have you done this thing?"

Karl spun around and saw Saurav, looking real upset.

Shit, thought Karl. *Shit. Fuck. Shit.* Karl struggled to smile. "Hey, Saur—"

"Do not play coy. The kitten is out of the bag. You are the Moaner." Saurav's eyes were nailed hard on him. His voice was easily ten decibels too loud. He wasn't fucking around.

Karl tried to fake Saurav out. "Yeah. Real funny."

"Do not deny it!" Saurav answered. "'Ooh. Ah.'"

He was obviously trying to recreate what he'd heard, only he was pronouncing it better.

"You better stop saying shit like that if you know what's good for you," hissed Karl, trying to walk away, but he couldn't shake him.

"I saw you go in, Karl. The moaning began almost immediately. It sounded like an animal brought to slaughter."

Karl broke away from Saurav, taking extra-long strides down the hall, desperately trying to leave him behind. He was not having this particular fucking conversation. Not today. Not ever. He bobbed and weaved around AMICO employees like they were obstacles, as if everything would go back to normal if he could just put more distance between himself and the truth. Yet somehow Saurav caught up, grabbed a handful of his shirt, and pulled him to a stop.

"Why do you do this thing?" he asked. "At work?"

Karl wanted to shake him off, but he could see people starting to turn and watch. This was obviously what the end looked like. Karl had always imagined he'd say something snide, but no bullshit gag could prevent this embarrassment from happening.

"Answer me. Why?" repeated Saurav.

It had started with a Catwoman comic book, and it had escalated the summer he'd discovered a copy of *Cindy, a Very Private Nurse* in the night table at a friend's cottage. He could still vividly recall turning the thin yellow pages that practically crumbled in his hands and realizing all real-life sex would forever pale in comparison. Which it had. Real sex was sloppy seconds.

"What the hell do you want me to say, Saurav!? I'm sorry? Well, I'm fucking sorry, all right?"

"You must stop this nonsense," Saurav ordered. He looked fierce.

"Don't you think I've tried?"

"You must try harder."

"It's not a fucking switch. If I could turn it off, don't you think I would?"

Saurav stared at him. He was waiting for an answer to a rhetorical question.

"Of course I would fucking turn it off! Do you think I'm doing this because I want to? You think I *like* having to jerk off every couple hours?"

"You must join a group."

Karl hated groups.

Saurav read his expression. "Then you will be dragged out of the building with your pants around your ankles."

"Whatever. Doesn't matter anymore! They got me on camera, Saurav. Jerking off behind a dumpster ..."

"Who got you?"

"Security." Karl sighed deeply. "It's just a matter of time before they put two and two together. I appreciate you offering me a chance to make it all better, but there's only one way this is going to play out. Now if you don't mind, I'd like to finish the day because I need the money to make my rent."

Saurav hesitated before he opened his mouth. But as the words came out, he fully committed. "The brother of a friend ..." he said.

Karl's mouth went dry as he leapt ahead. "The brother of a friend, here? In this building? In security? Security here?"

Saurav nodded, weighing options, studying Karl.

"Jesus, Saurav. Do you think you —"

"I do not promise anything unless you swear to stop this buggery."

"I'll try, Saurav. I'll try."

"No. You must swear to stop. Forever. Or I will hand you over to the authorities myself."

Karl had seen enough late-night TV to recognize a once-in-a-lifetime opportunity when he saw one.

38

Wrong Answers Only

A THOUSAND DOLLARS WAS a buttload of money. And Becca wanted to pay it back. Truly. That's why the very first thing she'd proposed was reducing her weekly allowance for thirty-four months, but Caroline had lost it.

"That's not how this is going to be done," she'd said. "You're not going to hand me back my own money. You will pay me back using your personal money. Money you earn."

It was like she was speaking English but making absolutely no sense, because Becca felt she was fully earning her allowance money. Fully.

In the days that followed the "fakeduction" — which was how her mom now referred to the incident, using big, ironic air quotes — Becca had become a full-on house servant. Her mom stopped every objection with, "You owe me." She was seriously out of control, and Becca needed to do something about it.

Becca had tried calling the jobs she'd seen advertised on posters, but not one person would consider letting her sell lingerie, water filters, or protein powder if she didn't have deposit money.

Saturday morning, Becca went to the mall to find a job. She hadn't expected the process to be so hard. Caroline always talked about walking in off the street and getting a job as a night manager at a video store when she was fifteen.

Granted, perhaps Becca hadn't made the best impression in the first three stores because she'd had to start her applications over a bunch of times, but she honestly couldn't make her printing fit into the little boxes on the forms. No matter how small she wrote, there was never enough room, and they didn't give extra pages. Plus, there were so many things on the forms she found confusing, like which box was she supposed to tick if she wanted to work part-time on a full-time basis?

She quickly figured out that no one would hire her because she was fourteen, so she started to write down she was nineteen and a half. She also changed her signature so the only letter you could read in her first name was R. Like she was too busy to write out the whole word, or maybe she had close friends who called her R.

For work experience, she wrote down that she had bartended private functions, which in a way she had for her mom and whoever's pickup truck was in the driveway. And yeah, she'd never work-worked in a spa, but she could have done mani-pedis. She could have sold phone cases and cables in kiosks. Did people seriously think you needed to be a legal adult to know that if the thingy fit your phone, you had the right cable? She was so over being underestimated.

Becca signed off on her job application using a major R that went right over the date and some of her references, which were just versions of her and her mom's names. She walked back into Wilderness Fashions, through the racks of skinny jeans and leopard-print camis, head held high. She handed her application to a tall, thin saleslady looking like every mean girl ever: bored and revolted. The lady studied Becca, pressing her lips together like she was enduring a horrible moment. Then she squeezed a perfunctory smile shape out of her lipstick, put Becca's application in a drawer, and told her she shouldn't expect a call. Which confused Becca, so the woman said, "Maybe try the food court?"

Like that. Just nasty.

Becca thought of something to say back later, but by that time she was on the streetcar.

39

Practice Makes Perfect

THE TENSION COULDN'T BE too tight, and the wraps had to be evenly spaced. According to approved guidelines.

Katherine unwound the bandage from her hand and wrist and started over. It was amazing how it was becoming second nature to her, like breathing. Good thing too, because she actually had no time to waste. Her first year of nursing school was going to be really competitive. From now on, even bus rides were opportunities for skill sharpening.

Katherine had discovered a nursing thread online where ER nurses raved about a uniform shop in the west end, so she'd decided to go exploring on her day off. She loathed the wardrobe Cindy had picked out for Nurse Reeves. It was way too costumey. Totally wrong for her character. Reeves needed a uniform with classically tailored lines that suggested self-discipline but didn't draw attention to her figure because she was all about her patients, and Katherine was determined to find it.

She looked up from her bandaging practice to check the street numbers and noticed an old Italian lady in a flowered top sitting across the aisle from her, openly staring. It felt sort of hostile and rude.

"What is wrong with people?" Katherine muttered into her bandaged hand.

Like Brent. She might have been able to forgive him for being duped by her mom, but the self-doubt she'd suffered having her personal journey reduced to rich-girl privilege had not been great to deal with.

Brent and she were over. There would be no return visit to her parents' home, no crazy makeup sex in her parents' storage closet among the old fur coats. She'd deleted his messages. He was gone.

Despite her recent emotional upheavals, Katherine had managed to stay positive and refocus. She had a dramatic role to prepare and a transition into medicine to organize.

Katherine clucked as she noticed her hand felt a bit constricted. She unwound her bandage again and started over. Palm up, bandage tail inside the wrist. Go around twice. Then across, flip the hand down. Then wrist and palm, wrist and palm, wrist and palm. This training exercise would be so much easier once she was working on real patients. *If* she got into the program.

She probably would, but it was better to adjust to reality as it happened.

She was fortunate she'd given in to her urge to sign up for basic human physiology before she'd had any idea she had an official calling in medicine. It would give her a jump on the course load. She still had to find out whether she had enough science credits from her first-year psych classes to cover the prerequisites. She would probably be the oldest nursing student candidate. There would be awkwardness, but she'd make a point of showing up at a pub night, maybe paying for a round. Things would be fine.

The old woman across the aisle was watching her again, or maybe still.

"You can stop anytime," Katherine murmured. The old woman looked on, her bright red shoes dangling several inches above the floor. Her hands were latched on to her shopping buggy handle like claws.

Katherine shook her head lightly, rewound her bandage, and started again.

She needed a letter of recommendation to get into the program and kept coming back to the idea of asking Jason, but she feared it might be too awkward. First, they'd have to have a conversation about why she was leaving theatre. Second, she suspected he wasn't articulate enough to write a really persuasive letter. Maybe she'd propose writing the letter for him and asking him to sign it.

She flexed her bandaged fingers. This time, she discovered she could make a good fist. The crisscrossed beige folds seemed to stay perfectly in place. Bandaging 101: done. And she was a little over two hundred street numbers away from her destination.

Katherine rang the bell and got to her feet, stuffing the bandage into her bag. The old busybody across the aisle would have to find somewhere else to stare. As she moved toward the front of the bus, Katherine saw that the old woman's buggy was filled with wine bottles.

"I happen to know heavy drinking speeds the shrinkage of certain regions in the brain, so I understand you may have no control over some of your actions," Katherine told her. "But you're staring, and it's rude."

The woman frowned. "*Ma, che cosa?*"

The bus dropped her off on a patch of gravel. Katherine hiked back to the industrial park's entrance then walked another half kilometre to unit eighteen, a steady stream of dusty cars and loud semis roaring past her.

From the outside, Uniform Warehouse did not look promising. Just yellow bricks and vertical blinds. But its interior was spectacular. There were hundreds upon hundreds of uniforms, each the embodiment of a vocational or professional dream, each representing years of study and discipline.

Katherine moved through the racks, her arms outstretched, letting her fingers run over the fabrics, feeling the weights of the various synthetic blends, occasionally stopping to explore the detail of a pocket or the texture of a machine-washable garment. There were dresses and coordinates. Suits and uniforms. Solid-coloured and patterned — not to mention a huge section of surgical caps that looked exactly like those she'd seen in episodes of *Grey's Anatomy*. Katherine had found paradise.

"You're looking for a nurse's uniform. Am I right?"

Katherine spun around toward the voice wearing a radiant smile. "How did you know?"

The clerk, an older man with more hair directly above his eyes than anywhere else on his head, pooh-poohed her. "I can tell. I can always tell. Follow me."

He was small and slight, and his face was kind. The tape measure that hung around his neck was covered in tiny chalk marks. He turned to her.

"Where?" he asked.

"Excuse me?"

"Where are you a nurse? No!" he said, stopping her. "Let me guess." He gave her a long, appraising look. "Sunnybrook."

"No."

"Humber?"

She smiled. "I'm at St. Joseph's." It had just come out of her mouth like that. Unintentionally.

The old man nodded. "That was my other second guess."

She pressed her lips together to keep her smile from coming through. She supposed she could have corrected him, but she didn't want to. It was only a little fib. And he seemed so pleased to believe he was right.

"Where are you? Obstetrics?"

Katherine shook her head. "ER."

"Oh, well. That's a serious place. You must be especially level-headed."

Katherine smiled. She was.

Katherine followed the old man through the store past jump-suits, EMS coordinates, scrubs, and housekeeping uniforms, feeling all the possibilities of the universe passing through her outstretched hands.

40

Bedlam

AFTER BRENT HAD OFFERED his most effusive apologies for bothering the literary editor at the *New Fort Yorker*, he embarrassed himself further by pretending he had penned several short stories titled "Inert" and asked to have the pages he'd sent returned to identify the exact story the magazine was interested in reading. He was mortified by the length of the pause that followed his request, but ultimately the editor accepted.

Brent had imagined he would be able to pick up the story threads he'd set down and easily move the plot forward to its natural conclusion, but as he studied the first five pages of "Inert", he knew this would not be possible.

The story was simple and also stunningly complex. Brightness and darkness were intricately interwoven throughout. He could feel a breath of tenderness swelling gently in the writing as the chill of the distant woman abated it. The man would obviously come out of the encounter emotionally destroyed, but one somehow felt that he would not be defeated.

Brent could understand why the magazine was keen on publishing the story. "The" story, not "his" story, because another Brent had written it. A better Brent.

For hours on end, he'd hunted for the right combination of words that would add to the story's meaning and deepen what already appeared on the page but he could not reconnect. By the end of the week, it felt as though he'd composed and deleted an entire book. Not a single new word was worthy of print. His literary McLaren would forever remain in an underground garage.

While he'd been obsessing over his fruitless rewrite, karma had regurgitated. Every shred of kindness and help he'd received had transformed into a problem.

Initially, he'd been able to check Gary sightings and respond to all the messages his volunteer searchers had left, but as his post became more widely shared, his response time slowed, and the dog lovers' tone shifted. Now questions appeared on boards about Brent's suitability as a dog parent. A few people insinuated he was negligent. There were allegations that miracle eye surgeries for canines in the Netherlands had been roundly dismissed. Someone anonymously messaged him about a thread of people who were convinced they were being lied to. Brent would have liked to have had time to address these character assassinations, but there were also complications developing at work.

As Irene had hinted, the departmental chair had contacted Brent for a favour. He needed someone to sub in for him one day and host a grad conference. Brent had accepted the offer no questions asked. His role was minor. There was no paper to present, only lectures, questions, and the debate to preside over. But looking at the schedule he'd received that morning, Brent discovered he was hosting a day on "Breasts in Long Nineteenth-Century Literature: An Intercultural Exploration."

It would be a disaster.

There was no academic universe in which Brent should have been moderating the topic of intercultural breasts. His gender would be received as an affront to the mostly female assembly. Anything he tried to add to the conversation would be called mansplaining. And anyone who was peeved enough by his selection as host would go hunting through his early graduate work and find his old Hemingway papers. Sexism would be called out from every corner. It was conceivably the end of his career.

With that potentially vivid picture painted came the end of sleep.

He divided his time between pacifying the dog lovers and devising rationales for every word he'd ever written on Hemingway, while attempting to formulate a non-opinion on intercultural breasts in the hopes he could recover from his current situation. But it had all become too much. He'd come undone.

His mind was useless now, numb from overuse. It felt disconnected from his body, as though it had been sliced, set in a dish, and placed on an eternally revolving lazy Susan where others could choose what they needed. He desperately needed to stop thinking, to force his mind to rest and hope that when he awoke, there would be leftovers from his life to salvage.

41

Upon Further Reflection

NONE OF THE TENANTS in Katherine's building ever bothered putting up Halloween decorations, except for the one overly earnest woman on the second floor who hung a Hallowreath on her door for the whole of October, which no children ever saw because it was building policy to lock out trick-or-treaters. The wreath was made of dozens and dozens of empty toffee wrappers and had a homemade look, which probably had something to do with why the woman was always wearing sweatpants.

In Parkdale, Halloweeners went over the top with gory decorations. Katherine had seen skeletons and zombies and fluttering bats. Her biggest objection was to fake spiderwebs, more specifically with people who randomly spread fuzzy white string every which way over their greenery until their hedges looked like giant Rice Krispie squares. It was like no one knew what an actual web looked like anymore. She had absolutely no regrets about ditching entomology.

Katherine hadn't imagined she'd ever be walking down Brent's street again and yet here she was, going to his apartment. The truth was, she'd had a bit of time to process her feelings, and she'd come to recognize that her family held incredible sway over ordinary people. Although she was convinced the termination of their relationship had been the right move for her, she had to acknowledge that they *had* been a couple for several months. Until she'd invited him to dinner at her parents', she had respected him. Rather than continue to ignore his texts, she would end their relationship like an adult — in person.

As she neared the creepy neighbour's house, she felt herself tense. Her gaze fell on the dead vines and raggedy branches that poked through the rusted wrought iron gateposts. In semi-darkness, they looked like shadowy limbs begging passersby for help. The old guy was doing everything to keep people out. She wondered what gruesome secrets he was hiding.

As Katherine stepped off the sidewalk onto Brent's walkway, a gust of wind rose up and rushed her up the path toward the door. For a few harrowing moments, she was convinced someone was chasing her and threw back a panicked glance over her shoulder, then she realized the noise she'd heard was the slightly out-of-sync sound of her own feet.

She stood in front of Brent's door a moment, catching her breath. She hated that she'd let the old guy get into her head.

She took a moment to remind herself that she was in control of her thoughts and feelings and that she wasn't looking for chitchat. Just closure. She would explain to Brent how he'd hurt her feelings, tell him that their breakup had been positive for her, and then she'd leave. She could afford to be open to whatever he had to say as long as he didn't go on and on. She really had nothing to prove. For once in her life, she was in a great place.

Katherine put a smile on her face and buzzed the doorbell.

She waited.

She realized she should probably have called ahead, but he was home. She knew he was home because there was a light in the back room. Brent never left without shutting off all the lights.

She wasn't sure why he wasn't answering.

It had nothing to do with her. He didn't know she was coming. Anyone could have been at his front door. She buzzed again, starting to feel self-conscious. *Jesus*, she thought. *Answer!* She wasn't desperate to see him, but she *had* made the trip. Besides which, he was clearly inside.

The entire situation was starting to piss her off. She was beginning to text him when she heard shuffling footsteps approach and stop on the other side of the door. For several more moments, nothing further happened.

"Open the fucking door!" Katherine barked.

She heard the familiar fumbling of the chains and then the bolt slide. A moment later, the door yawned open, and Brent peered out. His face was pale, his eyes barely open.

"Jesus," said Katherine. "What the hell happened to you? Have you been on a bender?"

Brent shook his head. "I was asleep."

She checked the time. It was just eight. "When did you become a pensioner?"

"Took a pill," he said. Barely. He rubbed his eyes, trying to wake up. "Irene gave me. To sleep."

Katherine refused to feel guilty. If Brent didn't want visitors, he shouldn't have left his lights on. He didn't say her name or apologize for her wait but she needed to keep things moving. "Okay," she said, "I know you haven't invited me, but I'm coming in."

She moved with conviction, and Brent stepped aside to let her by. But only barely.

"You're being incredibly weird," she said as she slipped past him.

If Brent heard her, he didn't acknowledge it. He slowly shut the front door, plunging the foyer into complete darkness, then started to fiddle with the chains.

Katherine walked ahead. Someone's yard light was blasting through the living room window and illuminated a corner of the hall table. She saw the squeaky balls and tennis shoes that Gary had favoured lined up in a row beneath its legs.

Katherine turned back to say what she had come to say and

discovered Brent was still standing by his door. She could see him in silhouette, staring at the chains he'd only just slid and the bolt he'd locked. He really was out of it, trying to figure out what to do next. It was kind of intriguing.

"It's locked," she said.

"Yes," he answered in a drawn-out way. He paused, like what she'd said was still sinking in, then started to make his way toward her, his hand trailing along on the wall. At that point, Katherine debated leaving, but something about Brent's intensity and the way he was accepting whatever she said was making her stay, drawing her to him.

"I came to talk," she said.

He nodded, dozily waiting for her to continue. Normally, he would have filled the quiet until it was near to bursting with words. She had to admit his silence was kind of hot.

"I came to discuss the end of ... us," she said.

"Why?" he said.

His question was all sharp edges, but the honesty in it was beautiful. A single word kicked up raw from the earth.

"I wanted you to know I've stopped being angry with you," she said.

He sighed. Brent's eyes were dark and soft and trying to gaze directly into hers. He was deeply stoned, she sensed, but hearing and connecting.

"I recognize my wrongdoing. I haven't been as open as I could be in all my relationships. I've held back aspects of myself. I let my family and other people decide who I am ... or who I could be."

Brent started shaking his head. It was hard to tell whether he was upset or trying to stay awake. She jumped ahead.

"Bottom line is, I've had an epiphany. I know who I am now, and I don't need anyone to believe in what I'm doing to move forward. I'm in charge. My passions will take me where I need to go."

Now that Katherine had said it out loud, she felt alive. Electric. Exhilarated.

Brent could barely brush the hair out of his eyes. It was truly strange how lethargy made him more attractive. In the semi-darkness, his lower lip looked swollen and pillowy. The beard stubble didn't hurt either.

"Are we done?" he growled softly.

Before she could vocalize an answer, Katherine lunged toward Brent in the dark and, finding his lips, kissed them.

Brent pulled away with confusion. But she returned to him with even more passion.

He stumbled and fell back against the wall. She fell against him, pressing herself into him. She felt him give in. His arms came up to embrace her, but she refused to be controlled. She grabbed his wrists and pinned his arms above his head with conviction. Yoga had made her strong. "No. You do what I want. Understand?"

He nodded.

Clearly, neither of them knew where this was going, but neither was willing to stop it from happening.

Her hand slipped to his belt buckle and undid his pants with maddening slowness. "I'm going to fuck you," she promised, "like I've never fucked anyone before. Because I really, really want to."

He groaned.

"Show me how much you want it," she ordered.

She stood away from him. He stared at her a few moments, his brain still trying to decipher her request. Uncertainly, his hand slipped down under his waistband.

"Do it," she ordered, kicking his pants aside to make sure he knew she was watching.

He started to stroke, watching her watching him.

"This is surprisingly hot," she said, her hands beginning to move slowly over her own breasts, squeezing and twisting them through her shirt. He groaned again.

"Slower," she ordered.

"Then stop —"

"Shut the fuck up. Slow the fuck down."

He fell back against the wall again, slowing as bidden, watching her touch herself through the narrowing slits of his eyes. Soon, his lips parted. His breath became audible. He closed his eyes one second, and the next instant she was right against him again. He could feel the warmth of her body reaching out to him.

"Are you close?" she asked softly.

"Yes," he answered with what breath he had.

Katherine grabbed Brent's hair and yanked his face toward hers. "You have to ask me permission," she said.

His eyes tried to refocus. "Can I —"

"No."

A look of surprised torment appeared on his face. It was delicious. She was so wet.

"Down," she said. He didn't understand.

"Down!" she repeated and pushed him to the floor as she pulled up her skirt and stripped off her panties. "Don't you dare fucking cum," she threatened through gritted teeth. "I do not. Give you. Permission."

She ground herself into him, and when she could no longer bear to feel empty, she dropped onto him, screaming more than she moaned. Her head fell forward as she savoured the feeling of him in her.

Brent moaned and slid his hands up over her thighs.

"You're ruining it!" she yelled, eyes still squeezed shut.

She made him pin his own hands under his body, and then she started to ride him. Harder and longer. Brent didn't know how much longer he could hold off when Katherine pitched forward, falling on one arm, which lay across his throat, to grind her way across the finish line.

Brent's brain began to rise through his drugged fog. He couldn't breathe. Not enough to say, "Stop." Not enough to throw her off, and both his hands were trapped under his body weight. His heart started to pound in his ears. All his muscles tightened, locked into heightened sensations of Katherine fucking him, killing him. He was going to die. To explode. To lose consciousness. Then:

"I'm ... I'm ... I'm ah ah ah ahhhh," she cried until her arm slipped off his throat.

Brent drew a full, deep breath, and with the surge of oxygen, he drew out his arms, found her hips, and pulled her violently to him, shuddering inside her with a sexual intensity he had never experienced before, discovering all he could say was, "My God. My God."

42

All In

IT HAD TAKEN KATHERINE eleven years of sexual experimentation to learn that when she ignored all the "giving sexual pleasure" protocols and focused on her needs alone, she could get what she needed. It was a gift she'd never dared hope for, and she'd given it to herself. It had been such a week for personal revelations. She felt intensely satisfied. This was the kind of lovemaking she'd explore from now on.

Brent moved quietly around the kitchen, his twinkles extinguished. His face was pale. His lips were the colour of a bruise. He'd slipped into track pants and stood bare chested, hair perfectly tousled in the light of the refrigerator, silently pouring exactly two fingers of Scotch over three ice cubes.

Katherine accepted the glass he offered, though Scotch wasn't normally her drink of choice. Brent sipped quietly but avoided her eyes. He was mulling something over. She really hoped it wasn't about them, because she'd rather take back her orgasm than have to endure another week of politely watching period films.

She pulled herself up onto the counter and sat, watching her own legs dangle below her for a moment. "If you're thinking about Gary," she said, hoping to curtail relationship talk, "I think it's safe to start saying he's dead."

Brent shot her a look. "It's not about Gary." His hand moved quickly to his throat. He took a swig of his drink, wincing, then stared into his ice cubes like the words he wanted to say might appear there. "It's about what just happened."

He probably meant the breath play. Brent had been a bit rattled when he'd discovered she hadn't intended to suffocate him.

"I'm sorry, but I'm not going to feel bad about what happened," she said, "given how it worked out for everyone." Besides, she knew CPR, and she could have revived him if she'd needed to. It was an overreaction.

"The thing is …" Brent cleared his throat, starting over. "A thing you might not know about me is …" He fell silent again, then gulped down the rest of his Scotch and reached for the bottle to pour another.

Katherine waited until she'd waited enough. "Okay. Say something or I'm leaving."

"I need to control," he confessed. "Everything. What I do. What I say. How I say it. How I look while I say it. I do everything in my power to control how I come across. And frankly, the hours I put into it are exhausting."

"Oh," said Katherine. "Right." She wasn't sure why he assumed this was an earth-shattering admission.

"Tonight," he continued, "I gave you all the control. I didn't have to decide how to be or what to say or do. And you choked me." Katherine flashed him a look. "But it was like I was breathing for the first time. For some reason, losing control made me feel free. I think … my need to control negative outcomes is crippling me more than I ever realized."

Katherine was feeling more than a little pissed. "Okay. Whatever."

Brent looked at her sharply. He needed some kind of reaction from her, apparently but she wasn't going to give it to him.

"What just happened was life-altering," he said. "It means I have to stop pretending I have all the answers if I want to get anything good out of life. To grow."

"Are you fucking kidding me?" she said. "I tell you about my personal discoveries, my hidden core, and suddenly you're learning things about yourself? Get a life."

"Excuse me?"

Katherine slipped off the counter. Done. Again. For the last time. "I have a big revelation, and you have to get a better one. Jesus, you're pathetic." She had forgiven him so much: his weird clothes, his incessant babbling, calling her someone else's name, his dog.

"I didn't expect any of this to happen. It's just dawned on me that something important has occurred," he said.

"Right!" she said. "Well, I'm happy for you, Brent. Really happy." Katherine fished her panties off the floor.

"You're not actually happy."

"No, I really mean it. I have to do the work for every success I get, but it's wonderful how everything miraculously comes to you." She wobbled a moment as the heel of her boot got caught in the leg elastic, and she reached out for Brent to steady herself. She pulled her panties up with a snap then dropped her skirt. "To say you've figured out how you're going to 'grow.' It's such a meaningless, passive statement. It's so like you."

Katherine brushed past Brent and strode to the hall to get her coat. "News flash, Brent: if you can't work up the nerve to go look for your dead dog in the neighbour's backyard, you don't have control issues. You're just gutless."

As Katherine bent down to retrieve her bag from the floor, Brent's Scotch glass sailed past her head and smashed into the door behind her.

Katherine looked back at him and pieced together what had just happened.

"You have officially fucking lost it!" she yelled.

Brent walked away without apology.

Katherine buttoned her coat and paused at the door. Sure enough, there was a dent in the wood, quite near to where she'd been standing. Scotch trickled down the mullion and pooled in the panels.

Katherine checked her pulse. Seventy-six.

Some ER manuals advised staff they might experience violent outburst from patients that might require counselling, but Brent's eruption appeared to have barely bothered her.

43

Consequences

CAROLINE ANNOUNCED SHE'D FOUND a job for Becca. It was delivering grocery flyers door-to-door a few nights a week after school. It sounded lame, but since Becca wasn't fielding offers from the mall, she had no choice but to accept.

"Work for who?" she asked.

"Her name is Jeanine. Or Jeanelle." Caroline considered a moment, then nodded. "Jeanelle."

It sounded super sketch. "Do you even know her?" Becca asked.

"I don't need to know her. There was this help wanted ad. I called. We spoke. She sounded professional. I told her you'd do it."

Becca was reeling. While other people's parents were all about keeping children safe, her own mother was sending her out to walk around strangers' houses.

"That's great, Mom. I've always wanted to live in someone's dungeon."

"Becca, you're delivering flyers that let people know when ground beef is on sale. Nothing is going to happen."

In her heart of hearts, Becca knew that Caroline didn't want her to get hurt, but she also knew that what her mom loved most was having a good story to share with a couple or thirty strangers. No personal event was out of bounds: the time she'd seduced a police officer, the time she'd woken up in Buffalo, the time she'd snuck a homeless guy into her grandparents' house and let him stay in the basement a few days because he looked like Brad Pitt. This could be the time Caroline had to buy back Becca off a pimp while she was trying to teach her a life lesson. Now that she understood what she'd really wanted to happen in the motel, she didn't want to tempt fate again, but no amount of arguing could convince her mom.

CAROLINE SET UP BECCA'S meeting with Jeanelle for four o'clock.

Becca was supposed to stand in front of a pet store and wait for a pearlized white van to show up. Whatever pearlized was. It was totally sketch. Caroline would never have trusted an accountant who worked out of a Dodge Caravan, and yet she seemed to have no problem delivering her only daughter to some random stranger who did.

A super thin guy was hanging out in front of the pet store, ten feet away from where Becca was standing. She'd clocked him in a reflection on the down-low. He wasn't bugging her, but, he paced a lot. She wished he would leave.

Becca stared hard at her phone, pretending to look at interesting stuff.

Her mom had so many pictures on her phone, she could scroll forever. Caroline's love of selfies was legend. Pictures of family vacations were usually a million shots of her mother in a bikini or halter top with her arms draped around a complete stranger. In fact, most pictures of Becca growing up included Caroline with her arm around someone who was important to Becca. Her science teacher, her fencing teacher, her swim coach. There were pictures of Caroline with a collection of camp counsellors at Camp Ipiwachonga. Sure, sometimes Becca was in the shots, but it always seemed like a mistake. It was the way she felt about it too.

She briefly considered texting Dylan, but they hadn't exchanged two words since that night in the park. It didn't feel right to lean on him, especially since she didn't know how she felt about him. Besides, imagining Caroline standing next to him when he'd come to look at the house had freaked her out. Becca was sure something in her would break if she ever came across a picture of her mom with her arm casually draped around him.

Becca looked up from her phone. The skinny guy was still standing there. He nodded, smiled. Becca rolled her eyes.

A few moments later, a grimy-looking white van pulled up. All of Becca's instincts kicked in and told her it was probably pearlized. A woman with bleached-blond hair and long, dark roots lowered the passenger window and stuck her head out.

"Becca?"

"Yeah?"

The woman looked past Becca to the guy who'd been lurking around. "Thomas?"

He nodded. Becca instantly felt bad for thinking he was a creep.

"I'm Jeanette."

44

Baby Steps

HOLDING HER CLIPBOARD HIGH, Jeanette drove a meaty hip into the van's passenger door. It thudded shut, making a terrible grinding sound. Jeanette had a final brief exchange with the driver. The driver put the passenger window up, and the van sputtered as it pulled away from the curb.

"Phil has to find a parking spot," Jeanette explained, although no one had asked the question. "Okay," she sighed. "Let's go fill out some forms."

She gave them no indication of where they were going. She just started walking ahead alone, juggling a bunch of keys, a handful of pens, and the clipboard. Becca and Thomas fell in behind her like a procession of ducks noticed only by the dark faces and suspicious eyes inside Friends' Sports Tavern.

Jeanette had a remarkably large, square ass over which she'd pulled a pair of mauve track pants. Her size didn't seem to be a problem for her, though. She walked at a good clip like she was used to leading people down the sidewalk. She never even glanced back once to make sure they'd kept up. She was that confident.

Jeanette swung open the door to the Country Style Donuts with practised ease, beelined over to a table for four by the window, and set down her clipboard to indicate this was where Becca and Thomas should sit. As they reached the table, she crossed back to the counter to place an order.

Thomas sat down, looking slightly pissed, but said nothing. He kept checking the time on his phone and clucking.

Jeanette stood in front of the donut counter, studying the menu board. She didn't seem worried about what anyone was thinking about her pants, and she didn't seem to care how the counter staff kept trying to get her to order because she wasn't ready. She was going to take all the time she needed. She jiggled an extra-long key chain with a thing on it that looked like the state of Florida as she considered her options. Joseph clucked again.

When she was good and ready, Jeanette pulled up her Hollywood sunglasses. She had a super plain face, but she wasn't wearing a stitch of makeup.

As she waited for her order, Becca saw Jeanette glance back at her and Thomas. She squinted. Maybe to see if they'd left with her pens. Becca waved hers lamely.

Jeanette eventually came back with a large double-double and some kind of treat in a bag. She tossed her keys down as she settled heavily into her chair. The keys slid across the table toward Thomas, but she didn't make any move to retrieve them. Maybe it was a trust game, or maybe it was to let Becca and Thomas know that it was her table. She sighed long and hard like she'd been working since before the sun came up, then, after she'd had her first loud, soul-saving sip of coffee, she asked who'd delivered flyers before. Thomas nodded. She turned to him and asked if he was legal to work. He nodded again, and then she found out he had a car. She told him it was thirteen dollars an hour and gave him a form to fill out. He picked it up and moved to a different table to fill out his paperwork privately.

Jeanette pushed an application and a pen over to Becca. "Get started on that."

As Becca stared at the empty squares on the form, a familiar panic started to rise. "I don't drive. I mean, like, I probably could, though."

"That's okay."

"So where it says driver's licence ...?" Becca let the question hang in the air.

"Don't put anything down." Jeanette looked out the window.

Becca started filling out the form. She didn't like the pen she was using because it kept cutting out, but she didn't feel she could switch to one of hers without coming off as judgy, and she could feel Jeanette watching her.

"I remember being your age. What I'd give to be fourteen again," she said.

Becca said nothing. Fourteen sucked, and from where she was sitting, she was pretty sure fifteen wouldn't be any great shakes either.

Jeanette opened her pastry bag and pulled out a chocolate chip cookie. Her fingers were tiny. They belonged more on a little baby's hand than an adult's. Becca watched Jeanette centre her cookie on a napkin and then tug it to a spot in front of her. Becca could tell she had done these moves before because it felt like she was executing some sacred chocolate ritual that had to be done before she ate.

"What grade are you in?" asked Jeanette.

"Ten. Just started."

Jeanette raised one of her practically nonexistent eyebrows. They were pale blond and barely transmitted expression, but Becca could spot shade clear across a room.

"Is that a problem?"

"No. It's just I thought I'd be seeing your mom today. Lots of times, parents come to the interview. They ask questions — you know — check out the job. Because I'm not going to lie. This work can be a bit hard for someone who's never carried before. A lot of the parents deliver with their kids until they get the hang of it. Am I gonna meet her tomorrow?"

"No. I have to work alone."

Jeanette whistled. "You must have pissed in her cornflakes."

Becca could feel her cheeks burning. She stared at the table.

Jeannette lowered her voice, suddenly a friend sharing a secret. "She told me you needed to make money 'cause you did something.'" She broke off a piece of cookie. "What did you do?"

Becca looked up. Jeanette delicately nibbled at her cookie and glanced back at Becca. She wasn't going anywhere, and she wasn't going to let Becca off the hook. She could wait all day.

"I broke a patio door."

"Uh-huh," she said, running her tongue over the half-melted chocolate. "Is that it?"

"Pretty much." Becca leaned further over her application.

"Pretty much," Jeanette repeated. She had another sip of her double-double and looked out the window. She could tell it was all the story she was going to get. "You sure did piss in her cornflakes," she said again, but this time her voice was far-off and dreamy. Maybe she was remembering fourteen.

Becca carefully reread her answers on the form, and when she was sure it was right, she handed it back to Jeanette. Apart from her name and her emergency contact information, the form was mostly blank. Jeanette looked it over and signed at the bottom to make it official.

"Delivery nights are Tuesdays and Thursdays. Either Phil or me will meet up with you to give you some flyers. It'll be me, mostly. I'll text you where and when tomorrow. You have to buy a carrier bag but you have to buy it from me. It's twenty-four dollars. I'll take it out of your first pay."

She unhinged her clipboard and pulled out a map, then picked up a blue pen and carefully traced the border of a square with the number thirty-one on it. "I'm giving you this section, okay?" She drew a line around the border three more times, but you could barely see the ink colour. "This part is what you're responsible for. It's three hundred and thirty-six doors. Mix of private residential and a couple of high-rises. It should take you about two hours to go door-to-door. I didn't want to give you too many 'cause I'm not sure how much you can carry yet." She slid the map across the table. "Umm, what else ..." She looked up into her mind's eye. "Wear comfortable shoes. Check out what the weather is doing ahead of time so you know what to wear. And your mom probably told you all this, it's common sense, but don't go into people's houses even if they invite you in. Especially if they invite you in. Even if they're women. You got any questions?"

Becca had plenty of questions, but she didn't ask them. She got the sense it would be like opening Pandora's box, that Jeanette had figured out all the answers the hard way. And if there was one thing Becca definitely didn't want to know, it was what she didn't need to know.

The sun was sinking down behind the barbershop and the windowless gospel ministry when Becca emerged from the Country Style. She located the bus stop, threw her schoolbag up on her shoulder, and made her way to the corner to wait for the traffic light she'd missed because she hadn't felt like running.

People always promised that life would get easier, but it never seemed to. Becca felt tired all the time now. Like she'd spent every day running through waist-high mud, trying to suck oxygen out of honey.

"Hey, kid."

Becca looked back. A heavyset man twenty feet away was talking to her. She turned back and hit the pedestrian crossing button a few more times.

"Kid!" he yelled.

He was hurrying toward her. Freaked out, she backed up a few steps and held her backpack in front of her. "Get away from me or I'll kick you in the balls!" she yelled.

He pulled off his dark sunglasses.

"Woah. *Woah*! Easy! Becca, right?"

Becca nodded.

"I'm Phil. I work with Jeanette! I was driving the van," he said. Becca relaxed, but only a little. Her mother had told her more than once that guys with vans were trouble because they were always expecting stuff.

He held out his hand to shake hers, but she didn't take it, so he dropped his arm to his side. There was a perfectly round red stain on his polo shirt, like a meatball or something had dropped out of a sandwich onto his belly.

"I didn't mean to scare you. I thought we'd get a chance to meet before, but I couldn't find any parking. I ended up way the hell down Eglinton. Must be a game on tonight. Look, Jeanette told me your mom's not coming out with you tomorrow night. I know she went over all the safety stuff, but I wanted to make sure you get this is physical work. Those flyers are heavy. You think you can handle that?"

Becca shrugged.

"We'll see tomorrow night, I guess. One piece of advice: do not listen to music while you're doing the rounds, okay? Stay plugged into what's going on around you."

"Okay." Becca rolled her eyes cynically.

"No. There's a ton of posters for missing dogs, missing cats in that part of town. You gotta stay sharp, right?"

She didn't know what he meant.

"Dogs and cats," he explained. "A serial killer's first steps. I don't want to scare you; I want you to be safe. Use your head. You'll be fine. And one more thing. If you're going to kick someone in the nut sack, don't tell them you're going to do it. Just do it."

"Okay." This time she meant it.

"Okay." He noticed the meatball or whatever stain and dropped his hand over it, making it look like it was a bullet wound. He looked a bit disappointed about the impression he'd made. "See you around," he said and walked away.

45

Drawing Lines

KATHERINE WAS FIDDLING WITH the IV tubes, considering whether she should tape them together to keep them properly grouped, when she peripherally caught the tail end of something Amanda said that involved the word *line*.

Naturally, Katherine extrapolated and explained. "You see, normally, the IV line should be completely separate from the oxygen and feeding tubes ... the theory being that in an emergency, you could push the rest of the tubes out of the way and inject whatever drug needed to be injected, stat."

There was an awkward silence. She looked away from her IV pole and saw Amanda trade glances with Theodore.

"No, I meant *line*, as in 'What is my ...?'"

"Oh God, I'm ..." said Katherine. She blinked at the work lights like an idiot, trying to figure out where she was.

Jason read out Amanda's line from the auditorium. "He never dared to hope —"

"He never dared to hope," Amanda repeated quickly, as though she were merely skipping ahead to the important part of the script, as if she'd known all along.

Katherine scrambled down the steps into the auditorium, wondering what the hell she'd been doing up on the stage without her prompt book.

"I am ... *really* sorry," she whispered to Jason the moment she sat down at the worktable. Jason held up his hand to shush her, intent on focusing on Amanda's performance or whatever it was he thought she was doing. A little rude.

Katherine flipped through the pages of her prompt book, trying to find where they were, and turned over at least a dozen pages before she found the scene. Jesus. Had she really been up there that long?

She shook her head, pissed with herself for being caught off guard and taking for granted the actors knew their lines. It was like they did it on purpose. Not that she didn't expect the occasional line drop, but seriously, they *were* three weeks into rehearsal. Previews started in a few days. Anyone who called themselves a professional actor should have been off-book by now.

She located Amanda's missed line in the script and put a check mark beside it in the margin. She liked to track the problem areas. Amanda seemed to have quite a few "issues" with this scene. She made a note to get her to run it later with the assistant stage manager.

They'd reached the part of the play where Theodore spoke to his family for the last time and Amanda mostly had to emote when Jason leaned in toward Katherine. "I'm confused," he said quietly. "Were you supposed to be on stage just then?"

Katherine felt her cheeks glow with embarrassment. She kept her attention on the script so she wouldn't have to look Jason in the eye. "I don't actually come in for another three pages. But I happened to notice that ... the IV was wrong? And I needed to fix it ..." She hated apologizing.

"*Line.*"

Katherine's eyes shot down to Amanda's response, and she started reading: "I'm tired of your questions, of the ..."

Amanda signalled for her to stop reading and picked up her line from the top. "I'm tired of your ... demeaning interrogations. Of the lies —"

"Sorry," interrupted Katherine. "It's 'questions.' 'I'm tired of your questions,'" Katherine made a second check mark next to Amanda's line.

Jason looked at her. "Let her get through it."

"Okay. But 'interrogations' means a whole different thing," she answered.

"*Line,*" said Amanda.

"I mean, the words are the words, right? If you want to change them, that's fine. I can change the line in the prompt book."

"*Line!?*"

"Yes, Amanda. I heard you." It seemed to Katherine that Amanda was starting to sound pissy. "'I'm tired of your questions, of the lies you've made us all tell one another ...'"

Amanda held up her hand to make her stop again. Katherine sighed impatiently because Amanda needed to hear the whole line, but she stopped and waited. She was a professional.

"I'm tired of your ..." Amanda said. Then she fell silent.

"Exactly," muttered Katherine.

Amanda stared hard at the ground. She continued to pretend she knew her line but was working out the beats in her head. She dug her fist deep into her hip and put on this fierce, focused face like she was some character from a Tennessee Williams play. Best. Acting. Ever.

It was strange how actors were constantly projecting different versions of themselves when they needed to get through embarrassing situations. Of course, lots of people who weren't actors put on airs too. It was just that actors, in Katherine's opinion, weren't very good at it. Probably because they weren't that great at being themselves in the first place.

The length of Amanda's pause had become awkward.

"What is she doing?" Jason asked Katherine. "What's going on?" he asked.

Amanda dropped the charade. "Sorry," she said. "I've *completely* lost my train of thought." She walked to centre stage and looked out at them. "I guess Katherine must have rattled me when she came up on stage early. I started thinking I was doing the wrong part of the play, and it ... pulled me *right out* of the moment."

"Bullshit," answered Katherine matter-of-factly.

She hadn't meant to say it out loud, of course, but she had. It appeared that Jason had also heard her. He was wearing that caught-in-the-middle expression men got whenever they realized whatever they were going to say next was bound to piss off a woman.

"Why don't we take a five-minute break to go over our scripts," he said, "and we'll run this section again."

Amanda gave him a cursory nod and left with Theodore.

"Back at ten after eleven," Katherine called after them. There was no response. Jason leaned back in his chair and sighed.

Katherine went through her prompt book to reconcile her notes on Amanda.

"Why did you leave her hanging like that?"

Katherine looked at Jason and squinted, trying to understand.

"Amanda. Just now."

"She didn't ask for a line. Every time she *does* ask, she doesn't let me finish, and then she gets the rest of it wrong. Whether I give her the line or not, she's going to say the wrong words."

Katherine could tell Jason knew she was right.

"She needs to run the —"

Jason got up abruptly. "Excuse me."

"Tex..." she said, her voice petering off. Jason had already jumped to his feet and left without listening to her answer. She wondered if he'd always felt so self-important, and whether she'd merely chosen to overlook it until now.

She didn't get why he was blaming her for Amanda's failings. Katherine knew her lines. She also understood that the ability to remember them was a prerequisite for acting work. She had offered Amanda multitudes of opportunities for betterment.

Katherine turned to her first aid kit and neatly snipped four inches from a roll of white adhesive medical tape. She hopped up the stairs to the stage and permanently secured the IV lines in their proper place while making sure the tape was out of the audience's line of sight. She'd always assumed Jason appreciated her thoroughness, but now she recalled how earlier, when she'd suggested that Theodore's character should be a little blue around his lips for the third act because it was a visual signal of someone's oxygen levels being low, Jason had pooh-poohed her. He'd said he worried it was excessive and might detract from the play's larger message of redemption. "This isn't *Coroner*" had been his exact words. Which Katherine felt was a little reductive.

If she was to be perfectly honest with herself, she was starting to find theatre's devil-may-care attitude toward facts irritating. No one was taking the play as seriously as she was, and if there was anything she truly detested, it was a lack of commitment.

As Katherine walked through the curtain legs to check on the props, she heard voices.

"She's *freaking* me out."

It was Amanda. Katherine peeked around the curtain and saw she was talking with Jason.

"Your character's focus should completely be on Theodore. Try not to let her get to you," he said. "You're the professional."

More than anything, Katherine wished she could bust in on their little lovefest and inform them that *she* was the only true professional among them, but it wasn't an argument she felt they were intellectually able to handle. She quietly retreated to her worktable in the auditorium and sharply re-underlined the stage directions in her script until she inadvertently tore through the page with her pencil.

Amanda resumed rehearsals with a great show of confidence. Katherine could tell she felt she'd finally won Jason over. Despite Jason's duplicity, Katherine was attentive for the remainder of the rehearsal and was quiet and poised and professional unless a line was called for. Jason acted as though nothing was wrong, giving Katherine no other option but to play along.

The post-rehearsal mood suggested there'd been a return to normality. Katherine stayed behind to clean up and put away the props, but as she walked into the wings to turn out the work lights, she was ambushed.

"Is this becoming too much for you?"

Katherine turned and saw Jason. He was trying to appear nonchalant. "What?"

"The nurse thing?" he said. "Because we could get someone else."

"Why? What do you mean? Am I doing it wrong?" Katherine was stung but determined not to show it.

"No, you're doing it perfectly."

"So what's the problem?"

"I think," Jason said. Then he lowered his volume like he wanted to erase his words as he was saying them. "I think you've become too invested in your role. I mean, I'm glad you're into it, but ... it's disturbing the actors because ..."

She waited for him to finish his thought, and of course, he didn't. She could see he wanted her to fill in the blanks. "... It's disturbing because they want to continue to see me as a stage manager first."

"Exactly!" he said a bit too loudly, looking quite relieved, like he'd birthed a bowling ball in one push.

"All right ..." said Katherine slowly to convey she thought he was being unreasonable, but also to indicate that she could be level-headed. "How about until previews, I call out my line from the audience. Will that work?"

"Yes. *Yes.* Thank you. From now on, that would be best."

She was about to broach the subject of Amanda's earlier back-stage theatrics when Theodore came forward to chat with Jason. He'd obviously been lurking backstage. He still held his script tightly rolled in his hand. It looked more like a paper napkin after a picnic than the work of a Pulitzer-nominated author.

It occurred to Katherine that Theodore might have been hanging around to report back to Amanda. Her eyes narrowed on the little twerp. He noticed. And quickly offered to walk out with Jason.

"Good night, Katherine," said Jason.

"Good night!" echoed Theodore cheerily.

Katherine felt too numb to reply.

Once again, she'd been singled out for being good at her job.

She walked around the fly rail to the main power panel, then turned off the work lights one by one. She stood a moment in abso-lute darkness, listening to the curtains swaying on the heavy pipes above her, thinking of how much she'd been limited.

When Katherine got home, she beelined to the bathroom, kick-ing off her shoes, peeling off her socks, and pulling up her sleeves as she took in all the places that needed to be cleaned.

Peeling the sticker off the holes on a new can of Comet, she dropped to her knees and started to scrub. The sink, the tub, around the taps. Big angry circles at first. Angry slashes around the drains. Then smaller but no less vicious diagonal stabs on the flat surfaces.

The tub was original to the building. It was clean but old. You could make out streaks of glaze in the finish. She remembered the first time she'd peered closely at its surface and seen the hundreds of fine grey lines left behind, like strands of steel wool. They bore witness to all the women before her who had scrubbed with anger, ache, and venom. They had left their marks, and tonight,

Katherine joined their ranks. She scrubbed until her fingers felt dry and hot, and when she suspected her fingertips might start bleeding because she'd denied herself the comfort of rubber gloves, she held her hands under the cold-water faucet until her palms went numb.

46

Surprises

IT WAS 7:30 AS Becca walked down the hill toward her house. Caroline was home. There weren't any pickup trucks parked in front of the house, but the garbage bins were still by the curb. Something was definitely going on.

Becca dragged the bins up the driveway and parked them in their spots toward the back of the house, then followed the patio stones into the dark yard.

She could barely see the path or the patio chairs because Caroline hadn't switched on the exterior lights. She half stumbled over something in the grass. It took her a millisecond to identify what it was: the blender lid.

Becca whipped it across the yard like a Frisbee and heard it hit something with a loud, satisfactory *thwack*. Despite everything that had happened, making blender drinks was going to be forever in her past.

The kitchen was dark, but there were a few lights on in the living room.

"I'm home," Becca called out.

"Dinner's in the microwave," her mom yelled back. "Could you put the kettle on?"

At the mention of food, Becca realized she hadn't eaten anything since lunch. She'd made a no-fat cheese sandwich on some of her mom's janky-looking organic quinoa bread, but the moment she'd sunk her teeth into it, Becca had semi-gagged. It was a recurring problem with her mom's bread. Caroline swore by it, but it tasted like hay held together with predigested corn and bird spit. She'd ended up pulling her sandwich apart to salvage the vegan cheese slice, which Caroline swore tasted just like cheddar but didn't. Lunch had lasted all of thirty seconds. Now she was famished.

The small plate in the microwave had couscous mixed with some sort of green veg and some dodgy dressing, but Becca was too hungry to question it further.

"How'd it go?" her mom shouted.

"Okay," Becca yelled back and shovelled a large spoonful of supper into her mouth, discovering too late that the kale hadn't been cut in bite-size pieces. She resisted spitting it out for a few moments because her stomach was screaming for food, but she was fairly certain she'd choke if she tried to swallow it. Reluctantly, she deposited a wad of half-chewed kale into her palm like an owl spitting out leftover mouse. Before she could reflect on her spontaneous act of grossness, she transferred the warm wad of green into the organics trash. She shovelled the few remaining spoonfuls of couscous into her mouth and chewed as long as she could because dinner was done.

Becca filled the kettle. "Water is on, but you have to get it," she shouted. "I'm going to my room." She picked up her backpack to head upstairs.

"Wait! Come in here a minute," Caroline shouted back.

Becca sighed and obeyed reluctantly. Caroline would probably notice she hadn't washed her hair to meet Jeannette and kick up a fuss.

Becca wandered into the living room, checking her phone for nonexistent messages, and stopped a few feet short of where she'd intended to end up.

There was a guy sitting on the sofa beside her mom.

Not a regular guy. A really, really quiet guy with tufty pale brown hair, a slightly crumpled dress shirt, and sharply pressed pants. He looked anxious.

"This is my daughter, Rebecca," said Caroline. "Becca, this is Mommy's friend Karl."

"Hey," Karl answered a shade too quickly. "Rebecca, how's it going?" He quickly looked down at his lap.

He definitely wasn't one of those self-assured types her mother usually brought home — men with warm, open, sun-kissed faces but "get that kid outta here" eyes. Karl was sort of pale. Nothing about him suggested he'd ever swung a hammer or visited a construction site. He was lean like a whippet. His shoulders rolled forward a little, and his shoes were polished but scuffed around the toes. In the Caroline landscape of men, he was a complete freak.

"So? How did it go?" asked Caroline. She didn't leave Becca any room to answer because she launched into the story of how her daughter had wrecked her door.

To his credit, Karl didn't play the "I'm a big softy" card and urge Caroline to forgive her daughter. Nor did he ask Caroline to remember the trouble they'd both got into in their youth and chuckle that she should go easy on her. Instead, he nodded.

"So?" said Caroline, turning back to Becca. "Tell me about Jeanelle. Did you like her?"

"Her name's Jeanette."

"Are you sure?" Caroline looked totally skeptical.

"Um … yes?"

Caroline told Karl how "Jennett" had sounded exceedingly pleasant on the phone, then she added, "Like some other people I know." Which Becca thought was weird. She noticed Caroline was stroking Karl's leg with the tip of her foot, and right away, she knew they'd done it.

Becca was ready to move on. "Can I go do my homework?"

"You going to be upstairs a while?"

"Yes. I'm definitely not coming back down," Becca answered, wondering why they were going through the bother of speaking in code when clearly everyone could understand what was going on. They were going to do it. Again.

If Karl had looked anxious before, he looked really unsettled now.

Becca made a note to plug in her phone and recharge the battery.

47

How I Met Your Mother

KARL DIDN'T KNOW HOW he'd come out of the house with his pants on under his own steam, but holy Christ, he was beat. He had nothing left. That Caroline had wrung out his dick like a washcloth. First order of business was to get home, replenish electrolytes, and sleep for at least four hours.

That is, once he found his bike. It was out there, somewhere, in the pitch-frickin'-dark. He'd leaned it up against a hedge because there hadn't been any obvious place to lock it out front. Though truth be told, he'd been too busy trying to remember how to appear interested in the conversation he was having with his new lady friend to pay attention to what he was actually doing.

Normally, when Karl was trying to calm or charm someone, it was on the phone. He'd forgotten about all the things that had to happen concurrently to seduce someone. Like the facial stuff. The "I'm listening" expression. And then actually listening, which meant maintaining an eye lock that would have provoked a cat to attack. It had been a bit much. Still, he'd made it through the day at work without touching himself. More important, he'd got off the traditional way. It was a step forward — a blazing fucking success.

His phone was dead, so the flashlight was not an option. He was going to have to feel it out. Karl took one decisive step in what he assumed was the right direction.

"Ow! Jesus! Fuck!"

It was a patio table or something. Nope. A long, horizontal thing with spiky things dangling off the end. Barbecue. It was going to leave a mark. Two more steps forward. He walked into something else. More gently this time. It had to be the table.

Karl leaned forward, letting his hand skim the lip of it, and followed its general direction until he reached the point where he had to let go. He wobbled as his right foot slid off the patio stone and onto the lawn. *Okay*, he told himself. *Progress*.

He took a few more steps, holding his arms straight out ahead of him, and made his way to where he thought the hedge or the shed had been. Then he remembered that the backyard sloped down sharply toward the neighbours below. He had no clue how close he was to falling into the abyss. He started to brush the top of the grass with his foot to try to detect any potential downward incline. And when it occurred to him he didn't one hundred percent know whether there was a tree in the yard, he started swiping at potentially existing branches at eye level. Just in case. This went on for several minutes until —

"Owwwwww."

Sharp metal corner.

"Ffffuck me gently," he said, rubbing the sore spot on his thigh. He'd discovered the gas barbecue again. Thank Christ he wasn't trying to cross the Canadian Shield.

Karl became conscious of someone's TV set playing nearby and decided to try to use it like a location beacon. If he kept the sound on his left side, then walked past it until the sound was behind him, presumably he'd be walking in a straight line. He walked forward fifteen or twenty steps, one arm outstretched, the other hand covering his eyes. Listening. He knew that music from somewhere, and he struggled a few moments to place it. Was it *Little House on the Prairie*?

Before he could start wondering what had happened to Bandit

the dog, Karl landed softly in a hedge. And because his instinct told him to go left, he went right.

Nothing about this motherfucking day had been predictable.

HE'D SPENT THE FIRST part of the afternoon at his desk, struggling to keep his mind on his work and his hands off himself. Every time he'd thought he'd lose it, his thoughts had circled back to Saurav, a guy he'd only just met who was going out on a limb for him. It was tough, though. Like going through the worst kind of break-up — the kind where you're constantly reminded of how easy it would be to get back with your ex, even though she was really bad for you.

Caroline had been looking for some general product information, considering an upgrade for her internet service. They'd been talking about modems and data speeds. She had a nice voice with a bit of catch to it, which was attractive. After a few minutes of playful banter, Karl got the feeling she had game and tested his theory.

"Caroline, I think the big question is: how fast do you need it to be delivered?"

There was a long silence. Long enough that Karl was sure he'd fucked himself. He was about to start backpedalling when Caroline found her voice: "I'd say it depends on the mood and whether I've had a few drinks."

Holy fuck, it was game on. Karl stood up, pretending to look for a binder but really on the hunt for Ed. "There are lots of factors to consider," Karl advanced. "I mean, every package has its pros and cons."

She laughed. Throatily.

He spotted Ed holding a laptop under his arm, which meant he was on his way to a management meeting. He could get his ass fired for talking to her like this, but she wasn't stopping him.

"So what does a professional like yourself think is the make-it-or-break-it package element?"

"I'd say," Karl said, quickly sitting back down, "it's user interface. A smooth, responsive, intuitive, and highly graphical user interface."

She burst out laughing. "Well, in that case ..."

Lucky for him, Caroline forgave him his shit banter and asked if he wanted to meet up for drinks. He went all out and bought some new underwear after work.

When a silver Lexus pulled up in front of the building and a strawberry blond called out, "Karl?" from behind the wheel, he knew he'd hit the fucking jackpot. Sure, Caroline had gone around the block a few more times than he had, but she was easy to look at. Nice smile. Fit. She did a lot of talking at first, which he didn't respond to as much as he should have because he was trying to remember how to get around the bases.

But it turned out baseball wasn't important to Caroline. He'd barely finished his drink when she dropped to her knees and gave him a blow job. It had both surprised and scared the hell out of him. Karl closed his eyes and thought of porn and came hard, calling her a slut. Which he apologized for — after — but she hadn't taken offence. She'd slapped the tops of his thighs and said, "I'm giving you twenty minutes to recharge your battery, and then it's my turn."

At some point, Caroline mentioned a daughter. For some reason, he'd imagined a six- or seven-year-old, but it turned out she was a full-on sullen teen. Karl had pasted a smile on his face through the hellos because he had no idea what to say. It had been awkward, and in all honesty? The daughter made him nervous. She stared at him like she knew something. Like she'd picked up some signal that something was off. He could feel the doubt coming right off her. This kid was not his friend. Maybe she resented him for stealing her mommy's attention. He'd have to keep an eye on her.

He didn't like complications, but right now, he needed Caroline more than her kid did. At least until he had himself under control.

There was too much at risk. If he got caught as the Moaner, he would never be able to get his career back on track. No one would help him. When people knew you were a falling dagger, no one wanted to catch you. So the minute Becca went upstairs to fold her day-of-the-week underwear or whatever the hell it was that teen girls did, Karl went to town on Caroline.

Following several action-packed minutes, they had a rest. There was a third round, and then they made another date.

It had been one hell of a day.

Karl was almost out of hedge to explore when his hand hit leather. Jesus Christ. Finally. His bike. He grabbed the saddle and flipped the bike around so it pointed toward the carport. Behind him was absolute darkness, but ahead he could see the faint glow of a streetlight, so he knew he was pointed in the right direction. He just had to keep moving.

Karl hopped on his bike and gently pushed off when something hit the back of his leg. He reached down and discovered something jammed in between the wheel spokes. He rolled forward a few feet and held the object up to his face to inspect it.

It looked like a blender lid.

48

Destiny for Beginners

IT WAS A LITTLE after 6:00 a.m., but Becca had been awake for hours. She'd had a vivid dream about Jeanette trying to show her where to deliver flyers by pointing at the map, but with *actual* baby hands. Mega disturbing.

All night, she'd felt her anxiety turning around and around on itself, every new doubt tossing her dread into a fresh tumble. Around one in the morning, she'd heard the patio door slide open. Desperate for a chance to think about something that wasn't a feeling, she got up to see what was going on. It was Karl, leaving. Or trying to. Becca watched him walk into the barbecue. Twice. "OMG," she'd said each time.

He was such a weirdo. She didn't know how he'd got on her mom's good side. She just knew that at some point, he would resist something Caroline really believed in, like low-calorie meals or subtitled movies, and then he would never come back.

Around the third time he started around the yard, Becca started feeling guilty about spying on him ... until he started windmilling his arms. Which was hilarious. She could have shouted directions out to help him, but something about his willingness to keep moving was compelling. It was like he thought every fresh problem he encountered meant he was gaining ground. She wondered if in the end, all the struggle was worth it.

Around 5:00 a.m., when it was clear she wasn't going to sleep, she'd decided it was time to abandon her bed. Becca had loosened the drawstring on her PJ bottoms and let her fleecy baby sheep travel down her legs to her ankles. She turned in circles, assessing the different clothing piles, trying to guess which was the one with the clean underwear. As she scouted, her foot slipped over something crinkly. She squatted down to have a look. It was the red carrier bag Jeanette had forced her to buy to make deliveries. Becca hacked its cellophane wrapper open with her cuticle scissors and was immediately rewarded with a huge whiff of chemically caustic spray.

It looked like the carrier bag had been hot when it got packaged, because it held on to its folds like it was in the grip of rigor mortis. Even after she'd stood on it awhile to flatten it, it sprang back to its original shape. But it had cost Becca two hours' pay, so she was going to use it.

As she padded downstairs, Becca couldn't help but notice how everything looked wrong. Sure, it was earlier than normal, but that didn't explain why it felt like she'd walked into a parallel universe that was exactly the same as hers except not. Sunlight was weirdly all over the place. And the sounds! She could hear actual birds outside and music in the kitchen. All she normally registered were car alarms, a super annoying garbage truck, and, of course, the blender.

Caroline was in the kitchen in a crazy joyous mood, chopping, quartering, and singing whatever parts of Taylor Swift's "Shake it Off" she remembered. It was like the beginning of a Disney movie. All it needed was a few animated bluebirds.

Her mom's head swivelled as she heard Becca walk in.

"Good morning, Rebecca!"

"Sure is," Becca answered cautiously. This full-on early-morning joy stuff was uncharted territory.

"I didn't hear you come down," Caroline said, reaching for the quart of strawberries. Her wood bangles clinked together musically.

"No. You were singing to all the little forest creatures."

"The last time you were up this early," she said, "you were ten, and it was the first day of band camp."

"That's so random, Mom."

"My God, I slept like a log."

Becca noticed a disturbing half smile appear on her mom's face as she dropped half a dozen strawberries into a brand-new blender. "You know how normally it takes two of Mommy's blue pills to knock her out. Not last night. I feel so relaxed this morning, I don't even think I need to do yoga. It's crazy." Caroline giggled to herself, then gestured toward the celery root.

Becca bowled it down the counter to her mom, unsure how to respond. "I didn't sleep much," she volunteered. Becca waited a moment for Caroline to ask her about it. When she didn't, she prompted her, "Do you want to know why?"

Caroline glanced up from the cutting board. "Okay, Becca. I'll bite. Why couldn't you sleep?"

"I had nightmares."

Caroline's phone buzzed. She reached, tapped, and swiped.

"Jeann..."

Caroline snorted with laughter at her text message and immediately started texting back. Becca stopped talking.

"No, go ahead. I'm listening," said Caroline. "I'm listening." She bit down a snort.

"You're not."

"Okay," said Caroline. She was too busy texting to argue. "Just ... hold on a minute. Let me finish this, then I'll give you my undivided ... attention." She tapped out a long sentence, a smile growing on her face.

Becca picked up half an apple off the counter. "I'm eating this apple."

"Mm-hmm," Caroline answered, still not actually listening.

Becca bit into the Granny Smith as she watched her mom type. Caroline smiled right up until she hit "send." Then she made a big show of setting her phone down like she was the most attentive mom in the history of attentive mothers.

"There. Done. Okay?"

"Right." Becca started over. "So yesterday, while I was talking to —"

Caroline's phone buzzed. She snatched it up like a hawk picks off a mole. She clarified, "It's Karl," as though it was necessary. "I'll text him back in a minute. Go on."

Becca stared at her mom in utter shock. She could remember Karl's name without issue. Becca had been remembering men's names for her mother since she'd mastered the white Russian.

Caroline blushed. Even *she* knew she was being weird. "What? I think he's nice! Don't you think he's nice? He's so easy to talk to. He texted me this morning and said he'd been thinking of me. No one's done that in years."

"Uh-huh."

"You want to hear something funny? Like funny-strange? Karl's last name is Reynolds, and my boyfriend in middle school had the same last name." She cocked her head and raised one eyebrow. "Isn't that weird?"

Becca shrugged.

It wasn't the answer she wanted, but Caroline's sense of serendipity demanded a connection. "You know what's really weird?" she said, leaning in. "The last four numbers of Karl's cell phone are the same last four numbers I used to have when I was at O&Y."

"Freaky," said Becca. She didn't mean it, but if she didn't feed the dragon, it would never listen to her.

"Right?!" her mom shouted with relief, like she'd proven something immense. She reached a bangled arm up into the cupboard to fetch some whey powder. Her bangles slid down her arm and made a sound like set of a wooden wind chimes dropping onto a porch. "I mean, I doubt I would have even noticed a link before I started doing meditation, but it's like I've started receiving all this extra information from the universe, and I don't think I could turn it off if I wanted to. There's just something about me and Karl." Caroline quickly picked up her phone, flicked through the photos, and handed it to Becca. It was a selfie of Caroline with her arm draped around Karl's shoulder. They were in the living room. She was smiling really hard. Karl sort of looked like he was some mail room guy who'd inadvertently walked into a CEO's photo op by mistake and was trying to make the best of things.

Caroline took the phone back and studied the picture. "He's a little rumpled, but it's nothing a few good shirts and a decent belt can't fix." She held the phone closer to her face. "He's very assiduous otherwise." A smile appeared on her lips. "In every regard."

"Ew! TMI, Mom. Seriously."

Caroline flashed the picture on her phone again. "Don't you think he and I would make beautiful babies together?"

"Could you stop, please?"

Caroline appeared both surprised and disappointed by Becca's lack of enthusiasm and vision. She let her phone slip through her manicured fingers and caught the top, making a practised connection with the sleep button. It was a sign she would not discuss Karl further for the time being, which was fine with Becca.

Caroline crossed to the refrigerator to start packing her carrots.

"Can I finish telling you what I have to tell you?"

Caroline let out a sharp sigh. "Becca, either say what you have to say or don't. You don't need permission, and you don't need to introduce every topic you want to talk about. This isn't debate club."

"Jeanette is expecting you to deliver flyers with me until I know what I'm doing."

"No. Absolutely not."

"All the other parents do it!"

"I'm not a lemming."

"But there's a reason!"

"This is your lesson, not mine. I already have a job and a date."
Caroline poured her green juice into a tapered insulated cup to
keep her slime fresh and elegant. "Besides which, Jeanelle assured
me it was a job a twelve-year-old could handle, so trust me when
I say I believe you're more than qualified."

"There are serial killers in the neighbourhood. Did you know
that? Even Phil said to be careful."

"Remind me. Who is Phil?"

"The guy who drives the van for Jeanette? I was coming home,
and he told me there were serial killers. And to stop listening to
music so I could hear them coming."

Caroline did not look concerned in the slightest. She nodded
and kept right on calmly counting her baby carrots.

"Becca, have you asked yourself if there's a reason why this Phil
character might want you to be scared?" Becca stared blankly at
her mother. Caroline sighed like the answer was obvious. "When I
was a teenager," she said, "I had a boss who liked to tell girls how
dangerous the night shift was so he could put his arm around them
and say, 'There, there' whenever they got afraid."

The final piece of the puzzle dropped into place.

"Oh my God, Mom. Phil drives a van!" Caroline had always
warned Becca about guys with vans. She had never been clear as
to what happened in them, but for sure, if Caroline had a warning
for it, it wasn't good. "What if he wants me to get into it?"

"Tell him your mother says you're not allowed."

"How is that even going to work? It barely makes sense."

"If it looks like he's going to try to touch you, tell him you're
underage and you're going to call the cops."

"But —"

"Becca, I don't have time to stand here and go through every conceivable scenario with you. This is part of growing up. You're just going to have to figure out how to handle it."

"You're supposed to be raising me, you know."

Caroline seemed surprised by her words, but she was staying the course. She pasted on a mindful Buddha smile. "Becca, I'm speaking calmly and rationally." Caroline was enunciating again. Her voice was smooth and dead flat. It was her controlling tone. "I'm not forcing you to react emotionally. You're doing that. You're choosing to get upset because you don't like my answer."

"That wasn't an answer."

"Maybe you should do twenty minutes of meditation before you go to school. Figure out what the universe is trying to tell you."

"Yeah, thanks. I know what the problem is, Mom." Becca hoisted up her schoolbag onto her shoulder.

"If you hang on two minutes, I'll give you a ride."

"I'd rather get on a random bus and let the universe decide where I'm going."

Before Caroline could pretend to care more, Becca opened the front door and slammed it behind her.

49

Second Opinion

CAROLINE'S "PARENTAL ADVICE" ABOUT what might be Becca's first and last night of work had only added to Becca's dread. She needed specifics. She wanted to know what to do. How to handle things. She needed to know how to prevent everything that could happen from happening. Almost barfing with worry, Becca walked into the counselling office. She didn't care who saw her.

The pretty, popular counsellor she'd initially wanted to talk with was standing in the front reception area, alphabetizing the STD pamphlets. She smiled at Becca like it was the first time she'd ever seen her.

"Can I help you?" she asked.

Becca sailed right past her — because she'd had her chance — and continued toward Greeley's office. She was just coming out with a pen and a notepad.

"Becca! Shouldn't you be in homeroom?"

"Yes, but Mrs. Greeley, can I talk to you?"

"I was about to leave. I have a staff meeting in ten minutes. Could we talk tomorrow?"

"It's just — I really need to ask you about something personal."

"Oh, I have appointments scheduled all day. What about after school? Could we talk around four?"

Becca shook her head. "Please, Mrs. Greeley."

Greeley studied her for a few seconds. "Without knowing what this is about, I have ten minutes before my meeting. Is that enough time?"

Becca nodded.

"Okay, then. Let's go."

Greeley took off like a rocket. Becca followed her out of the office, inadvertently getting a good look at what she was wearing: a green checked skirt made out of a car blanket, hemp wedges, and brown tights. Caroline would have told Becca not to take her seriously, but there was a lot Caroline said that didn't make sense anymore.

Greeley walked at a pretty good clip, as if she had some sort of urgent task to accomplish. Becca noticed a few kids looking at them, trying to figure out what they were doing. It made her feel oddly grown-up. She'd never been in school doing something that was so obviously not school, so she decided to pretend they were walking fast because they had to go to Greeley's meeting together. She sped up until she was walking beside the counsellor.

"We'll talk in a minute, okay? It's too noisy out here."

But it felt awkward to walk in silence beside her, so Becca asked, "Did you always want to be a counsellor?"

"No," Greeley answered. "That was an afterthought." She deked down a truncated hallway and advanced to a door Becca hadn't seen before. She fumbled around, patting herself down until she found her fob in her skirt pocket. "What I really wanted was to be an architect, but I discovered I wasn't a natural fit." She pressed the fob against the security box, and the door unlocked. "To be an architect, you need to be able to sense what people want because clients can't always verbalize their needs. It turns out, I'm sort of deaf to that."

Greeley pulled open the door.

Becca followed her into the teachers' lounge. It was a bit of a letdown. She had expected it to at least have leather armchairs and maybe a pinball machine like at her mother's office. But it was a long, windowless room with many weird decorative touches that could not disguise it had once been a school science lab.

Greeley walked toward the counter and selected the world's ugliest coffee cup from a cupboard. It was brown with a bumpy glaze. As she polished the inside of her cup with a dry paper towel, she nodded to one of the small, random tables. "Let's sit there."

The door banged open loudly, startling Becca as she sat down. A janitor came in, pushing a cart. She thought for sure he would tell her to get out because she shouldn't be in there, but he just crossed toward the garbage receptacles and emptied them.

Greeley returned, setting down her coffee cup. She produced a pack of gum she'd secreted into her waistband like contraband and punched a piece through the foil. "I'm not being rude," she said. "It's nicotine gum." She popped the piece into her mouth.

Becca shrugged like it didn't matter.

Greeley took a bunch of short, chomping chews. "It's a ridiculous habit," she said, her features starting to relax as the nicotine smoothed off the edges. "I can't seem to kick it." She switched gears, as if she'd suddenly remembered she was with a student. "You don't smoke, do you?"

"No."

"Mmm," answered Greeley, which presumably meant, "Good." Greeley inhaled like she was taking a deep pull on an invisible cigarette. Becca thought she could almost hear the paper and leaves crackle and pop.

Finally, Greeley checked her watch. "Okay, so what's up?"

Becca felt her panic level rising like she always did whenever she had to say something important. Greeley leaned in toward her, waiting.

"I would like to know what you think about a situation, like if it's dangerous or whatever, given my age and stuff."

"Is it something you would normally discuss with your parents?"

Becca nodded, feeling a bit embarrassed. "Yeah. Except my mom is the one who's making me do it."

Greeley looked concerned and glanced at her watch again. "Are you sure we couldn't talk tonight after school? I could call you if that's —"

"No!" Becca blurted out. "It has to be now. Because I have to go right after school, and I don't know what I'm supposed to do. She's always telling me I have to be nice to guys, but ..."

"Who tells you?"

"My mom."

"I don't underst—"

"Smiling. Serving drinks and nuts and things? I hate it so bad. It's just better if I pretend I'm not there. And tonight, my mom is making me go work for this guy, and I can't be alone with him because I think he's going to try to do something, but she says I have to deal with it."

"Oh, honey," said Greeley, her face increasingly transformed by concern.

That's when Becca knew she'd been right to ask a responsible adult about her situation. Greeley's expression unlocked a torrent of words. Before Becca could even order her thoughts, all her worries started to spill out of her mouth at the same time like bad clams. All jumbled together.

"I have to wait on this corner in the dark in this super sketch place for a van. And this guy might want me to get in it. And he's going to try to scare me so he can touch me. And I don't want him to, right? I begged my mom to come with me because I'm scared, but she says this is my lesson and I have to grow up."

"A lesson? Why is it a lesson?"

"Because I owe her. So much money. She says I have to work for it."

Greeley frowned. It occurred to Becca that maybe she was talking about too many things.

"How do I not go in the van if he asks me? I need money, right?"

Greeley shook her head. "I don't believe this."

"I know, right? But what would you do?"

Becca could see something changing in Greeley's features. She wasn't sure what was happening.

"Who told you to ask me?" Greeley said. Her voice was all hard now. Cold, grey steel.

"I don't understand," said Becca.

"Who told you to ask me for money?"

Becca shook her head. "I — I don't — I'm not ask —"

"Was it Webster? The Findlay kid?" Greeley angrily squished her gum back into the blister pack with her thumb. "I go beyond what's expected of me at work," Greeley said. "I do things no one else in this school would even consider doing. I volunteer to chaperone at dances. I've opened up my home to kids rather than see them tossed out on the street. I've given some of them money when they had nothing to eat. And you vultures keep coming around with your hard-luck stories so you can tap me for whatever it is your rich parents won't give you because my generosity is a laugh riot."

"Tch," said a voice behind Becca. She spun around. It was the janitor. He had the same look as Greeley on his face.

"Mrs. Greeley, no. I broke a —"

Greeley stood up. Whatever Becca said afterward got buried under the screech of her chair. "I have a meeting now. In future, if you want to discuss anything with me, please book an appointment."

As Greeley walked away, Becca felt her heart go numb. Maybe it was hope disappearing. All she'd wanted to know was how to get through the shitty parts of her life so she could she get to the better ones, but every time she asked for help, people got angry.

Becca saw the janitor look back at her, muttering. She picked up her bag and hurried out. Once she was in the hallway, she kept her head down until she found the girls' washroom.

While the Juulers got their vape pulls in by the sinks between classes, Becca struggled not to give away she was in a toilet stall, watching herself cry on a cracked phone. She had never been a pretty crier and today was no exception. There was nothing remotely cute about the snot bubbles or the rivulets her tears had carved through her foundation. It was worthy of a picture, but she couldn't find the energy to snap one.

She was such a mess. Her life was like a huge out-of-control SUV she didn't know how to drive. All she knew was she was headed for a cliff, and the brakes were for sure going to fail. It was like she was meant to smash through the guardrails, bounce off the rocks, and turn into sea foam.

Becca opened her bag and felt around the long side pocket for the cuticle scissors she normally carried around, but then she remembered she'd used them at home when she'd unwrapped her carrier bag.

Desperate to find anything that might work, she upended her bag onto the bathroom floor. She ruled out a Popsicle stick, a marker, and a lead pencil. Her feelings had moved past scratches or welts. She needed something sharp.

She spotted her pencil sharpener and laid her thumb on the metal bit to test the blade. It had catch.

"Just one," she promised herself as she swept her junk back into her bag. "Just once."

She placed the pencil sharpener on the floor and smashed her heel down hard on top of it, busting the plastic. Picking up the blade and dusting it off, she tested its flexibility and found a grip she was comfortable with.

Her go-to had been the top of her thighs, but something about cutting herself there seemed wrong now. She knew some people who cut their stomachs, but she could never do that, so she decided it would be her left arm.

The sleeves on her shirt were tapered and a bit hard to roll up, but eventually she managed to expose the inside of her elbow.

Becca stared at her perfect, unblemished skin and then rested the blade on a spot right above the crease and the veins where the nurses drew blood. She asked herself if she really needed to do this, although she already knew the answer.

Becca dug the blade into her arm and pulled it out immediately because it felt weird and it hurt and it was wrong. Just pain on top of pain. She was so tired of her uselessness she almost started to cry again.

She picked a different spot and drew the blade two inches across her arm. The cut stung, but she pushed back. This time, she was in control. As she drew the blade a third time, her deeper pain began to slowly leave her. She felt quiet sinking in. The deeper pain didn't completely disappear, but being Becca was bearable for the moment.

After a few minutes, she opened her eyes and saw blood. A lot of it. Dripping onto the floor. Maybe it was a normal bleeding amount for an arm, or maybe she'd cut herself a bit too deep. She didn't have a reference. Becca unspooled some toilet paper and pressed down on her cut to stop the bleeding. She wished she could wash up, but she couldn't chance anyone walking in.

She tore a second strip of toilet paper and wound it around her arm like a bandage. She tucked the ends in so it would stay in place and carefully pulled her sleeve back down over it.

Becca came out of her stall: earbuds in, music on, head down, arm hooked around her books. She stole a look at herself in the mirror while she was washing her hands and noticed her reflection didn't make the slightest impression on her.

She walked slowly but steadily through the crowded hallway, moving as space opened up in front of her. All she had to do was keep her eyes thigh-high. If you didn't make direct eye contact, people seemed to move out of the way for you.

Until one pair of legs refused to move. She stared at them a moment longer than felt comfortable. It occurred to her to look up. It was Dylan. He was talking to her. She tugged out an earbud.

"Hey. Welcome to earth," he said.

"Sorry," she answered. She wondered why she couldn't make herself smile. She toggled the volume control switch, and the other bud fell out. "I didn't ... I wasn't, like, focusing right," Becca offered.

Dylan nodded. "I haven't seen you around in a while."

"Yeah. I've sort of been dealing with stuff. My mom."

They both nodded. She wished she had something more to add. Dylan found a way to keep the conversation going.

"Where are you off to now?"

"Math," she said, looking down the hall in the direction she was going. "I should probably go. I'm almost late." She shifted her books to her other arm.

"Right. Okay." She was about to go when he stopped her again. "Hey, wait. Wait a minute. What did you do to yourself?"

Becca was not following. Dylan pulled up her arm. Spots of blood had seeped through the toilet paper and into her sleeve.

She crinkled her face in her practised way, trying hard to look puzzled by it. "Wow. Umm. I don't know. I guess I must have scraped up against something."

"Don't you think you should take a look at it?"

She shrugged. "No. Not really. It doesn't hurt."

"It doesn't?"

"No." If she really thought about it, she felt nothing.

"You're being really strange."

"Stranger than usual?"

Dylan didn't even crack a smile. "Seriously," he said. "You okay?"

He looked concerned. She hadn't meant to cut herself so deep. Now she felt bad for worrying Dylan. But she couldn't say any of that. "I really have to go," Becca repeated. This time, she dropped her eyes and started moving. Dylan stepped aside and let her pass, but she felt him watching her all the way down the hall.

50

Connecting the Dots

CINDY, THE WARDROBE MISTRESS, was pissed. Not a huge surprise. Once Cindy had stomped back to whatever dark sewing cave she lived in, Jason explained that although Katherine's new nursing uniform was perfect, the production didn't have the budget to buy it, the stethoscope, the white leather Dansko shoes, the watch, or the medical staff badge.

While Katherine understood the six hundred dollars she'd spent was probably the entire wardrobe budget for the show, the production's reluctance to kick in even a few hundred bucks to support her character bothered her. Clearly, the Prodigious Moments Theatre Company was not as serious about creating "connected experiences" as she'd been led to believe.

So Katherine offered to absorb the cost. Jason reacted with such surprise, she was embarrassed. She told him she needed a watch and that she'd find a way to wear the rest of the costume again. "You know, like, for Halloween." She'd decided she wasn't going to tell him she was going back to school. If she couldn't totally trust him to write a letter of recommendation on her behalf, why would she share one of her deepest personal decisions?

The bottom line was that Nurse Reeves had a real uniform. She'd undeniably be the most authentic person on stage. Her family would see her natural shine. Then they'd have to acknowledge she'd made the perfect career choice.

Katherine decided to keep her costume at home. It was a big theatre protocol no-no, but she couldn't fully trust that the wardrobe department wouldn't try to sabotage her.

Having her nursing uniform close by had actually been great. Initially, she'd just worn the shoes around her place to break them in, but then she got the idea to wear the whole shebang. It was such a lark. Like she was Nurse Reeves coming home after a shift in the ER, opening her mail and making coffee.

It was amazing how she could look at her own reflection and believe she was really an ER nurse. And her hips looked good in uniform. They really did.

She'd started cleaning and tidying up in character. Nurse Reeves had transformed her apartment into a neat and spotless living space — so much so that Katherine had actually gone ahead and cancelled Consuela's monthly housecleaning visit.

She realized some people would think her playacting was a little odd, but seriously, who was it hurting?

Nurse Reeves had gone through all of Katherine's things and turfed out all the stuff she'd been hanging on to for "sentimental" reasons. She'd also classified and reorganized all of her belongings in deep, opaque plastic containers that were clearly labelled. It was the way nurses accessed sterile instruments, drugs, and bandages, and it made a certain amount of sense. An emergency was not the time to be scrambling through a drawer looking for hypodermic needles.

Of course, Katherine's apartment had different types of objects that were not found in an ER — clothing, food, household objects, and so forth — so Nurse Reeves had modified her approach. She'd moved the half-empty bags of spices into a box and organized them alphabetically. She'd prewrapped sets of knives and forks in paper napkins and stored them in a clear canister. She'd become so immersed in her pen reorganization task that she'd have probably gone on working through the night if it hadn't been for the soft knock at the door.

Though Katherine didn't relish having to engage in potential chitchat at the door, the diligent part of her knew she had to answer in case it was an emergency and someone had come for help.

Katherine slipped the chain on, unbolted the lock, and cracked the door open.

"Brent!"

"Katherine. I'm sorry I didn't buzz. Someone let me in downstairs. I hope it's not a problem?"

"Well, it's a little weird."

He stood there expectantly. She sighed. "You can come in, I guess." She undid the chain then opened the door to let him stand in the foyer.

"Who did you say let you in downstairs?"

"Brunette with streaks? About yea high." He gestured vaguely, suggesting a woman who could be anywhere between 4'9" and 5'7". It had been a stupid thing to do. She'd definitely bring it up at the next tenants' meeting.

"I guess I don't look like a serial killer," Brent chuckled.

"Well, even serial killers don't look like serial killers until after they're caught."

"Is that ... for the play?" asked Brent.

The change of topic threw Katherine off guard. Brent was referring to her nurse's uniform.

"Yes," she said. "I was just trying it on."

"Well, I must say it suits you to a T. You look very professional. Play opens this week, doesn't it?"

"Previews."

Brent nodded. "You must be very excited."

"Sure. I mean, I guess?" Typical Brent. Trying to tell her how she felt instead of asking her straight out. She was glad she wasn't with him anymore. He could be exhausting.

He had started looking over her shoulder, noticing the plastic tubs in the living room.

"Are you moving?"

"I'm reorganizing," answered Katherine. She started to feel herself bristling at his fucking pointed comments.

"Did you put your remotes in a ziplock —"

"Okay, why are you here?" asked Katherine point-blank.

"Yes. Right. I'm not happy about how we left each other."

"Throwing a glass of Scotch at someone can have negative effects."

"I wasn't in my right mind. I wanted to apologize. I've started to see a —"

She had to stop him. "Brent? Sorry. I really don't want to hear it."

"That ... that ..."

He was going to say, "That's not fair." She could see it on his face, but something stopped him. Instead he said, "That's your right."

Interesting. She'd have to email him later and ask for the name of his therapist.

"I'm not here to ask you to reconsider our breakup."

"Good," she said, starting to feel a tinge of regret. Brent had a sexy new messed-up quality. He reminded her of Nicolas Cage in that movie about the writer who decides to drink himself to death. It was a bit of a turn-on, although for the life of her, she could not explain why.

Brent was still talking. "— if I came to see you in a preview this week? If it puts you in a terribly awkward position ..."

Katherine shrugged. "Do what you like. It's a free world, right?"

He nodded, looking slightly lost. She needed to be clearer. "I'm definitely not going to comp you."

Brent nodded. "Of course."

"Also, I'd prefer you didn't sit up front. I don't want to look out and see you and then lose character and all that."

"How far b—"

"Row M and further." She swung open her front door to invite him to leave.

He graciously took the hint and walked through, turning to glance back. Katherine quietly nodded at him and shut the door. He was no longer part of her evolution. His coat had been returned to the rack.

51

Reality Check

BECCA HAD BEEN STANDING on MacDonnell nearly twenty minutes, waiting for Jeanette's dirty white van to appear. The sky was almost dark. Sunlight was becoming that friend who could only hang out a little while because she'd made plans with other more interesting friends across town.

Becca rubbed her arm to smooth away the hurt like she was trying to iron out a wrinkle. She was feeling pain from her cuts now. Definitely. She'd taken a look at her arm after math class, and one of the wounds looked raw and puffy. It had mostly stopped bleeding, but it was still leaking. She'd rebandaged it with toilet paper before she left school. She'd clean it up when she got home.

Of course, it had started raining the minute she'd jumped off the streetcar. It was really coming down now, drops making loud *plop* sounds as they hit the slick cement sidewalks. The shitty rain cape she'd bought at the dollar store turned out to be more of a tinted plastic dry-cleaning bag, and the hood made her head sweat. But while the cape was keeping her dry, Becca's wide-leg jeans were wicking up water off the sidewalk, and her blue suede runners were soaked black and covered in the pulpy things that were falling off the trees.

At some point, it occurred to Becca to take refuge under a leafy oak. She felt weird just standing there, so she pretended to look through her phone to find some music. She wasn't listening to any, obviously, but on the off chance someone asked her for something, removing her earbuds and getting them to repeat what they'd asked would give her some time to figure out how to respond.

Luckily, it was supper time, and Parkdale seemed to be ignoring her. People were whizzing past. Everyone seemed to be in a hurry to get someplace else — the cyclists, the speed-walking commuters, the moms — all moving past the broken-down shit and the homeless people asking for smokes and cash. Urging their dogs to poop faster.

Becca noticed a woman walking out of an alley that ran behind the stores on Queen Street. She was dressed like she'd just stepped out of her girlfriend's apartment to pick up some gum or whatever, really pretty and cool, except she was spinning around on herself, twisting then dropping into a squat. She reminded Becca of one of those snakes she'd seen in videos. The ones that were writhing on the side of the road because they'd been poisoned. At first Becca suspected the woman was sick, but then she understood she was either too stoned or not stoned enough.

Some dodgy guy who didn't look like he could normally talk to girls like her was following five steps behind. He kept saying her name over and over again. "Kelly. Kelly." Becca could make out that much of the conversation because the rain carried it to her. "Kelly."

His voice got calmer and calmer, and she let him get close. Then he said something, and she started yelling, "Fuck *off*!" over and over again and stumbled away. Maybe he was trying to keep her safe. Maybe he was trying to get her to do something she didn't want to. Maybe she needed to be alone to twist out of her skin.

Becca felt like she should do something, except she didn't know what. She never knew what to do and she hated that so much. She watched Kelly wander back down the alley until she disappeared; she waited, but she never saw her again. Four or five people were huddled under a covered back entrance, trying to keep out of the rain. She hadn't noticed them before, but suddenly, they were watching her watching them.

Becca quickly looked up the street for sign of the van. It had to be way past seven. When she glanced back at the group, everyone had disappeared. For the next few minutes, she fully expected an ambush. Her phone was no help. It looked like 4\:11 on account of the glass being cracked. If it was a sign, it was a bit arch. But everyone left her alone.

Just as she started to wonder how much longer she needed to wait, she spotted the pearlized van coming down the street.

It stopped right in front of her, its headlights lighting up the rain, which was coming down pretty hard. Becca could see that the front bumper was tied on with wires. It was weird that she hadn't noticed that the other night.

The van changed sound as it shifted into park. The windshield washers stopped, then the headlights went out and the interior dome light came on. That's when she saw there was only Phil, unless Jeanette was already in the back of the van getting her flyers ready, which was highly unlikely. She was probably nice and warm in a coffee shop, her baby hands wrapped around a double-double.

Phil lowered the passenger-side window. Becca stood on the sidewalk waiting for whatever was going to happen next.

"Sorry I'm late," he called out. "Traffic was a mess."

"That's okay," Becca yelled back politely.

"Why don't you get in for a minute and warm up?" He wasn't looking at her. He was looking at some papers.

"Nah," Becca called out. "I'm okay."

"Well, we have some stuff to get through, so get in."

Becca hovered on the sidewalk, looking around, pretending she hadn't heard him. It was raining so hard, it was like the drops were being hammered into the ground.

"Look," he said, definitely sounding more irritated, "I want to show you your route, and I'm not going out there to explain it to you."

Becca opened her mouth, about to say that her mother had said that she couldn't get into vans, but Phil had pre-emptively raised the passenger window.

She could feel her body wavering, getting ready to obey him. Her feet shifted. As she edged toward the van, she looked around to see if anyone would be able to help in the event she was walking into a trap, but there was no one. Not Kelly. Not the others.

Becca's fingers grappled with the van's passenger door. She tugged at the handle with both hands until the mechanism moved and the hinges gave way. The door opened with a heavy screech. She felt a short, sharp pain in her arm where she'd cut herself earlier. It was probably going to start bleeding again.

Becca pulled the van door fully open and got a waft of warm vanilla scent. She lingered on the sidewalk, looking in, still trying to find a way to avoid climbing in.

Phil glanced up at her.

"Well, come on. I haven't got all night."

"Where's Jeanette? "

"Something not agreeing with her," Phil said, staring at a clipboard. He rubbed the stubble on his face, the way men did when they were tired and trying to concentrate.

Becca climbed into the van and perched on the right side of the vinyl seat, as far away from Phil as possible. Water ran off her rain cape and gathered on the floor mat below her feet, becoming instantly transformed into liquid dust beads.

She hadn't completely closed the door — just in case — but Phil hadn't noticed. He was busy looking through some big envelopes for something. Becca waited in silence.

The inside of the van was nowhere near as shitty as she'd thought it was going to be. She noticed an empty coffee cup with a wadded-up napkin in the cupholder. Other than that, it needed some Windex. She couldn't turn around to see what was in the back.

Phil found the envelope he'd been looking for.

"Okay," he said, pulling out a bunch of loose paper. He flipped through photocopies of maps. "Jeanette told me she gave you section thirty-one."

"Yes."

Now Phil was thumbing through his photocopies. Every other second, he would hold up his index to his mouth to lick it and get more traction in his page turning, but it didn't seem to be helping much. "At some point, I need to go through all of these and put them in order," he muttered. "Okay," Phil said suddenly. "Here we go."

He clamped the map of the neighbourhood to his clipboard. It was a copy of Jeanette's. If hers had been illegible, Phil's was a graph of ordered blobs: row after row of incomprehensible black-and-white squares representing houses and buildings. There were some legible bits of letters, but they didn't seem to matter in the big picture.

Phil tilted the clipboard toward Becca and uncapped his pen. "Okay, the best way to do this, in my opinion, is to start at the apartment buildings up on Northern so you can get out of the rain a bit and get rid of a few pounds of flyers. Up here." He circled some blobs. "Once you do the buildings, go like this ..." His black pen started moving around on the page. "Then you go here," he said, tracing his way back over all the black lines he'd already drawn. "That way," said Phil, assuming she was keeping up, "you get the north part done, then you can snake your way back down, and you go between Lansdowne and Brock. Go back and forth."

He leaned away from the clipboard to be able to see the clip. He pressed, and it sprang open. Phil pulled out the map for Becca to take. "That's the way I'd do it, but you can do what you want, okay?"

Becca was silent. She was looking at the blobs, trying to under-stand which way she was supposed to go after she'd started. Phil asked, "Do you want me to show you again?" He paused a few seconds. "Ask me. I won't be mad."

"No, thank you," Becca answered quietly, but on the inside, she was totally freaking out.

"Are you sure?"

Becca nodded.

The more Phil tried to be nice, the more Becca's panic grew. Clearly, he could see she was going to mess up. He was going to get a call, and she would get yelled at. Everyone could tell how much of a freak she was just by looking at her.

"Could I have my flyers, please?"

Becca was surprised that her voice came out sounding like it was ready to pop like another lame rain cloud.

Phil started shaking his head. "No. I'm sorry. I don't feel good about this. I think this is too much responsibility for you. I think we should call your mom."

"I can do it. Honest!"

Phil kept shaking his head. Becca hadn't seen his big hand com-ing in for her shoulder, coming down for a pat. She screamed, kicked the passenger door open, and leapt out. She turned, looking back at Phil from the rain-drenched sidewalk, bug-eyed.

·"Don't touch me!"

"What did I do? What did I do?" Phil asked.

"Give me my flyers," Becca screamed with as much fierceness as she could muster —although it really was just desperation.

A businessman walking past with an umbrella slowed down and looked at them both with great suspicion, but he kept walking.

"Go around the back. Go around." Phil had had enough. He wedged himself through the small space between the seats. Becca walked to the back of the van and waited in the rain for the rear cargo doors to open.

Phil pushed one of them out. Becca cautiously stood a few feet away but peered into the back of the van. It didn't have carpeting or a mattress or any of the things her mother had suggested might be there. She felt like she should explain to Phil, but maybe it was too late for that.

Phil pulled a box toward him and tore the top flap open. He counted out flyers, tossing them near the open cargo door in bundles of twenty-five for Becca to pick up. They were not single sheets as she had imagined. They were bunches of grocery store flyers that came bundled in plastic.

Becca awkwardly stuffed them into her carrier bag, which kept trying to fold back on itself, while Phil hung back and did busywork like checking things off clipboards. He was not smiling. When she was done, he addressed her.

"Look," he said, his nose whistling as he breathed. "What you just did back there was not cool. I am not into neurotic fourteen-year-old girls. You got me?"

He was really upset. If he'd had the room to pace, he totally would have.

"Boy, I don't know what your problem is — and I don't want to know — but you are one messed-up kid." He grabbed the handle of the cargo door. "I'm coming back to check on you later, all right? Because it's my job, and I am your boss. So when you see my van, do me a favour and try not to lose your shit."

Becca started to nod to show that yes, she understood, but Phil slammed the door before she even got through nodding a second time.

Without further ceremony, he put the van into drive and pulled away.

The rain felt brutally cold on Becca's face. This was the real world.

52

Message Received

IN THE TIME IT had taken her to walk a few blocks, Becca had lost her map. She remembered the basic area she was supposed to cover and that she was supposed to start with the apartment buildings in the distance, so she decided she was going to do like Phil had suggested and go there to get rid of a bunch of heavy flyers first.

Now that they'd been on her shoulder a while, they felt like they were sawing into her flesh. Becca slung the bag across her chest, tearing a few new holes in her rain cape in the process, but at least her shoulder felt better.

As she reached Northern Avenue, Becca came to a full stop. She'd had no sense of the size of the buildings until she stood right in front of them. The complex was massive. One of the structures was the size of two normal-sized buildings.

Someone held the front door open for her. She walked in.

Becca had never been in an actual apartment complex before. Most of the people her mom knew lived in either houses or condos. This building didn't look anything like those.

The lobby was all old-person colours, empty and dull. There were two slightly mismatched peach leather wing chairs turned in toward each other like an invitation to sit and have a conversa-tion — except for the fact that the chairs were off-limits, kept behind a long, white plastic chain like a museum rope. They didn't look special, but how could anyone know for sure.

While she waited for an elevator, Becca pulled off her plastic hood, letting her head breathe a bit, and became conscious of how hot and cold she was everywhere else. Her left arm had started to throb.

By the time the elevator arrived, she'd decided to start at the top of the building and work her way down. Becca punched the button for the fifteenth floor. Nothing happened. She punched the floor number a bunch more times until the doors finally closed. The elevator was finished in real plastic "wood panelling" and made her think of the motel and Wayne. She probably shouldn't have burned his clothes.

As the elevator reached the top floor, the door crabbed open. Becca stepped out into a hallway that felt like she was walking into a game of *Doom*.

The lighting on the penthouse floor was dim and flickered. A glaze of desperation clung to everything — the walls, the places around the doors. It stuck to people's stuff too — the baby carriages, the shopping buggies, the umbrellas in the hallway. Nothing looked pretty or bright or cheery. It was all asphyxiated by a fine layer of poverty and a cloying old-lettuce smell that seeped out under the apartment doors into the hallway.

Phil hadn't exactly had a chance to go over all the details, but Becca was pretty sure she didn't have to knock at every individual door and say, "Here's your flyer, sir." She'd drop one in front of every door so it could get discovered, like an unexpected gift.

Behind one door, she heard a TV set. At another, an angry conversation in some Asian language.

When she'd finished the floor, she started down the stairs.

Big mistake. She walked right in on a furious white dude with dreads shaking down a scrawny, scared-shitless guy. The dreads dude turned on her all fierce, and though his lips didn't move, she definitely received his "Get the fuck out of here" message.

Becca accommodated his request and ran back to the world's slowest elevator, punching the call button repeatedly until it arrived.

It took her almost an hour to finish the first building on Northern. She was less meticulous with the others, but still, it was past nine o'clock when she started to criss-cross the streets with just the houses.

It had started raining again, even harder than before. Becca's sneakers were gurgling like they had pneumonia. She felt so hot under her plastic wrap she started poking extra holes in it to create some ventilation until she got too cold. The pain in her arm was starting to kill her.

Around O'Hara Avenue, Becca noticed a crazy number of missing dog posters in all kinds of colours and sizes. It started to creep her out, particularly since she remembered Phil's warning about serial killers.

She wondered if there was any truth to it. It was hard to know who was on the level when it came to adults, because they all lied. Like, they'd say how something wouldn't hurt when it did, or how good something looked when it didn't. Becca was beginning to suspect her mother's warning about vans had been completely wrong. Thanks to her, talking to Phil would undoubtedly be awkward from now on.

He probably hadn't meant anything by putting his hand on her shoulder. She imagined he'd gone home to watch *The Bachelor* with Jeanette.

Most of the houses along the residential section of Becca's route were old, narrow brick buildings with pointy roofs. Halloween looked good on them. It seemed way harder to get a horror vibe happening on a modern house, especially when you could look all the way inside it and see bored people staring at their iPads. The other thing she noticed was that the further you got away from the buildings on Northern, the more jumpy the people became. Like, yes, it was a little late, and maybe one or two dogs had started full-on baying while Becca was trying to stuff flyers into mailboxes, but some people were totally losing it. One man made her take her flyer back. And one woman had lurched out her front door in snowflake pajamas and boots, barely managing to hang on to her dog's collar, screaming, "What the fuck are you doing here?" Like Becca had ruined her life. Like no one had ever delivered flyers after nine before.

Since she'd lost the area map Phil had given her, Becca had decided to deliver until she was out of flyers. It was a decision she was beginning to regret. As she wondered whether she could go home, she noticed a dilapidated house the next block over. It had a legit Addams Family creep to it, except more serious. A few small windows on the third floor were busted and looked half-assed patched. Becca couldn't see anyone living there, and yet she could feel the house watching.

The grounds were guarded by an ornate metal fence with aggressive spikes that were partially gnawed out by rust. Grasses and leaves and tall, dead flowers were pressed right up against the wrought iron curlicues as though the vegetation itself was looking for a way to escape. Something grabbed the back of her rain cape. Becca swivelled back fast, on the absolute verge of screaming, when she realized the cape was snagged on a branch. Her heart still pounding in her chest, she stood by the front gate contemplating the overgrown path to the house.

She could have tossed a flyer into the front yard and moved on, but something compelled her to ignore her fear and walk right up to the house.

She pulled up the latch and pushed the gate in.

There was a well-worn groove in the flagstone path where the rod had scraped it hundreds of times before. Becca started up the walk, past a deep thicket of plants that edged the property. She thought they might be irises or lilies gone rogue. It was hard to tell. The rest of the front yard was returning to its natural state. Creepers and low, flat bushes spread out all over the yard like a scratchy quilting pattern. She decided not to think about what she could hear rustling around in the spaces beneath the leaves among the headless flowers.

As she paused under the branches of a gigantic oak that partially blocked the downpour, Becca could hear the rain trying to penetrate the leaf canopy overhead. The oak also seemed to have a strange sound-dampening effect, because now she could barely hear traffic noises.

Vines grew rampant over the front of the house, only autumn had turned them into long, rusty snail trails winding through the peeling grey paint. As she climbed the stairs to the front door, Becca saw at least a dozen ancient flyers on the landing. They'd been rained on, bleached and hardened by the sun over time. They looked more like arm bones than announcements for margarine and green beans.

She peered in through the door's small, dirty window. The house was completely dark inside. For sure, it was abandoned. And then she heard a noise.

Before she could even understand what she was doing, Becca went back down the front steps to investigate the sound. It seemed to be coming from the back of the house. She stood under the oak tree looking for a way around the house until she could intuit the barest of paths in the vegetation. She followed it through the low shrubs, moving between barbed thistle plants alongside the house, past mottled patches of dark green moss, her feet straining to stay on the canting, slippery flagstones.

Up ahead was a wooden gate. The sound she could hear was coming from just beyond it. That's when Becca got a whiff of a strange odour. A dank, rotten smell.

Every instinct told her to turn back, but something else kept urging her to go forward. If her mom was right, if the universe was perpetually trying to send her a message she'd ignored, if destiny had actually been leading her footsteps from the "fakeduction" to a new way of being, it was leading her to whatever was happening in the backyard. She couldn't *not* look.

Cautiously, Becca pushed open the gate.

The grass beyond the gate was so wet it sparkled like it was covered in tiny diamonds. Deep in the yard, she could make out a heavyset man wearing black rain gear standing amid mounds of earth. The man tossed aside a few shovelfuls of dirt and stood back to consider the hole he'd created. With a grunt, he planted his spade in the bank and walked out of view.

He'd been gone long enough for Becca to begin debating whether she should leave when she heard something heavy being dragged, followed by what was probably a string of curse words.

The man reappeared and crossed the yard to fetch a wheelbarrow from a dilapidated shed; he pushed it back toward the house over the long, lumpy grass. He reappeared again a few moments later, pushing it with a Herculean effort. The front wheel kept getting gummed up in the long grass and sinking deep into furrows of mud.

The man grunted and pushed until the wheelbarrow sat right at the edge of the hole he'd dug. He stopped there a few moments to catch his breath. Becca could see something big resting in the bucket, wrapped in black plastic.

The man studied his load, then he picked up his spade, got into the hole, and removed several more shovelfuls of dirt. Tossing the spade aside, he climbed out of the hole and tried to slide the black garbage bag toward him, but he wasn't getting any traction. He walked around the wheelbarrow, looking for a better handhold. When he found it, his hand came down hard on the garbage bag with a *thwack*. Becca instantly recognized the sound of flesh hitting flesh, even through plastic. The man drew the heavy bag into the hole.

Shocked, Becca stumbled back into the gate, which creaked.

The man looked over.

Becca told herself to run.

This time, she listened.

Her legs carried her back up the path, past the dying lilies, and through the wrought iron gate. Her rain poncho caught on the speared tip of a post. She turned around and ripped it free. She ran and she ran, and stopped only when she'd run out of breath. Traffic whizzed past her as she bent over, wheezing and nauseous. She'd never seen death before, but she'd recognized its heaviness and silence as it fell deep into the earth.

The universe's message had been received.

53

Wearables

BECCA COULD CONFIRM THAT the ability to feel was overrated. She'd felt too much of everything before, and now, mercifully, she felt next to nothing. All her senses were dulled, overwhelmed by her recent experiences. Only the throbbing pulse in the cut of her arm confirmed she was alive.

Someone shouted, "Nice costume, loser!" as she crossed the quad, presumably for her benefit, but in view of what she'd witnessed the night before, insults no longer ranked as significant.

Besides, Becca hadn't worn a costume since grade six when she'd gone to school as a Special K flake. She'd put a lot of work into building it, spray-painting bits of foam just the right shade of orangey-brown and sewing them onto long johns. Then a kid had decided she looked like a scab, and the name stuck to her through junior high. Because, of course ...

Throngs of students were milling around, thrilled for a chance to play dress-up. Guys in rubber masks of mass murderers and girls pretending to be innocent childhood characters who'd accidentally grown out of their clothes overnight and became Cat Sluts and Angel Skanks. They were all going to hook up at the dumb school dance and pretend Halloween wasn't days away. It all seemed so meaningless now that she'd seen death. Not the sexy, provocative version with dark lipstick, smoky eyeshadow, and candles — real death.

The cuts on her arm had begged for her attention all night, but Becca had been incapable of tending to them. She'd become captive to her mind's eye, remembering how the man's skin had shone in the rain, how his hands had been creased with grime, and how his eyes had been dark, expressionless beads.

It was amazing how she'd held on to every detail. How the plastic had crinkled as the body slipped around inside the bag. How the body had plopped onto the ground. The complete absence of protest or expression of pain. Just the grunts coming from the dark-faced man. And the muted sound of rain sinking into the mounds of dark earth around the grave.

She replayed the events of the previous night over and over as she shuffled between classes, rocking the images backward and forward like a video. By math class, she'd started to wonder whether she'd seen the bag move. By history, she'd convinced herself she'd seen the outline of a face pressed up against the plastic. By French, she felt sure she'd watched someone get buried alive. She let herself slip deeper and deeper into the moments, imagining every second until she'd lived the stranger's final moments. Until she'd decided that death wasn't a release from the ugliness of living. It was a continuation of it. You were alone in it, and afterward, someone ditched you. Maybe the comfort death gave you was that you wouldn't have to be aware of anything after it.

The period bell rang. Becca needed to escape the darkening thoughts that were gathering in her brain. She would have liked some time to make sense of what she'd seen in the man's yard, but there was nowhere to go, no one to talk it through with.

She walked toward the bus stop, telling herself she had to get out of her gloomy headspace, but all she could see were people who reminded her of how she felt. People with long commas hanging off the corners of their mouths, women with heavy bags no one wanted to acknowledge. Old people in cars staring at traffic lights, opening and closing their mouths to breathe, like they'd just been yanked from a lake. She couldn't stand it. She heard a truck's brakes shriek and realized she'd stepped out in front of it.

Confused and embarrassed, Becca bolted across the street toward the mall, straight into the shitty consignment clothing store, and brought five random pairs of jeans into the fitting room. The instant she closed the door, she lost it.

The saleslady, who normally hated her because she never bought anything, gently knocked, asking if she could bring her some pants in a different size. Becca only cried louder. She could hear the saleslady hovering around the other side of the fitting room door, trying to determine what to do. When the woman asked if there was anyone she could call, Becca managed to answer that she was okay, that she was expecting her period and had found out her boyfriend was married.

After that, the woman left her alone.

When she eventually managed to get it together, she slipped her prescription Guccis over her full-on puffy eyes and bought a vintage seventies poncho using the credit card her mother had given her to use only in emergencies. The poncho was brown, gold, white, and orange and had a fringe all the way around. Becca walked all the way home, wearing her poncho in the rain, crying on and off, thinking that she'd eventually have to run out of tears.

She went up to her room and drew the curtains shut, utterly exhausted by crying. Shivering and sore, with a headache coming on, Becca stripped off most of her wet clothes, then burrowed deep into the rumpled sheets, seeking dark, quiet shelter under her comforter.

She wanted to curl up inside herself and disappear, like the snake that swallowed its own tail, only she couldn't figure out what to do with the last little bit of herself still left dangling outside in the world.

Becca picked up her phone, and the inside of her dark grey sheet cave lit up.

She studied the picture of the missing dog for several minutes. She wondered whether the man loved it enough to keep searching. Whether he would welcome it home, no matter how messed up it had become.

She wished Wayne Jennings had been more dangerous. She wished something different had happened in the motel. She wished she was braver. But she knew someone who could help her.

As she drifted off to sleep, Becca could imagine herself floating out from under her blankets and up toward something warm and dry. Toward a feeling she'd hadn't experienced in a while, but which she could identify as relief.

54

Follow Through

WHEN BECCA HAD FIRST started thinking about dying, death had had very little to do with it. She'd mostly thought through how she needed to look for maximum effect. She'd wanted the people who saw her dead to feel shock.

She'd imagined she would straighten her hair and wear makeup and clothes she still didn't own. She would be thinner, and her hands would be folded just so. She'd wanted her death to be called tragic because that's how beautiful people always died.

But although she'd skipped school to prepare, clearly, her last day on earth would not be her best. She looked grey, as though some internal dimmer switch had been turned down low, except for the cut on her arm, which was glowing. The red welt around one of the gashes had started to spread into a line up her arm. Maybe it would eventually point at something or spell *I'm with Stupid*. She didn't care. It really didn't matter anymore.

Shivering from her shower, Becca wrapped herself in the toffee-coloured bath towel her mother usually reserved for guests. She wished she could enjoy its super plushness more, but her skin felt like paper. She was afraid if she rubbed too hard, she'd tear a hole through herself, and her guts and bones would come spilling out in a jumble on the floor.

What she wanted most now was comfort. She dressed in the

peach-coloured bra her mom had told her to throw away, mid–wash jeans, and her softest beige cami that had an ancient balsamic vinegar stain on it. Over that, she slipped on her oldest, most favouritest hoodie. It was all raggedy around the cuffs, but she drew a lot of comfort out of the way the wristbands drooped over her fingers like velvety body armour. They'd been through a lot, this hoodie and her: scary movies, sad songs, long, dreamless sleeps.

Becca buttoned and zipped every item of clothing slowly, consciously doing every action. This was the last time she'd even out the pull strings in her hoodie, the last time she'd draw socks over her feet. The last time she'd put on clear lip gloss.

She called Dylan, not even sure why she thought she ought to, but he wasn't weird about it or anything. She noticed how even when she was silent, Dylan never hurried her. He waited for her to say the next thing. It's like he knew she needed the time to hear she was being listened to.

It was after one of those long silences that she surprised herself and said what she was thinking out loud. "I'm ready."

"For what?"

"To die."

He stayed quiet a moment.

"Back in grade nine," he said, "I wanted to serve a vampire and become immortal."

"That's not the same."

"I know. I'm saying people change their minds about tons of things. All the time. Situations change. No matter how shitty you think things are right now, maybe you'll feel differently about them tomorrow."

She didn't want to agree. "Did you ever find any?"

"Vampires?"

"Yeah."

"Not real ones," he said. He sounded a bit sad.

BEFORE SHE LEFT, BECCA emptied out her pockets and left her phone, her bus pass, and $7.65 in change on the top of her dresser so her mom would be able to find everything later. Caroline could sell her bed, her clothes, whatever, and put the money against her debt.

Caroline and Karl's voices were rising and falling in the living room. Hearing her mom laugh made her smile for a second. Then tear up. She clearly had no clue how to feel about anything anymore. It really was time to go.

She pulled her poncho over her hoodie and headed down the driveway, clutching her smelly red carrier bag. She kept her eyes on the road ahead. As she reached Parkside Drive, she saw how the sun was just starting to dip behind High Park, beyond the tree line, the hockey rink, the pond, melting into the edge of the world.

Becca turned toward Parkdale, determined to find the man who'd buried a body behind his house.

Phil's van appeared down the street just as she arrived. Becca walked down the sidewalk to meet it. This time, Phil kept the motor running and didn't bother lowering his window to say hello or to invite her in. He just headed straight for the back of the van. Once more, Jeanette was nowhere to be found. Becca was starting to suspect that she never rode around in the van. It was one of those things she told parents to reassure them. People were willing to believe anything as long as they got the outcome they wanted.

She walked around the van to the cargo doors at the back and waited for her flyers. She'd only worked one night, but already she knew its drudgery. She could anticipate the feeling of the carrier bag cutting into her shoulder.

The cargo door swung open.

Phil barely made eye contact. He kept his profile to her and started counting flyers, which he tossed toward her every fifteen seconds or so.

"Didn't think I'd see you here tonight," he said, almost as

though he was speaking aloud to himself.

Becca wasn't sure whether Phil was saying that she had a lot of nerve showing up or that he was surprised to see her come back a second night. She stayed quiet.

"Things go okay?" he asked. "After the ..." He stopped himself. He was clearly torn between wanting to make sure he was being responsible and wanting to stay the hell away from her.

"Yes."

He nodded. "Good."

"Can I get another map?"

Phil nodded. He tossed down the last bundle of flyers and waited for her to shove them into her carrier bag. When Becca was done, he gave her a copy the map and simply said, "Okay. See you next week." Then he pulled the cargo door shut and drove away. She started walking toward the big buildings on Northern.

Most of Becca's memory of her first night of work was a blur. Between the rain and her being so scared of screwing up, she couldn't remember where the man in the dilapidated house lived. She couldn't even be sure his house hadn't been in someone else's delivery zone, so she decided to retrace her steps.

This time, as she strode into the lobby of the first apartment building, she veered away from the elevators and dumped all her flyers onto the table near the mailboxes. The people who wanted flyers could take them. She did the same in the second building.

She followed the delivery route Phil had redrawn for her. She looked at the houses, hoping each one would tweak a memory of a person or a direction. Maybe if she saw the angry woman with the angry dog, she'd remember which way she'd gone. Maybe if it started raining again. Maybe, maybe, maybe. For hours, everything she saw remained vaguely familiar. And then Becca stopped in her tracks.

The house stood in the distance, looking as dark and dilapidated as she remembered it.

She crossed the street toward it and walked alongside the rusted curls and twists of the wrought iron fence. When she reached the gate, Becca did not pause. She lifted the latch and nudged the gate open. It complained loudly as she walked in and started up the flagstone path. It seemed as though the plants were trying to prevent her from making it to the house. Her feet snagged on vines. But she kicked through them or stepped over them, her eyes locked on the dirty front door. Becca wasn't afraid anymore. She was just impatient for the end to arrive.

She climbed the front steps and firmly pressed the buzzer. A loud electrical noise tore through the house.

Becca wondered whether the man would remember her. Whether he'd think she was there to start trouble. She needed him to know she wanted him to do it. To kill her. She couldn't do it by herself.

She waited several more minutes, then it occurred to her he could be in the backyard. Becca dropped the carrier bag off her shoulder and went around the house. She pushed the rear gate open and walked right out into the middle of the yard.

She could see the grass hadn't been mowed all summer. It was sopping wet and flopped over like a turbulent green sea frozen mid-swell. She crossed toward the mound of earth, walking by the rickety wheelbarrow where the black plastic bag had been. She pressed her hand inside the bucket as she passed, half expecting it to feel warm. Like time hadn't moved since the other night. But of course, it had. Only her thoughts had stayed put.

She stood quietly at the foot of the freshly shovelled earth shaped into a smooth mound. She pressed the toe of her dark rubber boot into the dirt and watched it sink inches into it, as though the black earth was predisposed to swallow whatever was introduced.

Suddenly, the back of Becca's neck went cold. She spun around and stared at the house. She could feel him. She was sure of it. But only the small, dark windows looked back. Why hadn't he answered the door?

Now she was worried. Becca walked back to the front of the house. She'd read once how serial killers had types. Maybe she wasn't his. Maybe she had to trigger him. If he told her what he needed, she would do it. She pushed the doorbell. "Come on," she said under her breath, pushing the buzzer again. "Please!" she shouted. He was the only person who could help her. Despairing, she rammed herself against the door. After the third thud, the door opened. Becca blinked with surprise.

She pushed it open the rest of the way and walked in.

The house was dark and smelled like earth and fried fish. After a bit, she could make out the details of some dull mauve wallpaper with a grapevine and trellis pattern on it, leading visitors down the hall toward the back of the house. In spots, the wallpaper seemed to sag under the weight of the grapes. The rest of the house was a mystery because anything that was a few feet from windows and streetlights fell into obscurity.

She walked into the front parlour, which seemed to be used as a place for storing broken tables and chairs. He'd covered them with cardboard boxes and random bags of junk. He was a hoarder — not to the level of walking on sacks of old food and clothes, but still, there was a lot. It took only a few moments for Becca to notice the things that the man didn't want to lose in the rubble because he'd lined them up on the fireplace mantle.

There was a fine gold chain. A hair ribbon. A children's book about a little red hen. And a dog collar. She was in the right place.

Becca heard a clatter of pots at the rear of the house. It sounded like someone in the kitchen was throwing things around.

She pulled off her hair scrunchie and set it down next to the other offerings on the altar. She hoped the dark-eyed man would be quick. Soon, it would all be over.

55

Lost and Found

AROUND 2:00 A.M., THERE was a sound.

It woke Brent just enough to make him wonder whether it warranted further investigation. It was an unfamiliar noise. As he lay in his bed, rising up through layers of consciousness, the noise repeated.

It sounded like scratching, he decided. A mouse trying to get in or a branch brushing up against the siding in the sunroom. It was nothing. He reminded himself he'd checked the doors, the windows, and the latches before coming to bed, and thankfully, he felt his worries beginning to recede.

Good thing too. He had a 9:00 a.m. class. Lecture on the Red Cross Knight.

As he began to lose track of the world outside his room, the noise returned.

Brent sat up, drowsy and discombobulated. Then he remembered he'd taken another sleeping pill. Damn his luck. He tried to focus on the sound.

If he'd had to describe it in a short story, he'd have written it as having a persistent quality. But hearing it more fully this time, he realized it sounded nothing like a mouse or a branch. The noise was bigger. There was heft behind it.

Threatening texts from a few angry dog lovers sprang to mind.

Holding the bottle of oven cleaner he'd started to keep by the bed, Brent staggered out into his living room to track down the origins of the noise.

It was coming from outside.

He carefully peered out the back bay window to investigate. The yard was dark, but he spied a muddle of white moving through a stain of moonlight on the lawn. Then, as suddenly as he'd seen it, the creature disappeared, absorbed by inky night.

"Gary?" Brent whispered.

Brent lurched toward the door, somehow made it down the stairs and spilled out into the side yard, barefoot in the cold, wet grass, but Gary had disappeared again.

He stood still a few moments, listening, hoping to catch a sound that might betray Gary when the noise that had woken him earlier, returned. Clearly, this time. Digging. It was digging. Which was puzzling, given the hour. Brent peered over the fence and could see the neighbour, working in a garden bed on the other side.

Brent drew slightly nearer, curious to know what was going on. The old fellow's face was glistening with sweat, his nostrils were drawn wide from the effort of moving what sounded like a high volume of earth. But it was his eyes which were most troubling. The whites of them shone too brightly. They almost glowed blue with manic intensity. Brent now understood why Kate had felt unnerved.

The man looked up and discovered Brent watching him. He'd been startled and looked angry.

"I'm sorry. This is not ... I didn't mean to disturb you," said Brent. "It's only that I just saw my dog out here."

The darkness in the man's eyes deepened.

"From my hou—" Brent stopped short as something in his neighbour's expression shifted. "My window looks onto this yard. I saw Gary right here. I don't know where he is exactly but I imagine he's wandered back into your yard." The man ran his thick hand along the top of the fence and wrapped his meaty fingers around the fence post. The other hand appeared on top of the next fence section.

"Gary is my dog," Brent said, suspecting Gary's ownership might be in contention.

The man's arms and shoulders tensed. He looked spring-loaded, like he was going to do something.

"Now, there's no need for this," said Brent, beginning to back away.

The neighbour's eyes twinkled even as he was prying open the fence.

"I want my dog back," shouted Brent, backing away while pretending he was in a position of power. "Gary!" he called. "Gary!!"

The neighbour pried the fence sections almost a foot apart, slipped his leg through the gap, and began to push his way into Brent's yard in earnest.

Brent stumbled as his foot slipped off the corner of the concrete landing. Realizing he'd retreated to his door, he turned toward it. His keys were in his hand. Within seconds, he'd jammed the wrong key into the lock. He flew into a panic, tugging and twisting the key until he wrested it back from the door to try again but no matter how hard he tried, he couldn't make the right key fit. Behind him, the fence's creaking and groaning grew louder and more violent until the neighbour was free of it, his face red and angry and glistening like a newborn from hell.

Brent regretted he was going to die in a T-shirt and track pants, without ever having distinguished himself professionally.

The neighbour was almost upon him.

Brent raised his arm over his face. "No!" he screamed. "*Nooo!*"

Brent's eyes popped open to the sound of his own shrieks. His heart still racing, his T-shirt drenched, it took him more than a few moments to understand he'd been dreaming. He was safe. In his bed. And he could still hear someone digging.

56

Still Life with Death

NASH HAD SAID IT before, and she'd say it again: Halloween was one of those holidays that needed to be celebrated on the day. You had to commit. Especially when Halloween was on a Friday. Celebrating it on a Wednesday when you had other options only made people second-guess your ability to run a school. And with a name like Mary the Immaculate, it was fair to say that people were second-guessing you from the get-go.

This year, Carmella was to blame. Long story short, the world's oldest secretary had strutted into the staff meeting with a half-eaten tuna sandwich, smelling like a day at the seaside asking to reschedule the dance because her nephew, the regular DJ, had booked a wedding on Halloween.

The administration caved to Carmella's request, but Nash dared anyone to push back on her right to wear a Raggedy Ann costume to work on the correct day. She also hoped the newlyweds who'd ruined Halloween enjoyed their evening of Monster Mash, Britney Spears, and all-80s hair bands.

Once the kids were mostly sitting, Nash looked at her clipboard. "Becca? Becca Chalmers?" There was an irritating silence in response.

"Has anyone seen Becca Chalmers?" she asked.

"She wasn't in math," said the kid with the unibrow.

"Jesus," said Nash under her breath. These still life projects were a complete disaster, and for that, she had the Ministry of Education to thank. Nash glanced back down at her clipboard again and found the next kid's name. "Can Krista Turnbull come talk to me?"

"She broke her leg."

"Of course she did," Nash said quietly.

"Does that mean class is dismissed?" some smart-ass asked.

"No, it doesn't mean class is dismissed," Nash answered. She put her hand on her hip. "Why would that mean class is dismissed? Art is all around us. You just have to open your eyes to draw inspiration from it." Comments like that bugged the hell out of her. Stupid kid. Round face. Eyes like a cod. She was tempted to dock him participation points for being an idiot.

"Somebody said this was supposed to be an easy class," he answered.

"That's an easy A," she corrected. "And no, it isn't." It was an easy C-plus. She knew what a bell curve looked like. "Remind me who you are again?"

"Josh Martins?"

"Right." Nash walked to her desk to write it down because she wouldn't remember it. That done, she turned to her collection of vases and found objects, trying to conjure up a challenging way to present them. As the year wore on, the students swiped the good stuff and left her with a shelf full of ugly. Nash sighed. She didn't remember signing up for improvisation classes in teachers' college, but here she was, turning a broom into a banjo.

She spotted her thermos on her desk and wished — not for the first time — that there was something stronger than coffee in it. It had a big, interesting pattern on it — definitely one of her finer scores. She'd spotted it laid out on a blanket on a sidewalk downtown as she was going in to get her streaks done, and she'd talked the old guy down to fifty cents.

It occurred to her that maybe she could group together a bunch of boldly patterned objects and get the class to draw them and fill out the pattern to explore balancing shapes using only one colour. Done.

She started pulling patterned objects from her shelves.

The Goth kid with the gigantic feet came in and nodded inquisitively toward the private little work area. She nodded. He was doing some independent project, but she was damned if she could remember his name.

She started rummaging through the box of good stuff she kept under her desk when she heard a buzz at the front of the classroom.

"Patterns, patterns," she said out loud, not wanting to lose her train of thought. "Things with patterns." She found a strange little rug. She remembered she also had an art book with an overdesigned cover, and then suddenly it hit her that if she was in the book section, she had run out of patterned things. Jesus. She'd have to rethink the whole shebang.

She heard the class suddenly go quiet. Something was wrong. Dammit. She hurried back around the partition and saw Becca, covered in dirt. Her clothes, her face, even her hands were dark and slicked with something black and oily. Her hair hung in long, wet, dirty ribbons in front of her face, and she was wearing some horrid homemade poncho thing that looked like it had been regurgitated during an acid trip. Her eyes stared blankly ahead, and she had a slight shake. She was a zombie. One of the undead. She'd nailed it perfectly.

"Nicely done, Becca. You look freshly risen from the grave." She might have been a kid with a dark soul, but she was making it work for her.

Nash pointed to the red carrier bag Becca had slung on her shoulder. "Please tell me that's your still life art project." Something in the girl's eyes changed. Nash decided to go with it. "Great. Put your stuff up either on the cube or the pillar and we'll see if we can guess how it reflects you."

Becca stepped up onto the riser. She looked a bit unsteady, but it was part of the spectacle. She was definitely getting an A for effort.

"Bitch looks like she needs some serious meds," Nash overheard a student comment.

Nash just hated the way the students tore each other up, so she wasn't about to let the comment go. "Remember when you wore an eyepatch through most of grade nine and everyone called you 'Lazy Eye'? Did you like that?" she asked. The kid went quiet. You had to shut the meanness down, or it would go on and on. She turned to the class. "You guys could all learn a thing or two from Becca. She has committed to her vision."

Nash remembered a green satin fabric sample that would prob-ably make a terrific drape or swag for Becca's Ode to Grimness. She'd barely turned around when one boy said, "What the fuck?" She heard chairs scraping the floor. Someone else said, "Beat it, freak."

Although Nash had a rule about intervening in the kids' inter-necine struggles, she couldn't fake not hearing the aggression. She stepped around the partition once more.

"What the hell is going on?"

She saw Becca pulling crumpled photocopied papers out of her bag. She was trying to hand them out to the students, but they kept shrinking away from her.

"What's the problem?" said Nash. "What is wrong with you guys? This is cool and different. Becca, good job."

"No, but Miss —"

"This is participatory art." The girl had obviously summered at art camp. "Becca doesn't want us to be only observers of her work, she wants us to help create it. Right?"

True to form, the kid said nothing, so Nash had to keep kicking the ball. "Okay, Becca, what do you need us to do with your crum-pled whatevers."

"Miss. Look at her hands."

Puzzled, Nash turned back and looked. What she'd assumed was dirty, greasy makeup was actually dirty, greasy blood. "Woah," Nash said quietly, pulling the red wool Raggedy Ann wig off her head.

Some uptight kid at the back of the class who'd stood up to get a better view started saying "Oh my God!" over and over again. Nash saw the cell phones coming out.

"Okay," she said. "Everybody out. Free period."

Of course, now she had to hustle them out one by one. The girl repeating Oh-my-God wouldn't let up. For kids who were all into TV shows about eating brains, some of them honestly had a seriously low tolerance for gore.

The gangly goth kid was making his way up from the back of the class. Nash could see him trying to wrap his head around what he'd stumbled into.

"Rebecca?" he said.

He knew her. "Can you stay here with her?" Nash asked, quietly closing the classroom door. "I need to find out if the nurse is in today."

DYLAN DREW CLOSER TO Becca, his eyes roving over her hands without understanding. "Oh. That doesn't look ..." His voice trailed off.

Becca studied her hands as though her fingers were part of a foreign landscape. She could tell they hurt, but the full pain wasn't reaching her through her numbness and the cold and the pain in her arm.

Dylan put his hand on her forehead.

"You have a fever. Becca? Can you look at me a minute?"

Her head followed his voice like it was on autopilot.

"I tried to call you back last night. I was worried."

Becca knew he was talking to her, but she was remembering being little, watching her dad carrying a box of trophies to the car and her mom following him, shouting, trying to take the box away. Becca was holding a bucket of flower petals, watching her mom and dad. They were really, really angry and being loud. Then her mom said something, and her dad swung the passenger door open, but he didn't see Becca standing right behind it.

And the door hit her in the mouth.

She remembered a gush of warm blood on her tongue that tasted like metal. The bucket falling, red petals all over the pavement. She remembered screams. And no one hearing hers because her parents were screaming louder, but at each other. There was so much noise, no one knew what to pay attention to. Like now. So much noise.

Then something clicked, and Becca could tell the noise wasn't just inside her head, it was on the outside too. And it was coming from her.

57

Bad Memories

I GO IN BACK for to work.

Man, he was out of practice speaking English, but even *he* knew that didn't sound right. Maybe he would skip that part and stick to the facts.

I hear bark. You dog was bark.

That much would be understood. It had to be. Barking was all the white dog did. Somehow, it had wandered into his yard. It had been the first time Coste had stood so close to it. He had spoken to it quietly. He'd never fully trusted dogs, especially big ones, so he didn't want to handle it. It didn't appear distressed. It barked once or twice. Once it knew it had company, it was quiet. Coste was sure the owner would eventually come outside, and he would wave him over.

Mister. I wait for to see you. Come please.

He kept an eye out for the man as he did yard work. The ghost dog followed him around, smelling all the different smells in his garden. The freshly turned earth. The fish fertilizer. The overripe tomatoes. The garlic. It fell asleep in his shed.

Eventually, he spotted the neighbour running around out front, and he went out to get his attention, but the woman was with him. He didn't want to talk to her.

Then he saw the dog posters everywhere, and it occurred to him he was the reason they'd been out all morning. The dog had been in the backyard with him the whole time they'd been searching. What was he going to say? *Sorry, mister?* He would come across as a simpleton, or worse, a thief or a liar. He decided he'd hide the dog and sneak it back into its own yard later that night.

He carried a chair into the shed and sat with the dog so it wouldn't bark. It seemed happy enough. Around 6:00 p.m., Coste opened a tin of sardines, which the dog persuaded him to share. Coste kept the dog at a safe distance. He wasn't thrilled about hand-feeding a monster with a gigantic maw, but the dog plucked the sardines from his fingers with the utmost delicacy. When the can was empty, it lapped up the salty yellow oil that had dripped on the shed floor. It took a few lumbering steps forward.

Coste wasn't sure what it was doing. But then it licked his fingers clean, and Coste realized he hadn't felt another being's warmth in a long time. The dog stood in front of him a while, like it was waiting for his sadness to pass.

Coste patted it. The dog seemed pleased.

Coste pulled out a large bar of dark chocolate and slowly peeled back the thin foil. The dog returned with great interest. Coste shared the chocolate too.

The dog seemed content and curled up to sleep. Later, when it was dark enough, Coste came back to fetch the dog and discovered it was dead. He didn't know why. He didn't know how. It was dead. He sat with it a while, hoping it was a mistake.

It was not.

He came out of the shed, feeling anxiety and anger burgeoning in him, wondering how he could ever explain to the man what had happened, when he noticed the woman spying on him, her face already saying she blamed him.

58

Sound of Silence

THE NURSE WASN'T IN so Greeley had brought Becca to her office to wait for Caroline.

Her office was small and smelled like cigarettes and old shoes. Classic Greeley. Her furniture was ugly and worn. It looked like she had brought a lamp from home to try to make her desk cozier. It had a plaid lampshade with a line of little felt Scotties running around the edges, but one of the dogs had escaped, leaving behind the barest outline of glue.

Becca could not escape. All she could do was sit in the office, cradling her arm while Greeley's door opened and closed and opened and closed. Caroline had said the school should keep her daughter until she could come in to assess the situation herself.

Of course, there had already been many questions. What happened? Did someone do something? What happened to her hands? Was she hurt elsewhere? The questions buzzed around and around her head with irritating persistence. Regrettably, now that people wanted to hear what she had to say, Becca didn't have the energy to talk.

And anyway, only one question mattered. Why was she still alive?

She'd heard smashing and walked down the hall to the dark kitchen, but as she'd reached the doorway, all had gone quiet.

The yard light streaming in through a soiled kitchen sheer had laid bare the ugly details of the man's life.

The kitchen floor was littered with the leftovers of easy meals: corn husks, cans of sardines and stew, boxes of saltines and cereal. The counters were cluttered with dishes and stacks of open boxes. She'd spotted two feature tiles behind the stove. A boy was painted on one and a girl on the other. They looked young and in love. Full of hope and set side by side in grout for eternity. Their prettiness would have been out of place had they not been covered in taffy-brown spatters.

Becca had stood waiting for the man to come for her when a mound of cans had started to shift and a large rat emerged. Before she'd understood what it was doing, it had climbed onto a chair, and leapt at her. She'd screamed and slipped on the trash, falling amid jagged can lids, rancid food, and dirty wrappers. The trash had continued to shift around her and because she had lost sight of the rat, she'd panicked, scrambled to her feet, thrown open the back door and rushed out. She'd fallen off the steps and landed on the toothy furrows of long, wet grass and pointy rocks.

She'd sat up slowly, cradling her arm and had just started to figure out that something had happened to her knee when the dark-faced man appeared at the kitchen door. He looked furious.

She'd tried to stand, to go to him and explain what she wanted, but he'd yelled at her and slammed his door shut.

Becca had fallen back to the ground in tears. She'd wanted so badly for her pain to end. But it seemed she sucked as much at dying as she did at everything else.

She'd lain back on the grass and watched her sobbing breaths rise and dissolve into rain.

The fine scratches of rain across the night sky had turned into long, wet ribbons. Eventually, she'd got to her feet and left, shivering, steadying herself against the house all the way out to the front walk. She'd made it out to the street but had no recollection of how she'd got there.

She'd seen the blind dog's poster on the telephone pole, and knew no one was looking out for him. She'd fought with the tape and got a staple caught in her finger. By the time she'd slipped his picture inside her hoodie, close to her skin, she knew they belonged together.

Later, she'd found other posters of other lost dogs. After that, everything had become scrambled.

Becca could hear threads of several conversations outside Greeley's office. Mostly, it was Nash saying things like "This kid is dark" and "It's a phase, they all go through it" and "I was pretty psycho when I was her age, but I turned out fine."

There was a lull in the level of chatter outside, followed by a chorus of low voices. Then a quick knock.

The door opened.

Before Greeley had a chance to announce her, Caroline entered, preceded by notes of Tom Ford's chic new perfume and followed by her voluminous cashmere coat, which seemed to gather up the dramatic momentum in the air and settle it around her. She dropped into a chair and let her huge, scarlet purse drop to the carpet beside her.

"Becca? What's going on?"

Greeley intervened. "Mrs. Chalmers —"

"It's LeFever. Actually. Ms."

Becca saw her mom's nose crinkle. She could smell the old shoes now.

"Becca's had some sort of a psychotic break."

"Really." Which was Caroline-speak for "bullshit," but she was trying to come off as professional.

Greeley faltered momentarily, taken aback by Becca's mom's brusque manner. "I didn't think it was necessary to call an ambulance, but as you can see, this is serious."

Caroline glanced at Becca's hashed fingers and hands, not fazed in the slightest.

"Right."

Greeley persisted. "She tried to talk to me about something a few days ago, but I didn't ..." She faltered. "I would strongly suggest you take Becca to the hospital and have her assessed —"

"Do you have children, Mrs. ..."

"Greeley. No."

"Well, this is what's known as a stunt," Caroline said, neatening random folds of cloth. "Becca never came home last night. Never answered her texts. And now, with the help of a little white glue and fake blood, she's ramping up the drama, hoping I'll go easy on her." She leaned in toward Becca. "She always gets needy when it's time for a detox."

Greeley stood up and waved toward the door. "Ms. LeFever, I think we should talk outside."

Caroline ignored her. "Right?" she asked Becca.

"Ms. LeFever, I really think you have *no* grasp of —"

"If I need to know what you think, Mrs. Greeley, I will ask you," said Caroline, rising to her full height in a perfumed sweep. "I may not be a perfect parent, but I am a parent. And I know when I'm being played. Maybe you should focus on your own problems, which, judging by the condition of this office, I'd say are probably numerous."

Becca started to laugh.

Caroline looked over from the stunned counsellor to Becca and back again, a smug smile spreading across her face as if to say, *See? She's full of it.*

For a moment, it looked like her mother was genuinely proud of her. Until she started to look worried.

59

Travel Plans

SAURAV WASN'T AT HIS desk, and he wasn't in the coffee room, but Karl was not done looking. He was a man on a mission, and the situation was critical.

He'd stayed true to his word. He'd committed to Saurav and to himself to end his chronic masturbation, and he'd gone cold turkey — his way. He'd given himself strict rules to follow. He'd put a porn blocker on his laptop and let Saurav set the password. He'd read up on addiction, studied couples in public places to normalize sexual behaviour. He'd even stopped saying the word *hard* because it was triggering. And when he wasn't going to group, he was with Caroline. For eight fucking days, Karl had resisted the siren call of his hand. Then, before lunch, a powerful urge came on.

He took his break early and biked over to a community centre for a willpower boost. In the rush to slip out, he'd forgotten his phone and the room number at work, so he ran through the hallways like an asshole trying to find his meeting because he sure as hell wasn't going to stop someone to ask where the perverts were hanging out.

It turned out his meeting was next door to a beginner French class.

Most of the students were seniors and seemed more intimidated by the technology than the mouth gymnastics. As he walked into his meeting, Karl heard them bleating, "*Bonjour, Madame Simone*" through the walls.

There were no social niceties at a perv meeting. No one said hello. No one was cheery. No one wanted a new friend. They all knew they were in the company of creeps. They sat with their chairs pulled in a circle around a counsellor whose job was to get people to talk quietly about how they'd been tempted or had succumbed. Then the group would talk about strategies for handling the next temptation. This was the part of the meeting that helped Karl most.

"Who wants to start?" asked the counsellor.

As a rule, people spoke around what they wanted to do — or had done — which was fine with Karl. He didn't need to know that old Jim needed to shove Lego blocks up his ass to get off. But the thirty-year-old Keg manager who called herself Denyse didn't get the memo. Within minutes, she was sharing details of getting banged in the washroom by the dishwasher while she fellated some guy who'd happened to wander in on them.

Karl remembered saying "Jesus" quietly a bunch of times. Some of the others pulled out their Nicorette, shifted in their chairs, or rubbed the backs of their necks. The counsellor was utterly useless and couldn't shut her down. Karl wouldn't have put him in charge of a drive-through window.

He was struggling not to form any mental images because it would be game over, but this Denyse woman was relentless. "He was old enough to be my father," she complained, "and I let him put his dick in my mouth."

In unison, all the French students next door asked, "*Où est le stylo?*"

And despite his best intentions, Karl started to imagine where the fucking *stylo* was hiding. "Aw, Jesus," he groaned, a chub waking up in his pants.

Fucking meeting that needed fucking trigger warnings.

He did what he had to do. He left the meeting and biked back to work, cursing the French and their fucking inane conversations about fucking pens. When he got back to his phone and saw Caroline cancelling their date, it wasn't good. He needed to find Saurav.

The elevator doors opened onto the ninth floor, where the senior boardrooms were located. The whole floor had a yoga centre vibe. Some executive's wife had convinced the board members to let her have a go at decorating. Words like *grace* and *ebb* and *light* were randomly stuck over the walls and doors. Karl imagined they were supposed to work on employees in some subtle way, but even shiny metal letters could not change the fact that everybody hated AMICO. Especially the people who worked there.

He walked past the receptionist — an older lady who handled boardroom bookings, coffee, and the asshole VPS. They kept her behind a dark wooden desk.

"Can I help you?" she called out after him.

"Just looking for someone, thanks," he said. He kept moving so she wouldn't get the chance to screw things up.

He spotted Saurav in the Empathy room, listening to a presentation some monkey in a tight checked shirt with French cuffs was making. Obviously, Karl couldn't barge in, so he planted himself by the window and stared until someone noticed him. Eventually, Saurav came out. He wasn't too happy.

"I'm in a meeting, man! Can't this wait?"

"No. I need a favour. A big one. Right after work."

"I'm driving my sister and mother to visit my Aunt Dimimi in hospital."

"No, man. I need your car. I have to get laid."

Saurav lowered his voice, but he was clearly outraged. "You pulled me out of a meeting for this?"

"Saurav! Listen to me. I have to control this, or it controls me. Stress is piling up on my back like a hump, and I'm *this* close to cracking. If I don't have an achievable plan in place, I will check back into the HVAC love motel, and then the last eight days will have been for nothing."

Saurav turned back toward the boardroom.

Karl had one final card to play. "You caught me, man. You stopped me. And technically, whether you like it or not, that makes you my sponsor."

It was low and manipulative, but Saurav had caved. By 5:35, Karl was on the road, but he still wasn't out of the woods.

Caroline's text cancelling their date night was a huge source of concern. "Something" she'd written cryptically, had "come up." He suspected the "something" had to do with catching him beating off in bed beside her. He'd told her he hadn't wanted to wake her, but he wasn't sure she'd bought it.

Whether it was that or a genuine kid problem, he couldn't let himself care. He had to convince Caroline she needed to see him.

60

Murphy's Law

TECHNICALLY, IT WAS THE first night of previews, which meant that whatever could go wrong, would, but the audience would forgive it because their tickets hadn't cost a whole lot. But it was an opening night of sorts, and one had to aim for perfection. Particularly as Katherine's parents would be in the audience.

They didn't normally bother with previews, but as the Radcliffes were going to Vienna for the rest of the run, they'd decided to put aside their biases for their daughter's sake. Katherine wanted nothing to detract their eyes and minds from her performance. She needed her parents to see and feel her as a nurse. This wasn't her looking for their approval. She wanted them to acknowledge she had a natural affinity for medicine and accept her emerging personal commitment to nursing.

The house numbers for that evening's performance were respectable, given that it was Halloween. One hundred and seventeen tickets had been sold, excluding last-minute walk-ins. It was a relief to Katherine, as an empty theatre would have been ruinous. Her family's spite for small, alternative cultural events was legendary.

Katherine had checked the set and revisited the props table not once but three times because she'd started to suspect the young assistant stage manager of messing around with the air pressure settings on the bag of blood. Contrary to what he had seen in movies, blood moved through transfusion lines slowly. It didn't come shooting out like water on a log ride.

She knew she needed to open the theatre doors soon. Earlier, she'd spotted at least a dozen people milling around in the lobby. Her glance had happened to fall on the row of cast pictures on display. Hers was there too, of course. She'd ended up using a photo taken by an ex-boyfriend who mostly did portraits of rock stars.

She hadn't been trying to show everyone up, but her portrait seemed to be the only one that said, *I am a whole, real person.* She was sitting on a carved stone block in Rome, near an amphitheatre. And by some miracle, her hair had come out right. So had her scarf. And her hand hung loosely over her knee, like posing was the most natural thing in the world to her. She was wearing Massimo's motorcycle jacket, and he'd snapped her picture while she was mid laugh. He was accusing her of stealing his jacket. Which was why she was laughing. He was spectacular. She'd told him her name was Gwen. She couldn't remember why.

Katherine did her final-final backstage visit. This time, she discovered her ASM sitting up on the props table, shooting the shit with a stagehand about longboards. She wasn't sure where the production manager had dug him up, but she didn't like him. He had a scraggly beard, which he scratched nonstop while he talked to people.

"Can you give the cast their thirty-minutes, please? I'm going up to the booth," Katherine said.

"Sure thing," he said. And didn't move.

She gave him the benefit of five seconds. "Now?"

He hopped off the table, making a face like she was power-tripping. So she stayed there and watched him leave to make sure, then checked the pressure on the bag of blood. "Just because someone likes torture porn," she muttered, "doesn't make them an expert in venous systems."

She cut across the stage toward the auditorium stairs, but as she hit the lip of the stage, she paused, struck by the realization that soon she'd be walking away from the theatre to a whole new life. She would never stand on a set again, captivating hearts and minds ... unless, of course, a roof caved in, and she happened to be in the theatre at the time. In which case, she *would* be up on the stage, not as a stage manager but as a medical professional trying to find the wounded, starting triage.

She'd say things like: "Those of you who can walk, help take those who can't out into the street."

The words came so naturally. Her voice sounded strong and clear. She felt totally buoyed by her confidence. She could imagine her father watching her organizing everyone in the room. "Take the children outside," she'd say. "Those who are near someone who requires critical care, raise your hands, and I'll come around."

"Are ... are you talking to me?"

The reedy voice cut her vision down like a ribbon at an opening.

"Is someone hurt?" the voice persisted.

Katherine shielded her eyes from the preset lights. "Who's speaking?"

A skinny, anxious man stepped out into the aisle. "Me. I — I'm a — an usher?"

Katherine walked down into the auditorium toward him. "For the record, it's bad form to interrupt people while they're working."

He swallowed hard. His Adam's apple bobbled.

"You can open front of house."

Katherine walked up the dark stairwell that led up to her booth, angry with herself at having been caught talking out loud. It was an annoying habit, but a private one.

She breathed deeply and let the earlier moment go so she could focus on the present one. She reminded herself she'd done every-thing to make sure it was going to be a great opening night.

Katherine sat in her chair, centred her prompt book on the small desk, and readjusted the black paper tape on her light because the gel kept falling off. She flipped through the pages of the script, silently reviewing some of the trickier cue sequences. As she did, she ran her hands over her uniform, fingers dipping into pockets to check for her pen: there. Keys to the dispensary, present. Thermometer. Watch. Name tag. Check, check, check. She tried to iron the one or two tiny wrinkles at her waist with the flat of her warm palm. There weren't many because it was really good fabric. She was glad she hadn't skimped like the wardrobe mistress.

She glanced through the window toward the stage and watched the audience drift down the aisles. Her heart raced when she spotted her father and mother sitting among the patrons in Row J, their shoulders almost touching other people's.

She noted that her eldest brother, Daniel, had come too. He sat in the row behind them and kept shifting in his chair, looking uncomfortable. Katherine wondered whether it was because he was conspicuously alone or because he thought her failure was imminent. Rather than second-guess herself, Katherine decided that Daniel's discomfort was his own problem. "Don't lay your insecurities on me. I will be fine. I am a professional."

"What?"

It was the lighting board operator. He was belly-up to his board at the desk beside her.

"When did you get here?"

"Call time? I said hi."

He had not. It occurred to Katherine he might have found the case of Steam Whistle she'd bought as a crew present and started early.

"Are you okay?" she asked. "To do the show?"

He looked puzzled by her question. "Yeah. I just had a nap in my car."

She let it drop.

Katherine glanced out her window to see how the audience was filling out.

The tide of humanity was starting to trickle off. Any minute, she'd get the "go" from front of house. From there, she would get through the show, the week, and the run, and then she would get on with the rest of her life. No more poorly trained volunteers, alcoholic technicians, or shoddy wardrobe labour to deal with. Theatre. God! What had she been thinking?

"Sorry?"

Now the lighting board operator was trying to undermine her.

"Maybe you shouldn't drink before a show ..."

"Excuse me?"

"House is closing," came the cry from Liz down the stairs. As Katherine leaned forward to make sure everyone was seated, she spotted the stragglers. Brent came rushing down one aisle, quickly finding his seat. A blond with a blunt haircut and a tailored camel hair coat walked down the other aisle. Katherine wondered if they'd come together.

"What?"

"I'm not talking to you."

"Can I give places?" asked the ASM on the headset.

The little shit imagined he was running the show. Katherine glanced at the time. It was 7:58. "Places," she said out loud.

"Places," confirmed the ASM.

Two minutes to showtime. It looked like Blondie had come separately. She was sitting with a girlfriend, but Brent had definitely noticed her. She had a nice neck, and she knew it.

"Did you just say 'bitch'?" asked the lighting board operator.

"I said stand by: house to half, house out and LX cue one, sound cues one and two."

"That's not what you said."

"Acknowledge the cues."

"Standing by."

She knew Brent was his own man. She had no claim on him, but she hadn't thought he'd be looking around for another woman on *her* opening night. It was so incredibly tacky.

"Still standing by, Katherine."

She was glad to be rid of him. "House to half, go. House out, go. Sound cue one go."

Like magic, the house lights slowly darkened, and the audience settled. Katherine could see the pointy tips of Blondie's blunt cut swishing around, glancing in Brent's direction. They were totally going to hook up.

"Should we turn the lights up and start the show?"

Feeling slightly confused, Katherine realized she had lost the plot. She would obviously have to stay single for the next four years if she was serious about wanting to save lives. She glanced down at her prompt book and called the next cue.

61

Curtains

THERE WAS A POP of light, then all the lamps faded to black, and the curtain lowered with gravitas.

Backstage, in the ten seconds that followed the curtain closing, the thrilled actors exchanged quiet, congratulatory hugs as they scurried to the wings for their curtain calls. It was clear they believed the show had gone well, and yet they held their collective breath for what was to come.

The music started, then the applause.

It was sparse at first, but it warmed as one by one, the actors emerged. The audience had been moved by their work, the vision, the experience.

Katherine's bow would come last, but she'd already lived the thrill of having an assembly of strangers believe in what she was doing. Only minutes earlier, as Theodore's pulse had faded, the audience had literally leaned in and experienced Nurse Reeves's discovery of his death *through* her. The silence that followed had given her goosebumps.

It was Amanda's turn to bow. She walked out to centre stage, smiling kindly. She pressed a hand to her throat as though humbled by the audience's reaction. The crowd clapped harder. Amanda lit up. Classic Pavlovian responses.

Katherine didn't need the praise to feel like she'd accomplished something meaningful. She was done with the role-playing that had plagued her life. It had taken her too long to realize that polite praise left her feeling hollow and unsatisfied. Now that she'd recon-nected with herself and her desires, she understood that what she craved was a deeper, more meaningful exchange of humanity. A true person-to-person bond.

Katherine saw all the actors on stage waving at her, beckoning her to join them, but she smiled and shook her head. She applauded the cast from where she stood in the wings, then retreated to the stage door, where she decided to walk out into the street, into the night, ever so eagerly toward her new life.

62

Reversal of Fortunes

NOISES. SOMEONE CUTTING SOMETHING. Not with scissors. Big cutting. *Big*. Karl couldn't figure out what was going on. Only that it involved cutting, and it was loud.

There was broken glass on the seat beside him. He tried to open his fingers to brush it off the seat onto the floor mat, but he was having trouble. It took all his concentration. He managed to reach a bit of it and flicked his fingers to brush it off. He hoped Saurav wouldn't notice.

Everything went black for a bit, and when Karl took another look around, he saw what was being cut. They were going through the dashboard. He'd never said they could. Right through the fucking leather and the vents and everything. Saurav was going to be so angry. He loved that fucking vent. No more driving his elderly aunts to the Dairy Queen with the air-conditioning on.

Karl tried to get them to stop. He could get out. He could wriggle the fuck out. He needed a minute. *What the fuck just happened?* But no one was answering, so Karl wasn't sure he'd managed to say the words out loud. There was too much goddamned grinding going on.

Then somebody started talking in his ear. A voice, asking him to stop moving. Voices were shouting at one another. Some were talking to him. There was a saw blade cutting right through the fucking dashboard. Saurav would be so fucking ... That saw was close — really close to his legs. He didn't like the look of that. He didn't like the look of that one bit. *Stop*, Karl thought. And he realized he needed to find a way to tell them they needed to stop, and stop now! But they cut through before he could say something, and everything went black again.

HE'D NEVER REALIZED HOW loud it was inside an ambulance. It was surprising, really. Couldn't they have done something? Like baffling. Baffles. Hang a few baffles. Why did they keep asking him shit? He just needed to catch his breath for a minute so he could find his ... Oh my fuck. How was he going to tell Saurav what they'd done to his car?

The ambulance slowed down, and then it stopped. Somebody flung open the back doors. Karl felt a blast of cold air. There were faces. He didn't recognize any of them. Then he was inside. All he could look at was the ceiling. He couldn't turn his head anymore because of the shit neck pillow. He had to look up.

Light.

Light.

Light.

Light. All fluorescent lights. On the ceiling. Too bright. They were flying past. Or maybe it was the other way around. Maybe Karl was sliding past them. Gliding under them. Like he was on a conveyor belt he couldn't stop. Or maybe he could stop, but at the moment he couldn't be bothered to find out.

They passed signs. *Exit. Entrance. Cardiology.* Lots of signs.

He remembered other signs, signs he'd seen earlier: Sherbourne, Jarvis, York, Spadina, Jameson. There had been billboards too. He'd really wanted to look at the sexy-times models. He'd wanted to. No. Wrong. Wrong-o. Something else.

Logos. Corporate logos. Good. The City of Toronto. CUPE. Canon. Made out of white stone. Lit up. And two people fucking.

Right by the logo. Right under a lamppost. Along the highway. Try-ing to get everyone to watch them. So fucking hot.

A truck leaning on the horn behind him. Trying to make him look at the road, but he was locked in. Flying over the embank-ment. Going through steel and fence posts. Drawn to the couple running up the hill. By the time he'd remembered he could stop, the lamppost had taken over.

"Where's Josie?"

"Maybe with the heart attack that came in ahead of you? I don't know. I'm in on a short call."

"Welcome to your shift. A car piled into pedestrians. They're working on the woman now. Older male is right behind us with severe lacerations, head trauma, complaining of chest pain. This is the guy who mowed them down. Both legs present as compound. And something that looks like a mandibular dislocation."

"Put the lacerations in exam six. Bring this one to emerg three."

Karl noticed he wasn't floating past the lights anymore. Now he'd stopped moving, he could feel pain. White-hot, pulsating pain, exploding. He had quasars for legs. He wanted to start moving again. He needed to sit up. He was going to hurl.

The voice came back. It spoke to him from beside his head. "Karl? Don't worry about a thing, okay, buddy? You're in good hands."

There was a loud tearing sound. Suddenly, the walls were mov-ing all around him, and the voices were on the other side of it. The woman talking to the man. Completely unaware that he was on the edge of a supermassive black hole, and all he could do was stare at the light.

63

Rhubarb, Rhubarb, Rhubarb

KATE HAD BEEN SPLENDID. She'd exuded medical efficiency from every pore and delivered a good, albeit brief, performance. It was an auspicious beginning to what would undoubtedly be a long, wonderful career.

Though the show had let out ten minutes earlier, the Mustard Extra Space's lobby was still packed when Brent emerged. Most people, Brent imagined, were waiting for the cast and crew to join them, to celebrate their first night.

Brent wandered through the lobby looking for Katherine, over-hearing bits of mostly positive reviews about the show. One man jabbered about the sorry state of the lobby carpet, and a woman's low voice replied, "Don't change the topic. She could be a hygienist in Prague. It's a profession that can travel."

Away from the glitter of the chandeliers and the glamour of the artwork in their foyer, the judge and Missus Radcliffe made a rather ordinary couple, which was probably why Brent hadn't noticed them during his first turn around the lobby.

"Judge Radcliffe! Missus Radcliffe."

The judge looked over his shoulder at Brent. His hand dropped on his wife's lower back, ready to usher them out if necessary.

Brent held out his hand. "Brent. Brent Dunn." The judge was

nodding but hadn't placed him. "I came for dinner a few weeks ago? Enjoyed a feast?"

Missus Radcliffe recalled him first. "Of course. Katherine's friend," she said to situate the judge. She held out her hand for Brent to take and shake. There was only so much wealthy people were willing to do.

"Did you find your dog?" she asked.

"It's very kind of you to ask," said Brent. "But as it turns out, no, I did not."

"Oh, dear," Missus Radcliffe answered with the barest hint of regret. "Well, maybe you can get another."

It was a preposterous thing to say, but he let it be said. The night was Katherine's, and he did not want to diminish it in the slightest. "How does it feel to have a burgeoning star in the family?" he asked.

The Radcliffes wearily glanced toward one another.

"I thought she was very convincing as a nurse," Brent advanced.

"How kind," said Missus Radcliffe without satisfaction. "Well, you must be sure to tell her when she comes out."

"That's odd! I couldn't find her backstage, so I assumed she was out here. We must have crossed paths. I'll go back and take another look."

The judge raised a hand. "Not on our account. It's fine. We'll catch up with her later," he said. "It's just as well," he added, leaning in confidentially. "It wasn't a good play. Maybe it won't stick." He winked.

"I very much doubt it matters to Katherine, dear," Missus Radcliffe remarked. "She appears to be oblivious to embarrassment."

"Meredith ..." reproached the judge.

"Why else did she use that tragic old photograph of herself?" They all turned and studied Katherine's actress photo in communal silence.

Missus Radcliffe sighed. "I need a drink."

The judge nodded in agreement.

"Well, it was good to ..." said Brent.

The Radcliffes were already moving. The rich needed no one's consent to depart, but Brent did wonder how long it was necessary for him to wait for their daughter.

"I'm sorry. Did I hear you say you recently lost your dog?"

Brent turned and recognized the arresting young woman in a tailored camel hair coat. They'd both arrived a few short moments before the curtain rose, and they'd exchanged a smile.

"Yes, that's right," he answered. "Three weeks ago. Would you like to see his picture?"

She nodded and drew nearer. Brent found a photo of Gary and held out his phone. As she looked at Gary, he noticed rich strands of gold and champagne in her hair. Her lips were a shade of a summer rose.

"How tragic!" she said.

Brent nodded with sad acknowledgement. It *had* been tragic. "My therapist suggested it might be good idea to hold a service for my dog. To help me deal with his loss, but ..." He sighed heavily, managing a smile. "Maybe next spring."

"What if I could help?" she said, pressing his arm.

64

Base Layers

SHE HAD WATCHED BLOOD and dirt and wavy strands of synthetic orange yarn travel down into the drain. It had taken almost twenty minutes to feel her arms and thighs again, but she still felt numbness inside.

Becca and Caroline sat on the sofa.

They weren't watching anything. They weren't talking. They were just sitting together. Waiting for the next thing.

Caroline had wrapped a cashmere throw around Becca after she'd said she still felt cold after her shower. The doctor at the urgent care centre had suspected she was fighting some kind of infection. He had given her cream for her fingertips but told Caroline to take Becca to a hospital if her temperature got any higher.

Becca started to feel her exhaustion and sort of leaned against her mom. And like it was the most natural thing in the world, Caroline let her. After a few moments, Caroline started to stroke her hair.

"You're hot," she said.

"Thank you," said Becca.

Caroline didn't laugh.

Becca went quiet and sank deeper into the comforting, felted silence, into whatever was going on. *This*, she thought. This closeness. It was a chewable vitamin for her deficient soul, the goodness and rightness of which could be immediately absorbed. They hadn't had a moment like this since her dad had left them and Caroline had gone contractor-loco.

"We should take your temperature," said Caroline. Becca didn't respond. Her mom gathered up a few strands of Becca's hair and let them fall, again and again for a few more minutes. "Do you want to talk about what happened?"

Becca shook her head.

Caroline nodded. "Okay. Later, then. But we *will* talk."

Caroline continued to run her deeply scarlet nails through Becca's hair from her temple to her ear. Over and over.

Caroline's cell phone rang, and she let it go to voice mail without even checking who was calling. Becca remembered: "You used to play with my hair like this when I was a little kid."

"Oh yeah?"

"When I was in kindergarten. We'd sit on the sofa and watch *Blue's Clues*, and you'd play with my hair like this. I liked it."

Becca could feel her mom trying to connect the dots. She wasn't a touchy-feely person by nature. It was something reserved for lovers or special occasions.

"Huh," Caroline repeated as though the idea of the intimate exchange surprised even her. Caroline used longer and longer strokes through Becca's hair as she thought back. The gentle jangle of her wooden bangles suddenly stopped.

"Oh," she said, remembering. Her tone was distinctly unpleasant.

"What?"

"I was checking you for head lice."

Becca sat up to make sure she'd heard correctly. "What?" She could feel the cold returning.

Caroline shifted and reached for her water. "Yeah. There was an outbreak at your school. They sent notes to all the parents. I found one, and you know how much I hate bugs. Of course, I was alone because your dad was — well, who knows where he was …"

She'd never touched Becca's hair again. Becca had convinced herself she'd done something wrong. "Why didn't you tell me?"

"About the lice?"

"How you reacted! I thought you couldn't stand to touch me."

"That's ridiculous! Jesus Christ, Becca. I made you."

"'I made you' is meaningless, Mom. I make snot. That doesn't mean I love it!"

"Okay. What am I supposed to say here? I'm sorry for keeping life real?" Caroline sounded more annoyed than concerned.

Stupid, angry tears started to sting Becca's eyes. "I'm so sick of always feeling like everything about me is revolting."

Caroline looked surprised. Shocked.

"I don't even know how you could think that."

"Really? You can't stop telling me I've got Dad's hands, his eyes, his feet. My feet smell like his. You say it all the time! I'm all the parts of Dad you hate."

"I hate your dad because he's an asshole. Not because his feet smell, you stupid kid." Caroline looked confused.

"We were having a moment, Mom. How often do we have those? Never. And you couldn't shut up about head lice. Why do you always make it so hard for me to keep one nice memory of us? One. Where you're doing something with me not because you have to. Because you want to."

It was Caroline's turn to look upset. "I don't understand where this is coming from," she said. "I kill myself so you have what you need. I make you healthy meals you refuse to eat, I force you to go to a school you loathe, and I buy you clothing you rarely wash. What am I missing?"

The phone rang again. Caroline let it go to voice mail.

"What don't you get? I can't stand being me anymore. Okay? But I don't know how to be anyone else. And you're not helping. I tried to die, Mom. Like twice. And it didn't work."

"Are you serious right now?"

"Jeez! Why would I lie about something like that? I couldn't. Ever. I'm not like you."

Caroline faltered as though she'd been struck by some bigger truth. "I thought you were ..." Caroline realized something. "Jesus Christ, I'm just like my mother."

Becca could see her struggling not to cry. Caroline hated her mother so bad. She was looking at Becca like she was completely confused. "I swore I'd never be like her."

Becca nodded, fully understanding her emotionality. "I never want to be like you either."

Caroline's eyes were shiny. Becca's answer seemed to sink in. For a minute it looked like she didn't know whether she was going to laugh or cry.

"Becca. I'm so sorry. I've been —"

"Yes," agreed Becca. "You have."

Because she had. And then she and Caroline fell into each other's arms, bawling their eyes out.

Eventually, they started half talking, half crying. Caroline said, "I thought if I gave you the freedom I never got from my mother, you'd run around and figure stuff out like I did. But without the hassles. Because you're smart, you know?"

Becca nodded.

"I just thought you were trying to be a pain," said Caroline. "That you were pretending to be stupid to get back at me. But you're genuinely ..."

Becca nodded gravely. "Yes," she said. "I am."

"I didn't understand," said Caroline. "I'm so sorry, Rebecca."

Becca nodded, crying again, hiccupping sobs of relief. She buried her face in her mom's shoulder. Caroline held her until she stopped.

"I love you, Mom."

Caroline's eyes teared up again. She half laughed and blew her nose. "I love you t—"

There was another buzz from the cell phone in Caroline's scarlet purse. She shouted, "Who the hell keeps calling? Don't they know I'm having a fucking epiphany with my kid?"

Her mom's voice was warm with emotion; she was laughing while tears were still squeezing out of her eyes. Becca reached for the Kleenex box. Caroline stroked Becca's cheek, grabbed a tissue, and wiped away her own tears.

She glanced at her phone. "Tch. It's Karl." Caroline blew her nose again. "I cancelled our date tonight. I think I was a little vague on the reason why. I must have worried him." She laughed again. "He should be."

She brushed a strand of hair out of Becca's face and let the phone ring one last time to give herself time to get the tears out of her voice.

"Karl!" Caroline said, then paused and looked confused. "No, you called me. Who's this?" She listened and brought her legs down off the sofa. "Yes. Yes, of course, I know him. Why? What!?" She listened for a few more moments and gasped. "Where? No. Where? I'm on my way."

She hung up and held her tissue at the ready. "Something's happened to Karl." She shook her head. "Some goddamned car accident. I'm the only number on his phone, so I guess I'm next of kin." She slipped her feet into her gold ballerina slippers and stood up. "Come on."

"I'm tired, Mom."

"I know, but get your shoes on anyway. You're coming with me."

"I don't feel up to it." It was like her skin was vibrating.

Caroline started rummaging through her big, red purse, looking for her lipstick. She sniffed. "Well, you really *are* crazy if you think I'm leaving you here alone after you've gone off the rails."

Becca didn't know if she ought to laugh or be insulted. Caroline must have seen it on her face, and she smiled at her own rudeness.

"Do I have to change clothes?" asked Becca.

Caroline applied a coat of matte red, recapped her lipstick, and shook her head. "It's an emergency room. No one comes dressed."

It was as good an endorsement as Becca had ever received.

65

In the Wings

KARL HEARD A SOUND and opened his eyes. The walls were moving again. No, the walls were curtains. Someone had come in. A nurse.

She walked around the foot of the bed to the cart beside him. He wanted to tell her about how much his legs hurt, but he couldn't make his mouth work. All he could produce was something that sounded like a long bunch of vowels and spit.

"It's okay. I'm right here," she said.

She leaned in toward him so he could see her better. She was wearing a lot of makeup. Her skin looked like all her pores had been sanded away.

"I'm Nurse Reeves," she said, pointing to something that presumably was her name tag. Karl tried to look but couldn't see the tag because the right side of his face had swollen up, so he nodded as best he could.

"You're at St. Joseph's Health Centre. You've been in a car accident. You're going to be all right. Are you in a lot of pain?"

Yes. Yes! he wanted to shout. But the sound that came out of his mouth was completely different. "Achsssh, achsssh."

"Yeah. I'm pretty sure both your legs are broken, and I think your jaw is dislocated. I mean, that's the best-case scenario. The doctors are dealing with the three-car pileup ahead of you, but someone will be here soon." She paused. "I mean, one of them

315

could actually be here this very moment if he managed his time better, but procedurally, CPR comes first."

Her voice was soothing, competent, but also slightly judgmental.

"Just hang in there a little while longer, okay?" she said. She went around to the IV pole and started to separate the lines and tape them together. "Sorry. This is the kind of mess that bugs me." She flashed him a smile.

The pain in his legs was unbearable. *Please*, he tried to say. *Please get a doctor*. But all that came out was "Peathe."

"Peathe. Peathe."

She stared at him a few moments. "I want to help you," she related in a confidential tone. "But we have procedures. We do things by the numbers to keep you safe. You have to wait. Of course, I personally don't think people should be left in unnecessary pain."

She stood in the curtain opening, looking out. Thinking. Nodding to staff walking past. He wondered whether she was looking for a doctor when she suddenly spun back to him and walked toward his IV stand. "Okay," she said. "I'm going to give you some pain meds. I'm not a monster."

Karl nodded in agreement as she reached into her pockets and pulled out several vials.

"I found these when I started my shift," the nurse said, setting a handful of little glass bottles on his chest. "I kept them because I just knew they could come in handy. Okay. Let's have a look." She squinted as she read the labels on the vials and shook her head.

Her eyes suddenly lit up. "Okay. This one is excellent."

Karl suddenly wasn't so sure he wanted immediate relief. She must have seen the doubt in his eyes because she smiled reassuringly.

"No. I bruised my shin bone once while I was skiing, and this is exactly what the doctor gave me. It was a godsend." The nurse peered at the label once more. "MDV. MDV ..." She smiled, remembering: "Multi-dose vial."

Something was definitely wrong with his nurse.

"Okay. I just have to find a syringe and then make sure there aren't any air bubbles." She sounded excited. She collected all the other vials and slipped them back into her pocket.

Trapped in his collar, Karl was trying to shake his head. "Peathe. Peathe," he said.

The nurse laid a calming hand on his arm and smiled.

66

Dénouement

"WOW. THERE'S A LOT going on with this guy."

Whenever a new patient came into the emergency room, Caroline commented on how they looked and whether or not she thought they were going to die. "Either a bladder infection or a knee problem. And obviously, he's colour-blind."

It passed the time.

It felt like they'd been in the waiting room forever. In reality, it had been an hour. Becca was trying not to think about the awkward plastic seat, trying not to react to people being sick, and trying not to breathe the air around her chair, but the layout of the waiting room seating made it difficult because it forced almost perfectly healthy people to sit next to other people holding their fingertips in a Tim Hortons cup filled with ice.

Behind Becca was a smelly guy barfing into a plastic bag. The other person of note was this girl who'd scored four seats in a row and was lying across them, but Becca decided she looked too much like a crinkled cafeteria fry to really be comfortable. She'd probably slipped into a coma and wasn't aware of the misery her body was in.

Caroline was trying to resolve the Karl mystery. No one knew where Karl was, nor could they confirm how he was doing. They couldn't even tell her who'd called. The admissions nurse promised she'd look into it when she had a minute, but she hadn't.

Becca suspected it wasn't that Caroline was worried about Karl so much as she was pissed she wasn't getting any answers. She was used to being on the inside of a situation with all the information. It was making her crazy.

Becca wondered what was different about Karl. Why had her mom decided he was the type of person she would do things for? He seemed all wrong, like stripes with plaid. But obviously, Caroline could see something in him that she didn't. And if there was something Becca had known for a while about herself, it was that she knew nothing about how everything worked.

When she'd been little, the world had been interpreted for her. Now she lived in a strange land.

Caroline suddenly stuffed her nail file and cuticle trimmer into her bag. Something had changed. Becca followed her mom's gaze and saw a new admissions nurse had arrived to replace the old admissions nurse. They talked for a few minutes and transferred over a bundle of keys. As they were wrapping up, Caroline leaned over to Becca, casually freshening up her hair. "I'm going to go see if this new nurse can tell me what's going on with Karl. Be right back."

Becca watched Caroline stride to the desk, clutching her scarlet purse. It seemed to bump up her level of concern by a factor of ten. In reality, she'd just spent the last forty-five minutes reshaping her nails.

Becca could tell she was getting better answers from the new nurse because Caroline was nodding and pointing and smiling. Yep. Something was definitely happening. Maybe they could go home soon. Becca was starting to feel like she should lie down.

Caroline walked back quickly, digging through her bag for more lipstick. It was like watching an excavator operator at work.

"Well," she said, "I'm glad I asked again because this nurse said she *could* see Karl in the system, but she wasn't sure which room he was in or whether a doctor had seen him yet. She's going to check up on him. Since I know what he looks like, she said I could go in the back to find him and speed things up. So I'm going to do that, and you stay put. I won't be long." She took two steps and came right back, lowering her voice. "Oh. I told them I was Karl's ex–common law wife. I'm just telling you in case they ask. But they won't."

Becca nodded. "Got it."

Caroline said, "Kiss-kiss" as she walked away in a fresh flurry of scarves, her words smelling like Forbidden Fuchsia lipstick. She walked past the nursing station and into the ER proper to find Karl.

Becca twisted around in her chair, trying to find a new way to mash her body into the plastic seat. One good thing about her infection was that she couldn't tell if her arm still hurt — mostly because everything else felt like such crap. But she didn't feel anxious. And that was strange.

Maybe it was the fever.

She looked at all the people in the waiting room through her narrowing eyes and realized they were alike: the crinkly fry girl, the barfer, the stressed-out nurse, the impatient doctors, the family, the friends. Everyone wanted to turn things around.

There were no guarantees that anyone would be happier. That the fixes they'd receive would address the problems they actually had. But people always wanted to feel better so they kept hanging around, hoping someone would eventually figure out what they needed.

Special Thanks To

Sioux Browning, Tina Cooper, Tanya Paoli, Andrew Kauffman, Corey Redekop, Ania Szado, Sarah Cooper, Marc Côté, Betty Jane Wylie's Blue Pencil Room, the OAC, NaNoWriMo, TWUC, and Mr. Brophy who read my writing aloud in grade 10 English and changed everything.

We acknowledge the sacred land on which Cormorant Books operates. It has been a site of human activity for 15,000 years. This land is the territory of the Huron-Wendat and Petun First Nations, the Seneca, and most recently, the Mississaugas of the Credit River. The territory was the subject of the Dish With One Spoon Wampum Belt Covenant, an agreement between the Iroquois Confederacy and Confederacy of the Anishinaabe and allied nations to peaceably share and steward the resources around the Great Lakes. Today, the meeting place of Toronto is still home to many Indigenous people from across Turtle Island. We are grateful to have the opportunity to work in the community, on this territory.

We are also mindful of broken covenants and the need to strive to make right with all our relations.